STOLE

- Annalisse Series Book One

"An irresistible page turner. With a splash of international adventure and plenty of surprises, Stolen Obsession is an entertaining read and a great beginning to the Annalisse Series."
—Self-Publishing Review, ★ ★ ★ ★ ½

"…Bell delivers a great, slow-building romance, gently examining her characters' painful pasts."
—Kirkus Reviews

"The villains are devilishly evil and diabolical. A highly entertaining read."
—InD'tale Magazine Review

Praise for
SPENT IDENTITY
– Annalisse Series Book Two

"…Bell keeps her well-paced story moving. Her use of dialogue to drive the narrative is excellent and she sticks the twist ending nicely, one of the harder tricks to pull off in this genre…"
—IndieReader Review

"…a riveting sleuth whodunit that has all the aspects of a brilliant murder mystery."
—Readers Favorite 5 Stars

SCATTERED
LEGACY

A NOVEL BY

MARLENE M. BELL

Ewephoric Publishing

This is a work of fiction. Names, characters, dialog, places, and incidents are products of the author's imagination. None of the events depicted in this book are real. Any similarities to actual events, locales or real persons, living or dead, are entirely coincidental and not intended by the author.

Cover design by Isabel Robalo – IsaDesign.net
Book design by Kevin G. Summers

ISBN: 978-0-9995394-6-0
ISBN: 978-0-9995394-7-7 (eBook)

For Grandpa Virgilio (b 1893), who emigrated
to the US as a teenager from Bitritto, Bari.
Although I struggled understanding his broken
English, I have fond memories of Grandpa's musical
skills in the mandolin, banjo, and guitar. Occasionally,
he'd let me win at cards when we played Casino!

*Grandpa, I felt as if you were looking in during the
research for this book...*

CHAPTER
ONE

Uncle Ted Walker killed himself on August 4, six years ago, in a swan dive off the Williamsburg Bridge, but that didn't stop him from haunting us. Because it's been three months since my dead uncle hired a man to kidnap me at gunpoint.

Kate Walker kept the truth to herself for seventy years while she hid a lover and my true parentage from everyone. She had her reasons, and some might say they were good ones. In her defense, keeping secrets prevented her from making a bigger mess of a strained marriage to a man I knew as Uncle Ted.

It's hard to separate feelings of love and betrayal by the woman who took me in so long ago. Kate's mysteries are tucked away because if they're allowed their freedom, they'll change the direction of so many lives. It sent her in a new direction. She's running, and in a way, I am too.

I slide an envelope across the jewelry counter and flip it over on the glass. The vibes coming from it are so unnatural it's hard to explain. Nate Adams, our security man, gave it to me when I walked into Zavos Gallery. The messenger gave him instructions to deliver it only to me. The envelope is an unmarked white number ten. My hand grazes the paper, touching subtle lumps under the surface. What's within this letter stops me from unsealing the flap. Undiscovered jewelry, artifacts, and Renaissance art during America's century of innovators is what I love and what our gallery specializes in, but fear keeps me from opening a silly envelope.

I'm known to have elusive instincts when it comes to places and historical relics. I can visualize who might have held a gem or picture them sitting for a portrait painted centuries ago. At times I imagine others who might have been in the room and their motives for acquiring rare oils and stealing personal jewels worth a king's ransom. The flood of information and imagery that flows from art is welcoming.

A year ago, anyone mentioning me, Annalisse Drury, and *successful* in the same sentence might have heard my old boss, Harry, laugh. Back then, my biggest worry was paying the rent on the brownstone and how to juggle work with weekends on Walker Farm. Westinn Gallery is where I cut my teeth as an in-house antiquities valuator.

I'm Generosa Zavos's friend and confidant—somewhat of a personal guru who listens and makes suggestions. She brought me in as a business partner after we rescued her from kidnappers months ago. I'm crazy in love with her son, Alec.

Nate opens the door for the first client of the day. Red, red everywhere, enough to make a London phone booth envious. From her lips to her stilettos, the brunette wears a bloody ensemble. Only the streaks in her hair and the plume in her hat are pink. It's not unusual to see plenty of character in New Yorkers walking the shops of Wooster Street. Every now and then someone catches me off guard, like this woman of maybe twenty.

"Welcome. Are you looking for anything in particular?" I ask, moving around the glass case for a closer look. Brim and plume shade her in a veil of menacing gray. Something is off about her.

"Honestly, I'm looking mostly. Is your coffee free?" The melodic voice trails off as she motions toward the espresso machine. "Nice for the publics, do you mind?"

"Feel free." Taking the ominous, delivered envelope in hand, I smooth down my new silk blouse from a quaint boutique on the west side.

Her three-inch heels chirp along polished tile as she roams an aisle, stopping at a garden landscape painted by a local artist. Gen purchased the oil because it reminds her of Hogarth's *View of Chiswick Garden* 1741. An elderly couple stands transfixed at a railing overlooking a waterway with orange groves. The painting is one of my all-time faves.

"The Windstrand is a steal at that price. His work is reminiscent of the great masters, wouldn't you agree? All works in the gallery are included in our sale. We ship anywhere in the world," I add, catching a whiff of her floral perfume. Red Door, of course.

She continues a stiff walk on the balls of her feet while holding her full cup of coffee. It's hard to tell if she's uncomfortable in her shoes or trying not to make noise. The woman in red unnerves me for no particular reason. Certain speech patterns and sentences ending in pluralities give me a clue where she grew up.

I glance toward the office window where Gen sits in perfect posture, writing at her desk. She's an obsessive letter writer with an exquisite hand that most remark on after receiving one of her personal notes. We joke that she cloistered with monks while she lived in Italy. The flourishes and curlicues in fountain pen ink belong to those of an earlier era. My penmanship should be so lucky.

Roses and violets from Ms. Red's scent tickle my nose, and I move closer to the office and the comfort of Alec's mother. Gen sweeps at her bangs and catches me watching, motioning me to come inside. Her meek smile melts my heart no matter what, especially when I consider how close we came to losing her. I wonder if we could have changed what happened to Gen and her husband in Greece if I had been more alert and less concerned about starting a thing with Alec. A thought that stalks me when Gen drifts off into a trance during our long conversations.

"Nate, I'll be in Gen's office. Kayla should be in soon. Would you mind covering for me? I won't be long."

He nods, glances toward our visitor, and steps to the counter.

We have a silent mode of sending messages to each other when we're shorthanded on the floor. Gen and I have complete confidence in Nate. He knows less than zero about the selections inside the gallery, but he's capable of handling all manner of security issues.

Inside Gen's office, the air is filled with her citrusy perfume.

"Good morning, dear. I wanted to catch you before you left for Alec's place. Are you excited about your excursion to Italy?" Her smile gleams, making me blush at the thought of our romantic getaway. "I can see by your face you're ready."

"More than ready."

"It's overdue." Gen digs around in her Hermès crocodile bag. "When I was cleaning out my desk drawer, looking for Papa's letter opener..." She excavates deeper into her purse. "Alec is taking you to Bari, yes?" Gen asks, carefully cradling a leather pouch in her palm. "Many years ago, when I was a slip of a girl, Sister Mary Margaret gave these to me. I'd like you to have them."

"Just a minute." I set the envelope on the corner of her desk.

Gen unsnaps the top and pours dark beads and a large crucifix into my hands. Rosary beads from an earlier era in vintage condition. The metal crucifix on onyx is fatigued by daily wear and tear. Someone in a religious order might have owned them since the large cross is customary on such rosaries. The beads are uneven wood, maybe bone, and they're cool to the touch.

Decades are measured by medals of saints and the Virgin Mary between the beads. I'm oddly compelled to run the length of the strand through my fingers, but I don't dare because the connecting hooks are fragile. The raised corpus crucifixion workmanship and fine detail are worn flat from heavy usage dating back to the sixteenth or seventeenth century.

Closing my eyes and running my thumb over the center Madonna medallion, a warmth penetrates my skin, growing stronger by the second until it's uncomfortable to hold.

"Ow. That's weird." Faint lines shine from the back of the medal. "Can you read this?"

"Put them in the case, dear."

"But—" I deposit the beadwork, strand by strand into the pouch, sensing that these beads are important somehow. My suspicion is that this rosary used to belong to a priest or a cardinal because the dyed bone and worn metals have a masculine look. Monks and Anglicans use a thirty-three-bead rosary, one for each year of Christ's life. Catholics have a much larger rosary to include the twenty mysteries that represent the life of Jesus. This set of rosary beads is the fifty-nine-bead style.

"Gen, I can't accept them. The beads are Roman Catholic, a gift to you. I... can't."

She gently shoves my hand away. "Nonsense. The Sister who gave them to me had a special gift. She saw things. A little like your intuition, only stronger."

"A woman who had visions owned them?"

"I can't explain it, but she had a knack for guiding parishioners from danger. What she told them gave the people hope. Sister Mary Margaret helped me through a very bad time in my life. I wish I could thank her, but I can't go back to Bari. She may not be among us anyway. Please, *bambolina*, keep them for me. Take them with you to Italy. They will bring you good luck."

Italians believe in many small gestures that bring luck, like the number thirteen. Little things such as never wishing someone good luck because it may be a bad omen, or the spilling of salt, unless one tosses the salt over a left shoulder. That's the side the Devil stands on. Gen carries a nail in her pocket so that she can touch iron in the same way we knock on wood to ward off evil. Helga, Alec's housekeeper, rarely turns bread loaves upside down or cuts bread with a knife because it's disrespectful, and she always adds a cross to each loaf per Gen's instructions.

"If you'd like, Gen, I'll keep them. I won't rest until they're researched though. Do you know who originally owned them?"

"Always the historian." She sets her purse on the credenza. "The beads have a spirit to them. The truth is there. Where the senses fail us, reason must step in."

I've heard that saying somewhere. "Where did you visit the Sister? In a convent?"

"Let me think." Gen taps her chin. "The Church of Saint Anne. She was a novice there."

"She hadn't taken her vows yet?"

"There were circumstances. She had to be careful. Nuns who have visions are frowned upon. I went to see her for advice." Gen waves her hand dismissively. "If you and Alec have time, please stop by Saint Anne's and light a candle for her." She points to the envelope. "Is that letter for me?"

"It's mine. A messenger left it." As I study the white thing again, an image of a woman overwhelms me. She's lying on the floor in a pool of her own blood. "Someone is dead, Gen."

"Pish. People die every day." Gen rises from her chair. "You're shaking. Is that what it says?"

"Would you mind looking inside?" I give the envelope to Gen. "Whatever's in there isn't paper. Something lumpy that puts out a very bad vibration."

Gen slides a drawer open and draws out a pair of scissors. She reaches for the envelope and cuts at the short end, which is her habit when she can't find a letter opener.

Nate taps on the glass pane in the door, and I start.

"Annalisse, you're needed at the counter."

"Let me know what you find inside, Gen. I'll be out front."

There's happiness in my shoes as I spring through the office door, adding distance between the envelope and myself. The room was beginning to close in back there.

Nate stops me right outside Gen's office. "Saw the woman hanging around the back of the cabinet where your purse is. When I marched over there, she took off like a scared rabbit to another part of the shop. Looked kinda guilty to me. I didn't see her in your bag, but it won't hurt to check your wallet."

Great, gone two minutes. "I'll be right with you," I assure the client, who's becoming more of an annoyance. In a beeline to the shelf holding my tote, I flip through my wallet and make a quick tally of keys, loose change, passport, .38 Lady Smith, and the Day Runner kept for appointments. When all's in order, the leather case with the rosary drops into the zipper compartment, and I slide my purse into a pull-out drawer.

Impatient nails from Ms. Red click on the glass case.

"Can I see the ring on the stands?" The woman's berry lips are a beacon against her pale skin.

In a half dozen steps to the counter, I slide the glass pane and lay out the slotted velvet tray with a combination of bracelets and rings from Brazil and Australia. Some of the most precious gems on the planet.

The woman in red widens her eyes. "Yeah. That one." She points to the trilliant cut red diamond ring.

A gemologist brought it into the shop not long ago—a stunning find. Gen couldn't resist accepting the rare stone, quickly mounting it in gleaming silver for the sale.

"Honestly, it's so lit." She sings the phrase in a high-low cadence, laying her keys on the case next to me. "Can I try the diamond on? What about sizing? Or is that only at Nordstroms?"

"We size it here. Let me help you."

As I slide the ring on her finger, I wonder how she can afford expensive jewelry. I couldn't imagine such a young girl with press-on nails having that kind of wallet.

My patronizing stream of thought stops dead. Harry taught me never to judge a prospective customer's background by their clothing or manner.

People have surprised me before.

A large jasper stone attached to her key ring sparkles in the overhead lighting. The darkest ruby bloodstone I've seen, and I'd looked at plenty of them for Harry when shipments came in from India and Madagascar. In alternative medicine, it can be crushed as an aphrodisiac or worn as a talisman for its healing powers. This stone is said to have come into existence during the crucifixion of Christ. It's written that his blood dropped onto the jasper stone placed beneath his feet, creating the red variations shown in some stones.

My focus lands on the unusual setting and weird assortment of skeleton keys on the ring.

"Where did you find your amazing heliotrope?" I ask. "The color is so intense. I'd love to know its origin. I'm Annalisse, by the way. And you are?"

"I'm into rocks, and I like reds," she answers without fanfare or the courtesy of looking at me, but her smirk tells me to take a hike.

Nate opens the door, and Alec enters the gallery. What's he doing in Manhattan? In a few hours, my cat Boris and I are leaving for his estate. He should be at home, packing for Italy.

The duskiness in his eyes is a telling shade, and he's not smiling.

"Hey, Alec, this is a surprise." My wave meets his frown.

"Hey. Is Mom in back?" he asks without so much as his usual peck on the cheek.

"She's in her office. I thought we were coming your way this afternoon. Is there a change in plans?"

Alec's holding a newspaper. No, it's a tabloid rag folded in half.

My chest grows cold, recalling the last time we dealt with a tabloid. His ex-wife, Tina, tried to come between Alec and me with the fake story about an affair, using an old family photo. The near break-up experience left a tiny wound on my heart that's still mending.

Alec stalks past me in a determined stride.

Gen's waiting for him at the threshold as if she expects him, then shuts the door.

Ms. Red takes her keys and coffee. "Never mind." She speeds toward the gallery exit as if I had a contagious virus and had coughed on her.

The slot in the tray that had earlier held the red diamond is empty.

"Wait!" My voice echoes off the walls. "Nate, hold her."

The guard folds bulging biceps; his mass stands in her way before she can reach the exit. "Sorry, miss. Please leave your coffee."

"I'm not finished," she whines, covering the top of her cup and pulling it close to her body. "It's free anyway. What gives?"

"We can't allow you to leave the gallery with it." Nate slowly reaches out. "Give me the coffee."

"I told you. I'm not done. What kind of place is this?" The woman's voice wavers. "I promise to drop it in the trash. Chill."

She sidesteps, as does he.

"Naaate?" I draw out his name slowly, dreading another client walking into the shop at this moment.

He directs me to his side with a glance.

We pay him well to observe patrons during their stay inside the gallery. No small act gets past him.

In utter calm, I slide the jewelry tray onto its shelf, lock the door, and meet him next to Ms. Red.

"Where's the ring you tried on?" I send a questioning look to Nate when the girl's finger no longer shows a ring.

A shuffle, a flick of her wrist, and *splash*. The coffee inside the woman's Styrofoam cup sprays the front of my blouse.

"Ack." I stiffen, holding the dripping silk from my skin.

Nate grabs the woman firmly by her padded shoulder while I run for the tissues.

"Nice of you to wait until the coffee cooled." I bite back a curse in time to save what's left of my business etiquette. "What made you do that?"

Warmth streams downward, soaking my slacks as I use the blouse as a bellows and absorb liquid from the fabric with a handful of tissues. While I rub, the added sugar sticks to my belly.

Nate motions at the floor, tugging harder on the woman's red jacket. The costly diamond from the case lies at my feet in an espresso puddle. Earlier, my eyes swept toward Alec for barely a few seconds but long enough for her to slip the band with the diamond into her cup.

"Nice save. Thanks, Nate."

My new Donna Karan blouse is going to the trash heap. No amount of cleaning will remove a coffee stain from sand-washed silk.

"Goodness. Did you spill?" Gen's manicured fingers raise the ring from the muck on the floor. "Will someone tell me why this priceless stone is in filth?" Her cocoa-brown pageboy flips wildly against her cheeks.

Alec remains behind, inside Gen's office with his phone next to his ear.

"Please don't turn me in. It's a big mistake." The woman swipes at Nate's hand. "My record's clean."

"Not anymore. Tried to take the diamond out in her cup of coffee, Ms. Zavos," Nate said.

Gen shakes her head at Red and pauses in Nate's direction.

"Wanna call your PD friend?" he asks.

"Colum's wading through enough burglaries these days." Gen looks at me once again. "I don't think we can save your white blouse, dear. Such a shame."

Gen went for the cleaning cloths in the case, tossing a roll of paper towels to me, then wiping off the ring on the way to her desk. It's possible she plans to call Detective Mooney after all.

"There. All fixed. Now can I go?" Red has the audacity to ask.

"Nate, would you show her to a seat while we check her identification?" I motion to the sofa.

"I'm late already. Yeah, just great."

The woman pounces on a fragile Queen Anne-style settee and crosses her legs, allowing one shoe to drop to the floor so that she can rub her feet. The same peach sofa where Alec and I briefly sat the night of Gen's grand opening party. The night I was introduced to Colum Mooney, one of New York's finest from the First Precinct and a personal friend of Gen's. I like to think he sends officers on an extra patrol of Lower Manhattan because he's watching over Gen. They share a special bond that strengthened after Pearce's death. It's a comfort knowing someone from the department is nearby should we need them day or night.

"What's your name?" Her refusal to tell us her identity is beyond irritating.

"Your ID, please. Take your license out of your wallet," Nate booms, and she does a jaw drop.

He opens his hand and waits while she thumbs through her little red bag.

"Honestly, I don't have to, ya know. Here, bro."

"May I see that?" Gen returns, and she's carrying an envelope. She stops and hands it to me, reading aloud from the girl's license. "Gwendolyn from Staten Island. Were you sent here to steal or here of your own volition?"

Why is Alec still in the office when the action is out front? The gossip paper must be in rare form this issue.

"Do you own the store?" Red asks Gen. "No one sent me. I don't know what came over me. The diamond was—is—beautiful."

Biting words rise to my tongue, but instead, I pucker my blouse like an accordion and stare her down with the sharpest daggers I can muster.

"I'm no criminal. You're taking my license? I need that. Please. I won't bother you again." Her gaze follows Gen, who's now halfway to her office.

My partner is on the trail for her office scanner. She uses the heck out of it for photos and sending notes instead of texting. I expect she'll scan a copy of Red's driver's license for the police department.

"Why did you bother us this time, whatever your name is?" I ask.

"Honestly, all right, they call me Tie Dye."

"Who's that person on your license?" My patience has worn thin.

"You're in big trouble, I hope you know, *Tie Dye*." Nate lifts his lip, exposing a few extra teeth. "Grand larceny and twenty-five years in jail. Who calls you Tie Dye? Your handlers?" He knew how to hold back comments with customers, but put a thief next to him and he loses it.

When appropriate, I like his brash way of handling criminals. Since we joined Gallery Row last year, a few have tried to take small trinkets like decorated hairpins from the shop. Nothing as costly as the red diamond. Having Nate at the entrance and the way his arm flexes his inked blue biceps is enough to keep most con artists from trying anything.

"I can't stay here; don't you get it? I'll get messed up," Red cries out in earnest. Her nose matches the rest of her, red and running from trouble. This woman invites more than her share.

I walk over with the tissue box and offer it to her.

"How much will a replacement blouse cost you, Annalisse?" Gen asks from her office as a desk drawer locks with a snap.

"How much?" The red purse, the size of a cabbage head, makes another appearance with her wallet. "What do I owe? I'm sorry about your shirt."

"Two-fifty ought to do it." I don't want to take her money.

The woman offers two dollars and fifty cents to me without thinking too hard on what a couple of bucks would buy. "Take it."

I turn away to hide my smile. Once in a while, the book *is* exactly as the cover describes.

"If you have two hundred and fifty dollars in your wallet, please pay her. Otherwise, *peccato,*" Gen says, returning to the main floor.

As a rule, Gen uses her native Italian to tease, but this time finishing with "too bad" feels more like intimidation.

Her sharp wit and business mind comes from her dad, I've heard. Alec tells me he had a penchant for getting into mischief. They lived in a coastal town called Bari near the heel of the boot in Italy, where they'd worked a small inland farm before she married Pearce Zavos. This is where Alec is taking me for a few days once he finishes with business. Shortly after her marriage, Gen's father went to prison—for what? I haven't a clue, because Alec leaves out all the details. He keeps much of his youthful past to himself, to my frustration. The best time for me to gather intel about his family is during casual talks on horseback at his estate. Harriet, my mare, is a gift from Alec. He gave her to me after our ordeal in Turkey while rescuing Gen in Bodrum Castle.

Gen's petite figure strolls toward Nate, and she hands him the girl's driver's license and whispers something in his ear too softly for me to hear. He nods and takes the woman in red to the door, who turns to mouth an "I'm sorry" on the way out. Nate follows her into sunlight and escorts her down the sidewalk.

"Gen. You're going to let her go? Shouldn't someone question her?"

"Bah." She waves in disregard. "There's a squad car waiting for her on the street. Nate's delivering her to an officer. No one steals from me without consequences. Now, do you want to know what is in that scary envelope?" Her big smile gleams mischievously at me. "It's nothing, really."

"I should've caught her palming the ring. I really blew it."

"No harm done, *bambolina*."

I flush from her endearment. She began calling me a baby doll when I worked for Westinn and appraised for her on the side. It's Gen's way of soothing over tense moments.

"Go ahead. Look inside."

As I bow the envelope open, a black feather floats to the counter. There's nothing else inside.

"What does it mean?" I ask Gen. "From a blackbird or a crow's wing." Shoving it back inside the envelope, I toss it into the garbage can behind me and shudder. "Someone's sick joke. I'm sorry to bother you with it."

"Disinfect your hands after you wash them. Who knows where that jailbird's been?" Gen's shoulders quiver.

I dismiss her strange comment since she's had a lot on her mind lately.

"What's Alec doing here? Did he tell you?" The office is quiet, and Alec is no longer on his phone.

"He went straight from answering calls to sending texts. I thought you were going to his place today."

"Me too. Something changed."

17

That penetrating stare of hers shoots past me to Alec.

"I'm sure he has a good reason to come to the shop. Why else would he drive two hours to get here?"

Gen leaves for the coffee machine, and I wash my hands. She fixes me a coffee and one for herself, beckoning toward the steps that lead upstairs to marble busts, masculine figures in their armor, and more exotic artifacts of the Roman Empire. From there, we have a solid view of Nate stepping through the gallery entrance.

"Thank you, Nate." Gen motions to him below.

"All taken care of," he says with a thumbs-up.

"Come up here, Alec." Gen uses her motherly voice, and he appears. His stiff, robotic gait and set jaw bother me a lot. The prospect of canceling our trip is in the back of my mind; I'm trying not to focus on that. Alec is selling his car company, Signorile, and we're going to Italy to finalize the sale. We both need this time abroad for different reasons—him for business and me as a sightseeing trip to get my mind off Kate and the uncle who raised me.

When Alec reaches us, he lays the same tabloid he brought with him on a display nearby. A guy wearing a blue racing helmet is on the cover, but his face is in the fold and hard to distinguish. The bold headline on *Reveal Reality's* front page I can't miss: Signorile CEO Takes the Money and Dies.

Glacial air raises hackles along my neck. "Is someone playing a joke on you?" I ask.

"I've missed you." His throaty words take me from the headline for a few seconds as he rigidly grazes his lips against my cheek, then glances downward, shifting himself in front of the newspaper. This is so not like Alec to make such a dry entrance. Twice. He's usually full of smiles and wildly animated with his arms flying about when he talks.

"Did I get my days mixed up? I thought we decided I was coming your way to Brookehaven and we'd fly out in the morning. Is everything on schedule?" I ask.

He focuses on the floor again, covering his thoughts with a bad smoke screen. Alec has expressive silver eyes that I've come to understand well. He knows I can read them. The tabloid from Satan's pit is behind some devastating news.

"Not again," I murmur while turning from Gen.

"Alec, tell us what's wrong, dear." Gen grabs my hand with frigid fingers before I can step far.

My heart stutters a few beats.

"What did you say?" she asks me.

We'd managed to keep the last tabloid scandal from his mother so as not to worry her. *Reveal Reality* pays people to stir up dirt on celebrities. Anyone being seen with Alec would invite the hounds to pounce on a regular basis. Two months since the last scandal is too often for my liking.

"This trash." Alec holds up the paper and allows the front page to flop open so that we can all see the man on the cover.

Gen gasps. "God forgive those people." She raises one palm and chokes up. "Excuse me, kids."

In seconds, Gen is at the bottom of the stairs, running for her office.

I haven't put the headline together yet, but it's clear the front-page photo isn't Alec; it has to be his dad, Pearce Zavos, during his racing days.

Alec manages a sigh. "Call me stupid. I should have spoken to her first." His shoulders sag. "I need to check on her."

"Wait." I touch his sleeve. "Before you do, can you give me the shortened version? What does 'take the money' mean?"

He snugs up beside me, rubbing my back, thawing the ice in my veins.

"Dad drove for Lanny Quicken Motorsports before he started his own business. This article accuses him of embezzling funds from the racing team to start his private car company. Not a good headline for Signorile now that we're seeking a buyer." His lips twist.

"Is there any truth to it?" I ask, breaking out of his muscular grip to get a better look at his expression.

"No way. Well, I thought that once, but..."

He's about to lift his arm for the hand-through-the-hair thing he does and catches himself. "I had Bill check a while back, but we didn't...finish." His eyes dart away from me to the stairs.

"Because you came across evidence? If there's a shred of proof to be found, let me help you. The Signorile buyers are going to see the story in *Reveal Reality*, or it'll be picked up in the Associated Press. Having the truth on your side is important, Alec. I want to help."

"Anna, it's not that simple. I wish it were."

"What then?" It's my turn to remind him of the pact we made to each other. "We're partners. You asked me to marry you, or have you forgotten?"

Alec snaps his arms over his chest. "Yeah, and you turned me down."

"Au contraire, my love. A mere hiccup in our relationship while I get myself sorted. Your family is *my* family." My smile is meant to divert from my trembling hands on my hips. I've taken the conversation to a place I didn't intend to go for a while. "This is about far more than us."

He nods. "You're right. It's about Josh Jennings."

"Who?"

"He joined Signorile when Dad asked him to. Josh was the financial officer for Quicken Racing, and he followed Dad to Signorile as its CFO. I fired Josh back in April when we found operating capital missing and strong signs of a money-laundering scheme."

"That's so not good."

"We believe Josh falsified invoices with certain clients and moved money to offshore accounts without my consent. I was so angry I removed him without hearing his side of it. As far as I'm concerned, he's totally responsible whether he was directly or indirectly involved. I wish I'd handled the situation differently. My short fuse got in the way when I felt Dad's business was being used illegally as a giant retirement fund for Josh. He would know whether Dad used illegal monies from the racing team. We're waiting on the board's decision to prosecute Josh."

"We have to find him."

"He found me," Alec grumbles. "Josh called me while I was in Mom's office. I haven't heard from him since I let him go." He shakes his head. "He wants my help."

"Will helping him help you?" The logical part of me wants a quick solution.

"Let's go into Mom's office."

"I have to watch the shop."

"It's important. Nate can watch." He takes my hand in his sweaty one and sees me down the staircase.

Gen's sitting at her desk in front of her favorite collection of astronomy books, staring at the wall. Her eyelids are rimmed red, and she's grasping a wadded tissue in her hand. My stupid fear of a blackbird's feather placed in an envelope pales against her sadness at the reminder of a lost soul mate. She witnessed her husband's head explode, as I did, when Pearce fought gunmen on the yacht. His small pistol was hardly a match against raining bullets from an automatic weapon. It's surreal when someone you know has died in front of you. Dreamlike, until their life jolts away and a body is left in place of a vibrant human being, like the man with his grin on the tabloid cover. Gen loved her husband deeply. No matter how many times I assure myself it wasn't my fault what happened, Pearce might still be alive if the Mushasha jewel—

Stop it. Samantha Freeman, my best friend, wouldn't give up her matching horse bracelet either. The curse was powerful, and it pulled us along.

Pearce's fate was sealed the day he was born. Only God knows what's in store for us. I have to show Alec and Gen that Pearce's short existence was meaningful.

His record must remain untarnished for Gen and her son.

"Has anyone been smoking? It smells like something's burning." I check the wastebasket for cigarette butts and find it recently emptied. "Alec, please sit before you fall down."

His chair squawks along the tile in front of the Victorian pedestal desk. "Mom, I'm sorry." Alec pats his mother's hand across the blotter. "I didn't think what seeing Dad again might do to you."

"He's gone, dear. There's no bringing him back. Believe me, I've tried." Gen smiles and dabs the corner of her eye. "Honey, how do we get in front of this bad press? Signorile's sale must go forward. It's decided. You and Annalisse are to be freed of the corporation to enjoy yourselves. Phooey on this bad timing, before your trip and all." She glances at me and points to the armchair.

"Have you heard from Global Star Class yet? What's the best move?" I ask Alec.

"Embezzlement matters. Serge LeBlanc is a straight-up guy, so he won't peddle the Signorile acquisition to his board while there's a scandal hanging over it." He rubs between his brows and takes out his phone. "We need Bill's expertise on this one."

The call is made via speakerphone so we can all be a part of it. It'll be great to hear Bill's voice again. After Kate's mysteries were solved a few months ago, Bill returned to his other investigations with his partner, Dan Chappell. Bill's a good friend to Alec, and he helped us both cope with Kate and Ted's nightmare at Walker Farm and in Massachusetts. The uncle I thought had committed suicide came back for revenge. Ted is being held in jail now for the plot to ruin Kate.

Bill doesn't know where Kate went, which was our hope when he dropped her at the airport, so she's in charge and determines when she makes a return. That mother-daughter talk will have to wait until she's ready. She left me with only a letter explaining that she is my birth mother, and I have a father who doesn't know I'm alive. It's little wonder my decision not to marry Alec at this time is frustrating for him. I'm so afraid something in my past will hurt Alec or his mother.

"Hey, I was about to call you. Have you heard mainstream news?" Bill Drake asks.

"You're on speaker with Mom and Annalisse. I'm at the gallery, and yes, we've read the gossip rag's trash." Alec lays the phone on the desk.

"Good morning, Generosa, Anna. I hope you're both well."

"Hi, Bill," I chime, imagining what color palm tree shirt he's wearing with his chinos. "Did we catch you at a bad time?"

"Not in the least. I'm in Connecticut, finishing up a case. What's up?"

"Can you break away to join us in Lecce?" Alec looks away from the speakerphone.

"Lecce... Where's that?" Bill asks.

"Italy," he says, staring at an imaginary spot above my head.

Gen whips around to glare at Alec. "Son, where are you going?"

I'm just as shocked. It's stifling enough to have Brad, Alec's bodyguard and chauffeur, along on the trip. Since there's already three of us, one more will ensure zero privacy with Alec. Not the trip of my dreams. *We'll put off the romantic venture for another time.*

"Do you want me to reopen the earlier investigation on the Signorile accounts?" Bill asks.

"What investigation? You never mentioned this before." Gen grabs another tissue.

Alec raises a palm toward his mother. "It's more complicated than that, Bill. I spoke to Josh already."

"Is that right? Wow. Surprised he'd take your call after being fired."

Alec erupts into mirthless laughter. "Bring all you've got on Josh Jennings before, during, and after his tenure with Signorile. Go deep, really deep into the slimy mud if you have to, and meet us at the Challenger hangar."

"Text me the address and gate. When and what time?"

Alec whispers to me, "What time will you be ready in the morning... six, seven?"

"Name it." This is Alec's mission, and I'm along for support, even though our beautiful, scheduled destination is a smoking pile of rubble blown up by an ex-employee I've never met.

"We don't have time to waste. Can you make it from Connecticut to the hangar, say, by seven thirty a.m.? You'll be able to get your beauty rest on the plane. Pack for at least a week. The ocean air is nice during midday and a little cool at night."

Lecce must be near the coast.

Alec notices my confusion because he walks by and sits on the arm of my chair.

"Anything else?" Bill asks.

"Yeah. A woman was found murdered in Josh's office, wrapped in concertina wire. He's the suspect."

Alec's admission triggers the weird visual in Gen's office. *Is that the woman I saw?* I don't know whose silence is more deafening, Bill's, Gen's, or mine.

CHAPTER

TWO

We lifted off from Syracuse at seven thirty a.m. with Bill Drake, the gifted gumshoe with great instincts who hails from the Florida Keys. In a matter of days, he and his partner uncovered Kate's whereabouts at the spa in Lenox and found Ted Walker, her deceased husband, definitely alive. Bill and Alec taped Ted confessing to the murder of the man found in the Walkers' barn by our ranch hand, Ethan. Bill is the reason Ted's awaiting trial, but no one knows where Ethan is. No one has heard from him. We're keeping my friend Ethan in our prayers.

There's no reason to be squirming and swiveling in my seat, yet that's what I'm doing in the comfortable captain's chairs of Alec's aircraft. In my haste, I forgot to bring reading material, and my fear of being thirty thousand feet high, where there's no oxygen outside, brings on my usual invisible crawling-ant syndrome. It's too early to get wasted on liquor, so I'll have to deal with the sensation for the next several hours.

As per his usual attire, Bill shows up in one of his swaying palm tree shirts and wrinkled linen slacks, ready to hard-charge Alec's fired CFO who awaits us in Italy. He's implicated in a woman's death, so we may already be too late to question Josh and have him help us. I don't know if Jennings channeled funds illegally for Pearce, but he's the logical person to clear Alec's dad. Pearce involved in a laundering scheme feels all wrong to me. We met only once, noting that Alec is so similar to his dad in looks and disposition. No matter how desperate the situation, neither of the Zavos men are morally capable of taking corporate money for nefarious reasons.

Bill and Alec have their heads together on the divan, planning strategies, while my fingers are leaving a sweat trail along the chair arm. I know every bump in the pebbled leather, fragrant and woodsy like a masculine cologne. Someone male must have sat in this chair before me.

Alec's phone interrupts my thoughts. "Good morning, Serge."

Serge LeBlanc.

My heart sinks.

Alec isn't ready with firm answers until he speaks to Josh. We can hope the tabloid news hasn't made it to France yet and the call is unrelated to the scandal brewing. Alec's facial contortions tell a different story.

"Yes, I heard. My father was an honorable man. Do you think Dad would jeopardize his company like this? Don't worry, I intend to clear him." A long pause strains their conversation from Alec's end. The sigh is unmistakable. Failure. "I see. Please give my regards to

Cici, and thank the board for their consideration." Alec cradles his forehead, staring at the carpet, and concludes with, "I understand your predicament, Serge. I'm sorry too." Alec's the color of pea soup. "That was brutal," he says to me.

"Can you resurrect the deal?" I ask.

"About the same possibility as remarrying my ex. Not a chance."

"Global Star tried to acquire Signorile for many years. People strive for the impossible. Doesn't an acquisition work the same way? This can't be over. Once Josh explains, Serge will negotiate with you."

"You're amazing. My glass-half-full girl. Always the optimist."

Glass-half-full girl isn't his usual nickname for me, but I'll take it as an upgrade from the cold reference as his Art Lady.

"Does Josh know we're coming?" Bill asks Alec.

"He asked for help but isn't expecting me." His gaze flickers to the wet path I'm leaving on the beautiful coffee-colored armrest. "Are you doing all right, Anna? Can I get you something?"

"Not much for flying, eh?" Bill faces me with honest concern.

"With our side trip to Lecce to see Josh, will we visit Bari? I hear the beaches are white as flour." I'm thinking about curling waves slowly rolling along warm sand—and me, lounging in a beach chair, crunching coffee granitas, and counting the seagulls through a pair of new sunglasses.

His subtle mouth twitch is enough of an answer. No one knows what to expect in Lecce.

"This isn't the trip I wanted for you, Anna. We'll get to Bari, I promise. Shouldn't be too long with Josh."

"I don't understand why we aren't going to Signorile first. Wouldn't it be better to start at your office in Sicily? Go right to the source of your dad's files again to see if you've missed anything? Josh won't implicate himself or Pearce because he's desperate for your help now that he's a murder suspect." If I'd been fired by the son of my friend, I'd be bitter and want revenge. Who knows what lengths Josh will go to save himself from prison?

Alec smiles at me. "We tossed that around. First of all, if I show at Signorile, I'll get tied up in other business matters. You wouldn't like that. Secondly, Bill has already made a deep-dive investigation into Dad's past. There's less chance now of finding more to implicate him or Josh. After Dad's death, Josh had plenty of time to move or destroy evidence. That's one of the reasons why I fired him without a face-to-face meeting. He had the means to hide most of the transactions, but Bill found a few he couldn't hide. I don't want a war with Josh."

"Seeing Jennings is the best chance we have of getting to the truth," Bill adds.

"Do you know why your mom can't go to Bari? She didn't explain."

"She wanted us to spend time together, away from New York."

"It's more than—"

"I should've taken a separate flight." Bill swipes his long blond waves down his neck. A habit to cover the burn scar he received in a fire rescue.

Mistakenly, I thought Bill was a surfing beach-comber who needed the job when he arrived on the scene to find Kate. He carries himself with an aura of pride and confidence in his work, yet there's a sweet innocence about him that an ocean of women would find endearing and worth investigating. I've caught him watching Alec and me interact, as if he were calculating whether we can make it long term as a couple.

Gen is my strongest link to Alec, and it's not always a comfort. My gallery partner is überprotective of her only child who consults with her on business as well as his private matters. There's a concern for getting burned when too close to a magnetic flame like Alec. An unsettling force is holding me back from accepting our engagement, so I balk, waiting for the perfect moment that may never arrive. Gen must know Alec has proposed, and I'm not wearing his ring, although she and I haven't spoken about it. It's curious why Gen gave me her precious rosary beads. *I'm making too much out of her gift.*

"Sorry I dozed off back there." Brad rubs a crystal-blue eye with his fist. "Bloody comfort I didn't expect."

Alec's and Bill's laughter echoes throughout the cabin. Leave it to Brad to feel bad about catching a nap.

We'd forgotten about Alec's bodyguard snoozing on one of the couches toward the rear of the fuselage. Bradley Edwards awakens from a deep sleep in the same picture-perfect shape as when he walks among us in everyday life. Hair's slightly gelled and combed, pants are pressed, and his button-down Oxford shirt is crisp and immaculate.

"We've been too loud. Sit here." I dislodge myself from the hole I'm making in the recliner and a seat belt that should've been taken off hours ago.

Alec beckons me to the cushion next to him. "We have a few more hours, Brad. Join us."

"Tell Anna about the time when you wrecked on that island." Bill nudges Alec.

My interest piques. I've been starving for any story from Alec's sheltered childhood.

"Alec had the school in an uproar when—"

"There's not much to it. Some other time." Alec gives Bill the look of someone who's said more than he should then glances at me. "Let's talk about something else."

"How long were you on an island?" I ask Alec.

"Once the granola bars ran out and most of the water was gone, I started to worry how I'd get back to Crete with one oar and a current moving against me. Fortunately, the next day, when my parents found my room empty, they searched and called everywhere and everyone. I'd been careful not to tell a soul where I went. Dad had a hunch where I'd be and checked the yacht, finding the dinghy missing. He called on a few buddies to motor out with him to our island spot we'd nicknamed Family Bay. I was so glad to see Dad and the boat parade he brought with him."

A startling fact flew at me. I might not have met Alec if things had turned out differently.

"When he saw me, Dad was both so scared and elated that he didn't know whether to scold me or kiss me. He did both." Alec wavers and bows his head as a tear splashes his pant leg.

My cheek presses against his strong shoulder as our hearts ache from memories. In daydreams and nightmares, I relive that terrible tragedy, helpless to watch as a bystander—shirtless men knocked out Alec on deck and destroyed their boat, looking for the necklace. We couldn't resurrect Pearce, but we found Alec's mother before the Gaucher disease could do her irreparable harm. At the time, I was unaware of the hereditary problem that caused her great bone pain and fatigue if deprived of her medication. Gen kept this secret illness from me, but Alec knew about it.

After a few quiet moments, Alec wipes his eyes and clears a frog from his throat. "What I'd give to go back to that day with Dad…" Alec chokes on his next words, but his regrets we've heard before.

"We were being hunted for the jewelry. As long as we sailed on the Aegean that day or any other, our fate was inevitable. They would have found us at the villa too. We were so outgunned and outmaneuvered. Pearce understood his chances were slim but fought bravely to save us."

"I remember they all carried AKs, and I woke up to the aftermath of a bloodbath." Alec gives me a peck on the temple and squeezes me tight. "One of them kicked the crap out of Annalisse, and she withstood it all. So did Mom. She was rough when we found her."

A shiver races through Alec, chilling my bones with his. We don't discuss that morning on the boat, and Bill hadn't heard details until now.

Alec checks his Rolex and scrolls his phone for messages, stopping to read one.

"You receive email?" Bill reaches for his laptop.

Aloud, Alec announces, "New York's letting prisoners out of Riker's Island due to overcrowding and health concerns. Crowding is making them ill. Really? What about how ill their victims are?"

"They're opening the doors for murderers and rapists too?" I ask.

"Low-level riffraff like car thieves, addicts, burglars—nonviolent types." Alec glares at me. "Like your coworker at the gallery."

I'm drawing a blank. "Your mom doesn't have those *types* working at the shop." It dawns on me whom he may be referring to. "Nate? Gen checked his background thoroughly. He's shiny spotless."

"*Westinn* Gallery. What's his name... the creep who assaulted you the day your brownstone was broken into." Alec snaps his fingers. "The Westinn manager."

My teeth come together at the visual of Alec getting shot and a bald head with a bad comb-over. "Peter Gregory. We didn't press charges— wait. He stole commissioned art and Harry's personal collection, much of it never recovered. Didn't he go to jail for that?" Turning to Bill, I finish my thought. "I can't begin to tell you the pleasure I felt when I emptied that can of pepper spray on him."

"I bet. But watch your back, Annalisse. Lowlifes have long memories." Bill snaps his laptop shut.

"Peter is in the past and no longer a threat to the art world. He deserves whatever sentence the judge gave him."

"Before I left for the hangar, I asked Dan to dig up the old information I uncovered on your dad, Alec."

Bill opens his laptop again. "I have the entire file and time to go over the data once more before we land."

"Mr. Zavos, I've called out a favor and made arrangements with an old friend to supply you with a firearm. In case we get separated or if you and Ms. Drury would like to venture out on your own." Brad settles back against the recliner.

"Is that legal?" I ask.

"Don't worry." Alec's jaw tenses. "We didn't have time to go through their permitting protocol. My permit is for Crete only. Hopefully, we won't have a need to use any weapons. The migrant activity makes the police jumpy."

"Have you considered what we'll do if Italian authorities already have Josh in custody? They won't allow us to question him without some... persuasion," said Bill.

Alec studies me and hesitates before answering, "I have that covered. Hate to say this, but their police departments are some of the most crime-ridden in Europe. The Mafia has feelers everywhere, so we'll plan on a little bribery if necessary. Euros, dollars, precious metals. We have plenty of options with us."

"I hear ya. We do what's necessary to make this scandal go away," Bill blurts.

Bribery? Payoffs? Alec may know these things from personal experience. I was naive not to have considered corruption in government. Signorile and its officials involved in an embezzlement scheme isn't far-fetched after all. Until this moment, I couldn't imagine Alec making deals with the police that weren't aboveboard. I hope Alec's problems aren't made worse by Josh, but deep down I know a murder suspect and ex-Signorile CFO will complicate our goal to clear Pearce.

"Excuse me, Brad." Reaching beside his chair, I unzip the pouch where the rosary beads are and receive a needle prick for my trouble. "Mmm, that hurt." I check for blood, then fumble with the pocket for the source of the sticker. Might have picked up a burr at Alec's estate. To my surprise, a brooch I haven't seen before lies near the seam. "Where'd this come from?" It's fused black and a little over an inch high, with enamel applied on a metal used by cheap Chinese manufacturers. My purse slips to the carpet next to Alec.

"Let's see." Alec extends his palm. "A blackbird brooch, huh. Doesn't look like Mom's stuff."

"It's stamped, not crafted. I didn't buy that pin, so how did it get into my bag?" My thoughts race to track where my purse has been until now.

"No big deal. Toss it," Alec recommends.

"Not yet. I received another bird reference earlier via messenger."

The wing-feather-in-an-envelope tale enlightens everyone, adding to the magnitude of the curious pin.

"Who had an opportunity? I zipped it and stowed it in a drawer when Nate mentioned that Gwen person was hanging around the counter." The cabin seats are scooting by me as I pace the carpet in search of logic for this game of bird body parts. It's like someone is toying with me for their own delight or trying to send a message. "Did the woman at the gallery have time to drop the pin when Nate found her near my purse?" She's the only possibility I can think of.

Alec analyzes the bird pinback further, rolling it between his fingers. "China is stamped in the metal. Nothing special there. Standard enamel process for a clutch pin. One color. It looks like a crow or raven with talons. Thoughts, Bill?"

"Two reminders of black birds in what... two days?"

Is Nate in on a charade to scare me? I won't believe that. Ms. Red, aka Tie Dye, aka Gwendolyn, had the best opportunity to set the pin in my tote or send the feather by messenger before she stepped inside Zavos Gallery. She wore a plume in her hat, so she could be behind the ruse if feathers are significant to her.

"Does a bird within the genus Corvus hold some significance to you, Ms. Drury?" Brad has some knowledge of scientific bird classification, winging me back to my zoology class days.

A pilot in proper navy attire and epaulets opens the cockpit door and strolls down the aisle. He makes eye contact with me and seductively smiles. Or did he? The altitude's effect on my buzzing mind is making me imagine things.

"Mr. Zavos, we're experiencing strong headwinds. It's going to get a little bumpy soon. I ask that you remain in your seats and fasten your belts."

When I spring forward, Alec tugs me down to the cushion beside him. No one has to tell me twice that we're going to bounce around and hit our heads on the ceiling in this metal coaster without rails.

"Stay here, Annalisse. There's room. I'll let you hold on, like you did when we had some bad weather in Athens."

He forces a smile to ease my nerves on their last end, but something else is lurking behind the platinum eyes encasing a black abyss.

My belt slides together, and Alec tightens it. "No, Brad. Corvidae are just large blackbirds. I'll look closer at the pin again. We might have missed something obvious." The brooch's shine is like obsidian glass at the base of a volcano. I feel an eruption brewing and examine the tiny beak and faint wing details for a specific bird family. It's not supposed to be a backyard blackbird, jay, or magpie. Alec's right; it's meant to depict something like a crow.

Bill breaks his long silence and snaps his seat belt, glaring at me. "Birds mean something to someone, and they're leaving you a calling card."

The aircraft drops as if it's at the top of a Ferris wheel out of human control, and I sink my nails into Alec's knee.

He hisses and winces as the sharp points bite his flesh. He reaches to secure my belt again, as we free-fall. *We're gonna die up here. I just know it.*

"Shh. Hold on to me," he whispers.

And I do.

CHAPTER
THREE

Generosa Zavos stares outside through the bay window of her son's Tudor estate, wondering why she let her guard down and told Annalisse about Sister Mary Margaret. She hadn't thought about her for decades. Withholding the information was safer for everyone that way. Silly to think that this holy nun of the Catholic Church with a checkered family could still be alive to help Alec find his true ancestry like she had for Generosa. If only her dear father, Antonio, hadn't joined the Cosa Nostra where committing a murder was part of the initiation to become one of them. The money-hungry beasts from Sicily live to cause others pain for recognition from the syndicate. Her papa wasn't even Sicilian. That's the part Generosa found so hard to understand. He was the ultimate outsider where normally the Barese aren't welcomed into a Sicilian brotherhood. The Mafia is a cult no one is allowed to leave unless they do so from six feet under or snitch to the police and hide out like Tony the Terror had. She'd shoved away the awful nickname they gave to Antonio and dared not think what it meant. Her imagination couldn't be too far from the truth. She was told to stay quiet and keep Cosa Nostra matters to herself. Her father paid heavily with a jail sentence to save them from Leo Manetti's wrath. Generosa would gladly have taken her father's place, but a woman can't. Remorse and all, it had to be this way.

Generosa couldn't take the risk and explain the past to Alec. How she longed to go with them to Bari and see her childhood home one last time. The burden of not being able to visit the homeland is a lead weight on each breath, but she takes her papa's warning seriously. To do so would mean an ending for Alec and eventually for Annalisse and her.

A pair of pudgy hands, strong and sure, sets Generosa's coffee cup beside her on the end table. Helga's cheerful yellow apron has creases left from the packaging. She'd broken into a brand-new apron to make a good impression; it was so like Helga to impress. That's one reason she was perfect to work for Generosa's son.

When Helga moved into the villa on Crete, Generosa and Pearce immediately liked her and her authentic German dishes. From the bowstring-tight bun to her clunky wooden shoes, Helga was genuine and reliable. A cook and housekeeper she could trust to run a Greek villa and, finally, an estate for a bachelor who barely had time to tie his shoes and wolf down a meal between business trips.

"I've whipped up a batch of lebkuchen. Would you like some when they're ready? Marzipan, hazelnuts… glorious spices. Oh my, the mouth waters just thinking about them." Helga smacks her lips loud enough to make anyone hungry.

"Nut cookies sound scrumptious, dear, but I'll pass. Don't let me stop you from baking. Eat one for me. My mind isn't on food."

As Helga moves aside and tromps for the kitchen, Generosa's left with a hint of flowers and apricot in her wake. Alec knew of her fondness for the rose scent and bought Helga the oddly named Dirty Rose perfume for Christmas. Helga had a good laugh at the title, but it doesn't stop her from wearing it around the house as her everyday favorite. She hoped Alec bought more than one bottle. Generosa brushes the frivolous notion aside, knowing full well her son doesn't have time to think about his maid that far into the future.

Helga returns with a cup of tea and settles on the sofa. "Gen, is anything wrong? Since Alec and Annalisse left, you seem to be preoccupied. What stopped you from going with them?" She crosses her thick ankles at the sofa in front of Generosa and slurps her Earl Grey the color of caramel candy.

The truth would trouble Helga more, so Generosa goes in a different direction. "Without Pearce, I'm floating in place. What do you think about me leaving my shop in Annalisse's complete control and taking an exciting world cruise? Wouldn't that be fun? Forty-five countries in 120 days. If it weren't for being stuck on a ship four long months. There are so many people who get sick on cruises. I'm torn about it."

"I can't imagine. Aren't you afraid to travel alone?" Helga asks, peering over her teacup.

"Do you think it's going well with Alec and Annalisse?" Generosa awkwardly jabs the cushion with her thumbnail.

"How do you mean?"

"You see them together more than I do. Does Alec seem less interested in Annalisse than he used to be?" Up to this point, Generosa hasn't been so bold as to ask Helga's opinion, but she's desperate to get another viewpoint to settle her fears.

Helga raises a brow and takes another sip, her blackening gaze burning a hole into Generosa. "Your son is mad for Annalisse. He's so caring of her, and I've seen him with a lot of girls." Helga starts an eye roll and stops short of a full revolution. "The way she looks at him too." She emits a dovelike coo. "Just because they don't fawn over each other like starstruck lovers in one of those fancy novels doesn't mean they aren't in love. If a handsome man looked at me the way he looks at Annalisse, I'd go anywhere with him. He's completely smitten, Gen. Are you worried?"

"Yes. Alec planned to pop the question months ago. Bought an exquisite diamond-and-sapphire ring—showed it to me when Marcello designed it exclusively for the occasion. It is stunning, and Annalisse isn't wearing it. Alec has said nothing since. It's absolutely frustrating." She slaps the clawed armrest. "Has he said anything to you?"

"If he has the ring, he's picking his moment. Miss Annalisse is dealing with a lot. I wouldn't be concerned. She's still finding herself after that experience with the man who drugged and tied us here. And then Kate's incredible news. I wasn't the same for weeks following."

She pauses and sips her tea. "Injury affects each of us differently. Speaking of… I overheard Annalisse mention New Zealand a few times. Alec must have business there, perhaps? Oh, this came yesterday." Helga picks up an envelope from the side table. "Usually I don't look over his mail when I lay it on the desk for him to go through. Look at the stamps, how colorful they are. Noticed them right away because they're so beautiful. See the Queen and her crown there?" Helga points at four stamps applied in a square, unique in blue and green, not unlike Hawaiian or Maori statues, then hands the envelope to Gen.

"This is definitely from New Zealand." Generosa flips the envelope over. "No return address. Who would leave that off? The young man who worked for Kate is from there."

"Would he send a card to Alec?" Helga asks.

"Not likely, unless there's something wrong. Alec doesn't care for Ethan. I think there's a little rivalry between them. Alec mentioned that Ethan had…what term did he use? Has the *hots* for Annalisse. A silly word to use. The card could be from a personal friend and not him." Generosa holds it up to the light, squinting.

"Would you like me to steam it open?"

Generosa shoves the envelope into Helga's hand. "Absolutely not. I'm not a snooper. Put it on the desk with the rest of his mail."

Helga jumps, wide-eyed. "At once. If there's nothing else then, I'll wrap the cookie dough in the refrigerator and begin dusting upstairs."

"Don't leave yet." Generosa extends her arm toward the love seat. "Ignore my childish outburst and sit with me, won't you? I'm worried what the kids will find in Italy. Have you heard that terrible story about Pearce? Alec is trying to mend fences with an old friend of Pearce's to get the truth, and now there's a poor dead woman clogging up the works."

"Really?" Helga lifts her cup of tea and resumes her seat on the sofa.

Generosa explains Alec's predicament and his reason for going abroad.

"This lie in the papers couldn't happen at a worse time. Pearce wasn't a thief, but Alec's word alone isn't good enough to clean up this mess. If he can't establish Pearce's innocence, the corporation will be too ticklish for an acquisition."

"Mr. Zavos would never have stolen from anyone," Helga says curtly. "It was not in his nature."

Generosa's phone vibrates on the table. "Excuse me, sweetie, I need to take this." She swipes the phone. "*Buon pomeriggio*, Oliver. How is Florence? Did you make it to the antique fair? ... Yes, it has been a while. The months seem to slip away." Generosa smiles at Helga, taking the conversation outdoors, allowing the warmth to soak her skin and the sunlight to lift her mood. Gen taps the speakerphone icon.

Oliver King clears his throat. "It's a treat to hear your voice, but a matter of importance prompts my call. It's imperative I reach Alec. Do you have another number for him other than an office phone?"

Generosa continues her walk along the cobbled pathway leading from the estate to the road. "He's on the jet, on his way to Bari."

"Bari? Do you know where he's staying?"

"I can get that information to you. What's this about? Is there anything I can help you with?" A drumming headache migrates to her temple. She should've eaten something.

"I don't know, Gen. This is a touchy... subject... and I don't want to spoil your day." Oliver's falter raises alarm bells. "The Global Star Class board met, and we are discussing a merger with Signorile."

Oliver, a Scottish national, stepped down from Orbacher Energy a few years ago. He had purchased several pieces of Renaissance furniture from the gallery, more so through a liaison since Pearce's death, either as a collector or out of compassion to help a widow make a few sales.

"A merger? How is Serge?" A churning inside Generosa eats away at her confidence to play ignorant of Alec's business. Her son requires her help with the deal, or it won't happen. News of the tabloid article must have reached Europe by now.

Generosa has to find a way to leave breadcrumbs for Oliver without being too obvious, like she has for Annalisse regarding an old foe. Hopefully, Generosa's clues are making sense to her future daughter-in-law. She must stay positive for her son's sake. Alec and Annalisse belong together.

"Oliver, I have a plan of mutual aid to us both. Would you like to hear it?"

CHAPTER
FOUR

After surviving our bumpy flight and touching down at Lecce Galatina Airport around two p.m. local time, Alec, Bill, Brad, and myself arrive via rental car at Josh Jennings's Fortuna Investimenti office in Lecce. I had to smile when Alec told us the name of Josh's company. Fortune Investments is the ideal venue for a money launderer like Josh *if* he'd taken Signorile's funds and schemed to do more illegal activity. Alec wasn't contacted for a job reference, which isn't a surprise. Josh could have used Pearce's reputation or more easily had an ally endorse him. We hope he's still inside where we can speak to him, or this will be a wasted side trip.

But the building's perimeter is swarming with black scooters and blue compact cars, *Carabinieri* and *Polizia* emblazoned in white on the doors, warning bystanders to stay clear of the square. Magnificent Baroque limestone the color of honey extends an entire city block on both sides of the stone road. Intricate gingerbread and cherub carvings seem to follow us from on top of each window for as far as I can see. A female traffic cop, with her hair piled inside her cap, directs sightseers on foot away from the entrance and motorized vehicles from being able to park near the building.

Brad slows at a side street and stops.

"There's no parking lot. What do you propose, Alec? I'd like to make the first contact. See if it's possible to get inside." Bill unclips his shoulder harness and sets his pistol on the floorboard, laying a jacket over it. Looking my way, he adds, "In case we're searched."

"Brad, stay with the car and wait for us. Drive around if you have to, if we're lucky to get through the door, that is. They most likely hauled him to the police station by now." Alec glances over his headrest at me. "Go ahead of us, Bill; Anna and I will hang back." Alec shows the same trepidation I'm feeling, then opens his car door slowly.

The sidewalk darkens from ominous passing clouds, enough to dip the temperature a few degrees. A woman with a short, dark pixie cut passes us in denim capri pants, sandals, and a tank top. I don't recognize the spicy scent she's wearing. She whizzes past us, head down, like she's late for an appointment. Octagon sunglasses in gold frames shade her eyes and cover most of her smallish face.

We approach the front of Fortuna Investimenti, and Alec draws me to his side while Bill speaks to an ultratanned officer who quickly shakes his head, guiding Bill to the street. Their discussion continues with Bill flashing his identification... and a badge? He doesn't use one. The policeman with a slight build and Raffa on his name tag stares at Alec for a few moments and shows us his mouthful of straight teeth. Finally we're

allowed to accompany Bill inside where we find ourselves in the midst of high winds. Literally.

"Uno momento." An Interpol official stops our
group from advancing, and both men carry on a
lengthy discussion in Italian. International police?
Either the victim has ties to another country, or Josh's
involvement has sparked their inquiry into this crime.

"What was that outside?" Alec asks Bill in a
whisper.

"He wouldn't let us pass, so I used your celebrity. I
took a chance your name is well known here and promised him you'd pose for a photo and provide autographs
for his entire family."

"Is Josh in the building?" Alec asks.

"I don't know. Can't be sure Officer Raffa knows
Josh. He just told me that hours ago, they cut the wire
away from the body so investigators could get prints
and lift evidence. I think the medical examiner had difficulties yesterday because of the razor wire."

The reception area is completely empty, and there's
a smell like metal in damp dirt circulating overhead.
Farther in, the ceiling fan is hovering on high speed,
and the windows are open.

A dead body inside a warm office leaves an unmistakable odor behind, as did the body Ethan found inside the stall at Walker Farm. Decomp is one smell that
sticks with you forever. Adding to the office creepiness,
who chose the interior's decor? We're surrounded by
limestone walls painted an ugly shade of ochre, slightly
more yellow and definitely more unappealing than the
building's exterior. The rooms will need another coat

of fresh paint to cover a harsh stench known to stick to the walls like cigarette tar does.

No one is nearby, not even the receptionist.

The office cubicles are silent but for a few flapping papers. Not a single desk phone is ringing. It's like the office decided to have a fire drill midday, and the employees left their computers on and didn't bother to close folders—open to anyone passing by. Frames holding pictures of sweethearts and children stand by as guardians for the people who are absent from their high-back swivel chairs.

Officer Raffa returns and mutters in heavy Italian brogue, "*Il signore* is waiting for his… *avvocato difensore*." He points to the room with a closed door. "Come, Mr. Zavos. Your friends stay here."

"Josh is in there waiting for his defense attorney. Back soon." Alec touches my arm and looks at Bill, sending him a private message.

Alec's led to a side office, and the solid door closes behind them.

"Is Alec signing autographs, or should I even worry about what's going on in that room? Has Josh been here the entire time messing with evidence?" I ask Bill.

"Alec's prepared for all contingencies. I'm surprised they haven't taken Jennings down to the station by now."

A few minutes later, Alec emerges by himself. "They weren't going to allow us to talk to Josh, but I *persuaded* him. It shouldn't be much longer."

For what feels like an eternity, we sit in ladder-back pine chairs with brown cushions while Alec keeps adjusting his watch. I don't know what Alec had to promise the officer. Autographs are fine with me, but if he had to pay him off, I'd rather not know.

"I hope Brad is parked in the shade somewhere." Alec looks at his watch for the eighth time in twenty minutes and turns to me. "Now that we're here, they seem to be in no hurry to get rid of us. I'm sorry, Anna. Hold on a little longer." His smile is an honest one full of regret.

I've heard the sentiment from him so often it doesn't even register with my brain anymore. We both have a lot of work to do in the I-promise-to-do-better department.

The closed door at the back wall opens, and a guy pokes his head out, surveying the room. He's fiftyish and, with his reading glasses, reminds me of Gen's studious accountant. Alec pivots, and his earlier smile vanishes.

"That's Jennings," Bill says quietly.

"Yes." Alec waves to draw the man's attention.

A confused Josh looks at us and then the floor as if he's embarrassed. Eventually he settles his eyes on Alec. "I wasn't sure you'd come. My attorney should be here soon. Come back to the conference room."

Bill asks Alec, "Is it okay to go on ahead?"

Alec must have compensated the officer well to allow us entry this close to the crime scene.

"Let's get this over with." Alec seems queasy.

The three of us move through the aisle between desks and toward the room with a door left open for us. Josh has already gone inside. For someone who wants Alec's help, he sure doesn't appear happy or grateful for his effort. A huge effort. This had better not be Josh's way of buying himself out of the woman's death. The disgrace of being fired from Signorile after Pearce's tragedy has to hurt his pride.

There's news of a deadly virus moving through Europe, and the typical handshake is no longer being used between business execs. Bill lifts his arm and catches himself.

"Mr. Jennings? My name is Bill Drake, an associate of Mr. Zavos. You've asked to see him, and we also have some questions for you on another matter."

"Wonderful." The man in a sweaty, slept-in polo isn't thrilled with us staring him down. There's frost in the room as testosterone flies between glances. No one wants to be the first to break the sheet of ice forming around the presumed blue-eyed killer. Alec hasn't made any assumptions yet until we talk to him, but Josh's cool facade feels calculated to me. A superior to Alec, or something like that. For an innocent, I don't like his peculiar behavior in the presence of a man who's here to keep his neck from a noose.

"I asked to see Alec. Who are the rest of you?"

He's behind a chair, using it as a shield to save himself from a CEO who wants to take his livelihood from him again. Or is it because he's guilty of ending a woman's life?

Alec pulls out the chair for me, and we all sit at the long conference table with a fancy letter *F* embellished in the center.

Josh's temples bead with sweat, and he's wringing his hands next to a wool felt fedora hat with a band. They seem to be popular in Italy. The guy's bloodshot eyes and dark circles are sure signs of insomnia and stressing to the max. Wet ovals hang beneath the arm-pits of his beige shirt.

Alec's unshakable gaze lands on Jennings, who abruptly turns away.

This meeting isn't opening well.

Bill addresses Josh. "We don't have a lot of time. Authorities aren't thrilled with us questioning you, but they were… let's say, swayed. Tell us what happened here?"

"She was tied and tortured in my office after I left night before last. I opened the building in the morning at seven and found her lying on her side, strapped to a chair and wrapped in wire near my desk. Lots of blood." Josh holds a paper towel over his mouth, then uses it to wipe away perspiration. "When I left the building, she was in the conference room. I have no idea how she ended up in the office. Maybe the cat went in there." He slides the fedora into his lap.

"Who is *she*?" Alec asks.

"Benita Alvarez."

Alec pauses. "That name's familiar. I heard Dad mention her a few times. Wasn't she a friend of yours?"

"She was a friend to a lot of us." Josh raps the table with his wedding band.

"Were security cameras running?" Bill asks. "If you left, the police will know that."

"The culprit shut down the cameras before he came inside. Police allowed me go to my apartment with a guard since their detective was out sick but told me I had to come back today. I saw Benita last when we met in this conference room around nine, two nights

52

ago. I would never do *that* to a human being." Josh flattens his lips into a bitter line.

"Do you have an idea what happened after you left?" I ask because the curiosity is killing me.

"Someone came in, tied her up with razor wire around her torso, then clubbed her. When I found her, she was dead, and a bloody bat was beside her. Her wrists were sliced up where she'd tried to free herself, I guess." His lips twist like he's chewing on a mouthful of bitter radicchio. "Can't imagine what she went through. I don't know if she died from bleeding wrists or the bop on the head. Either was enough to end her life. They'll figure it out. The wire makes things tough for the investigators." He sets his fedora on the table and pats the brim.

After seeing a spectacle like that, Josh seems detached, like a stranger, cold and uninterested.

He abruptly changes the subject. "Have you seen the news?" Josh focuses on Alec. "You must have, or you wouldn't have come here so readily by my request alone. Benita had the tabloid with her. She used it to scare me for money."

"We were coming to Italy anyway." I jump in at a place I didn't belong but couldn't help it. "She was blackmailing you, how? Is it that story about *you* stealing funds from the racing team, and she knew the truth? Was she going to expose you?"

A good motive for murder.

"Did Dad ask you to misappropriate funds, or was it you all along?" Alec breaks my trajectory.

He stealthily gets straight to the point and the reason for our trip to Lecce. Josh could take the question as open-ended for moving money from the racing team and Signorile. Either way, Alec will know what to ask next.

"Direct. I miss that tactic." Josh puckers his mouth painfully.

"You were his original partner. Who else should I ask, man? Did *Dad* knowingly take money from the team to start Signorile? I need to know."

"It wasn't like that and would take too long to explain. I don't have time."

Wow. He has nerve.

"You should make time." Bill stands, flexing his upper arms and increasing his presence.

An out-of-place, soft-sided pet carrier sits on one end of the table. What an awful day to bring a pet into the office for show-and-tell.

"Is that your carrier?" I scan the room in case we missed an animal.

"Belongs to Benita. Her cat escaped, and she was looking for it when I left."

"You left her alone inside this building and didn't check on her?" Bill asks. "She shakes you down for money, lets her cat run wild, and you leave?"

"Yeah, all that. I had the beginning of a mind-busting migraine and couldn't wait all night for her to find her crippled cat."

Alec looks at me with such disdain for Josh.

What a self-centered boob Pearce hired. I'm glad Alec fired him. In addition to his tendencies to grift, Josh has no sympathy for humans or animals, which instantly makes his possible crime less crucial to me. The poor cat must be starving by now.

"The cat isn't important." Alec's fuse shortens.

"Oh, uh." A fur ball grazes my bare ankles beneath the table, and I stiffen. "It is."

Slowly I reach down and pick up the most beautiful calico cat I've ever seen. Her markings are predominantly bright orange and a little white with a black blaze like a bandanna across her scared eyes. She's shaking and nips my hand.

"Ouch, bad girl."

"Be careful. She's got a broken leg," Josh warns.

Alec stands and inspects the cat. She yowls when he touches her back leg. "It needs to be set. She's in a lot of pain. Didn't you see that?"

"Benita was taking it to a vet. Aren't you one of those?" Josh sneers vacantly through the conference room window. "Sorry, kitty. I can't be bothered. You're on your own."

"We can drop her off at an animal shelter," Alec says.

"Why? They'll put a stray down if we leave her with a broken leg. Please, Alec, let's take care of that leg, or she may not survive her injuries." He's not thinking clearly. Faint cracks in his apathy appear as the vet training and oath to do no harm kicks in.

"Do whatever you want with her, but get her the hell away from me." Josh grimaces.

"Allergic?" I ask him.

"Yeah, to pistols. The cat's got a criminal history." It's Josh's turn to stand. "That schizo mafioso will keep looking for her."

"Huh?" I cuddle the cat against my breast, and she hisses.

"How did the Alvarez woman get it?" Bill asks, and we all stare at Josh for the rest of the story.

"This meeting is over." Josh's hands are in front of him like double stop signs. "You booted me out of Signorile. Why should I answer your questions?"

"Because you need my help. Isn't that why you called me?" Alec pets the cat and guides his chair under the table. "Be careful with her, Anna. She should be fine to ride in her carrier until we figure out her future. The authorities may not let us take her, so be prepared for that possibility." Concluding his words with Josh, he says, "Alvarez died in your office. Maybe you killed her, maybe not, but there's enough circumstantial evidence to zoom you to the top of their suspect list with a strong motive to want her dead. You and Benita were together in this building. You're a United States citizen in a foreign country. The Italian government doesn't need any *actual* evidence to lock you away. Don't you get that?" Alec folds his arms to stress his point.

"It's all about protection, my friend. Protection for Signorile and protection for your mother." The smugness in Josh's expression is full of loathing for Alec. "You're about to find out the hard way, dude."

The door behind Alec opens wide with a push from a fat hand. "Not another word, Josh." A man in a light sport coat, a bulging belly, and wrinkled slacks too short for his slip-ons rakes the conference table with his radar-like, bulbous eyes. He's looking for something. "You aren't Lecce police. Why are you quizzing my client?" The attorney scoffs at the cat in my arms like she's evil incarnate.

"What do you mean by protection for my mother?" Alec's lip curls at Josh, then he shifts his ire to the attorney. "Your client should explain that *before* I leave. How's Mom involved?" Alec starts for the other side of the table, and I grab his shirtsleeve.

"I'll put the cat in her crate." As I do, she mews but finds her footing in the soft padding.

"Mr. Jennings is finished yakking as we're expected at the police station. A good day to you, miss." Josh's lawyer sets his weird eyes on me and nods. Signal enough for our group to stop the inquisition and leave.

"We have more questions and no answers," Bill grumbles when he finds an officer waiting for us.

"Would you follow me, please? Through there."

Officer Raffa leads us to a small ten-by-ten office without the usual complement of desk and computer. Instead, a whitewashed table and four chairs fill the center of the hot, stifling space. A lonely parlor palm droops in one corner near the window; the shriveling plant is in dire need of a drink. The sweet stench of death is stronger in this room as it's closer to Josh's office where Benita was found.

"Please sit."

"Are you interrogating us?" I ask.

"How long have you been in this country?" The officer's heavy accent and piercing black glare are unsettling.

"Check the Lecce tower log. We touched down"— Alec checks his Rolex—"a couple of hours ago." He picks at the table end nervously. The last thing we need is to look guilty and be thrown into Josh's mess.

"Why are you meeting Mr. Jennings today? Are you with Fortuna Investimenti?"

Raffa has changed to all business and no smiles since Alec supplied the autographs.

"He has knowledge vital to Mr. Zavos's company," Bill jumps in officially. "I mentioned earlier why we're here."

"That's right. Josh was our CFO until recently. The chief financial officer," Alec adds.

Raffa writes something down in a booklet. "We check log books at the airport. You were in Lecce two days ago, yes?" The officer makes a lame effort to trick us into changing our arrival.

I glance at Alec, and we all tell him no.

Raffa clears his throat for another jab at us. "Did you know the *donna morta*?"

"What?" Bill says what I'm thinking.

"He's asking if we know the dead woman." Alec clarifies the Italian.

A photo of a longhaired woman with a cratered skull and bloodied face slides across the table in front of Alec and me. The visual is pretty gross.

Bill walks around to look but doesn't linger.

"I don't know her," Alec says. "Do you?" He waits for Bill as I turn away. "Who is she?"

"No next of kin. Not yet. Tell me about Mr. Jennings."

Alec breaks into Italian to hasten the explanation about Josh.

Roughly every fifth word is clear to me from my time as Gen's assistant. Alec is sticking to Josh's affiliation with Signorile.

"Why is he in Lecce and not your company in Sicily?" Raffa asks.

"We came to an agreement when he asked to pursue outside interests."

The quite good cliché response makes the officer sigh. He isn't going to get any details from Alec, and he knows it.

"May we go now?" Bill's making eye contact with me as he passes in front of the officer.

"One question to Mr. Zavos. Is Jennings capable of murder?"

Alec shrugs nonchalantly. "I don't know. Anything I say would be speculative."

"May I call on you again?" The officer adjusts the white harness holding his firearms in an effort to show authority.

Bill draws one of his detective cards from his pocket. "Call me anytime. I'm easier to reach than Mr. Zavos."

I grab the carrier and hold it up. "C'mon, sweetie."

"What is that?" Raffa meets me in the doorway and inspects the cat through the mesh.

Holding my breath, Alec answers him in Italian. We didn't arrive with a crate, so the officer has every right to question our leaving with one.

Raffa isn't swayed by the answer he hears and follows up in more stern Italian.

Doubt clouds my thoughts. We may not be able to leave with the nameless cat.

"Bill, please escort Annalisse to reception and wait for me there." Alec's face is expressionless, but I catch his hand digging in a pants pocket.

Payoff? It's hard to be indifferent to the way the police do business with the public in Italy. It makes me feel dirty in the midst of their cops.

I peek at the cat again. "Let's go."

While we sit and wait for Alec near the entrance, Bill explains, "Wish we had more time with Josh now that the murder victim ties back to the story in *Reveal Reality*. She might have been the one who leaked it to the tabloid since she needed money. We're so close to finding out Pearce's arrangement with his partner, although Josh might have been acting on his own. He's cagey with the body language."

"What do you think about his gibberish referring to Gen Zavos? He kept repeating the word protection, which is strange. If Benita had this cat in her possession, what's the Mafia about?" I stick my fingers inside the carrier. "Nothing makes sense to me."

"Maybe it's best I stay behind while the three of you go on to Bari. Once his attorney takes Josh down to the police station for more questioning, he may understand the depth of his situation better and be more receptive to our help."

We climb into the rental car with Brad and Bill waiting for us outside the veterinary hospital. Alec assures me that after the cat has surgery, we'll take her with us. She should be recovered enough for Bill to pick her up after he speaks to Josh again.

"You've been quiet. I hope I haven't fouled up your next client by having you stay behind," Alec says to Bill, checking his messages. "With me out of the way, he may open up to you. I'm a sore reminder of the cushy job he left behind for being stupid."

"I hope he comes clean. I'd like to find out more about the Alvarez woman before seeing Jennings to convince him that I know almost as much as he does."

"Why did the victim take a cat that didn't belong to her and bring it to a meeting with Josh? Was she planning to travel? I'd dig into that angle and find out who the mafioso is. What sick jerk uses razor wire on his victim? Is that a clue to who killed her?" Alec asks the questions for general discussion.

"What is protection for Signorile and protection for your mother? Did you figure that out yet?"

Alec barely looks at me, still busy on his phone.

"What could he mean by *you'll find out the hard way*?" Josh's last cryptic line to Alec raised my antennae at the time, especially the smug way he said it.

"How well do you really know Josh?" Bill asks Alec.

"I don't know him at all. Dad introduced me to him in the early days of Signorile. From what we gathered a few years ago, Dad allowed him to manage the finances as he saw fit. If corporate funds were moved into private accounts, I would like to believe Josh would've been stopped if Dad knew about it. Unless turning a blind eye was part of the deal to entice Josh from the racing team." Alec shook his head. "That's hard to believe, knowing Dad's ethics."

"What about the victim in the photo? Josh sounded as if he knew her intimately; at the very least he was friendly with her. Unless she's an Italian national, Lecce is a long way to bring a cat for a handout. She showed him the tabloid because she might have had firsthand knowledge of what happened to the racing team's money. It's a shame Benita's gone and we can't ask her. That's for Bill to figure out." I'm running at the mouth as ideas pop into my mind.

"I had hoped to get the truth out of Josh and drop this scandal in the trash bin where it belongs." Alec scratches his head. "I hadn't figured in a homicide with Signorile's ex-CFO at its heart." Alec gasps. "Man."

"What is it, Alec?" I ask.

"A text from Josh. They're on their way to the station. Listen to this." Alec reads from his phone. "Keep one eye over your shoulder for the Manetti family. The cat's name is Stella."

"Do you know this Manetti family?" Bill asks.

"Everyone in Italy knows them. They're Sicilian Mafia. Dad steered clear of them in Palermo, but they make their presence known everywhere. Sweet Jesus." Alec bounces his head against the headrest. "Protection for Signorile, protection for Mom. Did Jennings allow them access to Signorile?"

"So, that's a new wrinkle. Pearce orders Josh to pay the Mafia protection money." Bill grunts. "Or the Mafia got to Josh and your dad didn't know about it."

"If that's true, no one's paying them now. I haven't hired Josh's replacement yet."

"Protection, as in racketeering or extortion? Why did Josh link the two sentences with the cat's name? You don't think... That has to be it." I stop myself from going further.

"Stella must belong to one of the Manettis."

Bill finishes my thought, and I'm taken back to the vet hospital operating on Stella Notorious Kitty.

CHAPTER
FIVE

Manetti House, Palermo, Sicily

Leo kicks his dearly departed wife's crocheted blanket off his feet and wiggles circulation into his seventy-six-year-old limbs. His joints pop and creak like the dry floorboards in the attic.

"Ah, relief. I'm not dead yet." *Not soon enough.* "Open a window, Carlo. Bring some light in here. I'm smothering in this *bara*." In his condition, his voice doesn't carry like it used to.

They call him the Birdman.

He reaches for a deep breath and draws it halfway. A cough rattles from his croupy lungs and gags him. Getting air is harder today with the tumor growing more each week. He doesn't smell his food anymore; everything tastes like a stinky dishrag in the sink, so why bother? Doc Rinaldi's pills might be keeping him alive, but so what? He says Leo's got lots of time left, but he won't say how many weeks or months. He wrenches himself up against the pillow stack behind his head and coughs again, leaving a pink stain on his

T-shirt and cussing at the development. The pain is a knife plunging into his back. One of these days, the knife will drop for the last time.

"Leo. I'll help you." A pair of rough hands fluff and punch the pillows from behind. "How much light do you want? Shade up all the way or just a little? You decide. The screens are off outside. Mario's washing your windows."

"Lift them anyway. Shades too. Let me smell the lemons and blood oranges in the grove while I still can. I'll be in the coffin soon enough with the worms and cockroaches cleaning my bones."

"Hey, watch what you say." Carlo blesses himself and kisses the end of his finger. "You're gonna be good as new. You heard the doc. As soon as your pneumonia clears up—right as Papa's gold cross around your neck."

Leo looks at the smoky ceiling above his bed and wonders if he's giving him the evil eye from his perch in heaven, if he made it there. Maybe he's celebrating with Satan from below while watching Leo suffer in his bed. When he was alive, did Papa figure out Leo put the hit on him so he could take over the family? How could he have known? They got him from behind in the parking lot after he left the bar with a big Friday-night haul. Customers were gone. No shell casings. No snitches. No problems.

"Bring me a shot. Not the blended either. I want the good stuff for special occasions. I want to feel the burn."

"You just took a pill. Shouldn't you—"

"What? Wait a few hours? I could be dead."

Carlo nods and leaves him to his thoughts.

His ring finger is swollen and red, and it hurts to touch it. As he twists the ring in place, it pulls the skin and stings. The amber stone with the bird inside is laughing at the gold band cutting grooves into the skin. It's fitting because he cut down the *paisan* who gave it to him as a sign of friendship. He was such a phony. Stoolies pay a price, especially those brought into the fold from the outside. Loyalty is an oath to the Manettis every day of your life, not just when you feel like it.

He wanted Tony taken out with a bomb in his car, but Mario's attempts failed to detonate, and Tony found the bomb both times. Mario's no better at wiring than he is at talking. He's gotta fix that before he dies. Car bombs are the best: quick and clean. It's over in a matter of seconds.

Rat on the Manettis and you live in a cell with the rats. Tony ended up in the bug-infested Bari prison full of sickies spreading germs and syphilis to other inmates. No matter. With the help of Leo's connection working in the infirmary, a meth overdose got him in the end. He's the *capo mandamento* on the commission, and no one disobeys him without paying a price. Tony owed from his heist and bit the big one when he didn't return the treasure he took from them.

Antonio Giambruno was the Barese they called Tony the Terror because he terrorized the police and kept 'em busy while the organization made deals. A sweet talker from a fishing village in Puglia with a small farm and a couple of moth-eaten plow nags. Leo's downfall was being a softie. He felt sorry for Tony raising his kid without her mama. His temptation to steal from someone else was too great. That was *his* downfall. You can't trust the Barese. They're sneaky boogers. Still, Leo should've listened to Papa. "Stick with a Sicilian—your own kind—and you never go wrong," he'd said. Had he listened, the Manettis would be richer today. Tony stole something more precious than their accounts. More valuable than what's in Leo's strongbox. The holy keepsake he lifted from Carlo's safe behind the wine keg is as old as Michelangelo's Sistine Chapel ceiling. He who holds the strand holds the key to the stars.

His mouth puckers, anticipating the fruity red wine on the palate. He used to enjoy a good glass from the family's Nero d'Avola grapes… when he could taste.

"On second thought, bring me my homemade wine. Carlo? I feel like the Calabrese red instead. Last year's." Carlo doesn't hear him. "Where are you? It's in the cellar, Carlo." Leo's still alone, talking to himself.

"What did you say?" Carlo sneaks around the doorway with a tray holding the whiskey decanter and two glasses. "Imported good stuff coming up."

"Bring me the red wine from the cellar."

"You want to drink both?" Carlo sets the tray on the nightstand with a *plink* and pours the golden liquid into Lina's crystal tumbler. Leo and Lina used to share a nightcap in these glasses before bed. Before she left him with a couple of childish, hovering brothers. How can he leave the business to Carlo or Mario? They mean well but don't have a brain between the two of them.

His beautiful Lina; she was the smart one. No matter what problem Leo came home with, she would sort through the BS with no emotion and find the right solution. She was his confidant who stayed beside him and fought in his corner even when she felt he'd messed up. Lina denied to the family that he made mistakes. Instead, she'd make suggestions to him privately when she thought it would help. She was a loyal wife.

"Heavenly Father, in all your goodness, bless my Lina and tell her I'll see her soon."

They met in her family's lemon grove in Bagheria. Leo picked citrus with a small crew for extra money and worked in the vines on grapes the rest of the time. During a lunch break beside a stack of cartons, he was eating a hunk of salami on half a loaf of bread when this vision in a light summer shift walked over, barefoot. She offered him his first taste of chinotto cola. While he drank, he savored the spicy richness from the grove, the bubbles popping on his tongue with Sicilian orange, bitter and dark. Lina's beautiful face was as sweet as the honey in the Pignolata honey balls his mother made in their fryer. He fell in love with Lina right away. Her white floral dress and dark hair flowing past her shoulders, blowing in the noontime breeze, made him ache to know more of her. The way her profile caught the light, in a halo, turning her brown hair to auburn on top—his chest swells with old feelings of that day. They were innocent and perfect with their lives ahead of them fifty-four years ago. Leo smiles and swipes at the tear crawling down to the bed. She was his beauty then and as beautiful to him when the Lord took her away last spring.

On the wall, the cross-stitched family sampler with whole lemons and orange slices feels stale and worthless with his wife gone and children out of the house. Lina made this with her own hands when Joseph was born, named after Papa. Leo has three gorgeous daughters who look like their mother; God bless each of them. They moved away from Sicily, all married to Toscanas who own vineyards, and one of the girls has a hotel and restaurant. Sure, he'll admit their white wines are decent. He doesn't see much of Joey because he's running his own organization in Staten Island, a borough of New York City. He's still single with a lousy cat, probably because no respected woman will have him. He has a lot of his grandfather in him.

"What else can I get you?" Carlo enters with a dusty, dark bottle of wine and one glass. "How about some biscotto to go with the wine? I can take them out of the freezer." He sets the bottle on the little table near the window. "You haven't touched the bourbon. Do you want me to take the tray away?"

"Stop fussing. Pour the wine. Cookies are too dry and clog my throat." Right on cue, Leo starts another coughing jag, and Carlo appears with the box of tissues and deep furrows in his forehead.

"Don't talk. Rest your voice."

"My chest feels tight, like someone collapsed my ribs with a sledgehammer." He lays his hand over his sternum and presses his head deep into the pillow all the way to his ears, trying to breathe slowly as his heart races. The pain is different this time. Not the stabbing like usual. A squeezing pressure grabs him in a vise.

"Leo, you don't look so good. Let me call the doc."

He nods, taking longer, slower breaths. "Call Joey," he whispers. "Tell him to fly home. Fast."

"Doc Rinaldi says not to lie flat in the bed too long. You should sit up, Leo. Swing your legs over the side. I'll pour a small shot of bourbon. Take a few sips; it's good for the blood."

He struggles to change positions in the mattress rut where he's spent the past few weeks. Carlo's right. Doc warned him to sit upright if his heart gave him any trouble. It's bad enough he can't breathe. Now the pump is conking out too.

CHAPTER

SIX

Lecce Questura

Dirt cyclones spiral the path around the tall chain-link fence as Bill Drake pulls into the military police detention center on the outskirts of Lecce. With a tissue, he plucks grit out of the corner of his eyes and rubs them for good measure, clearing away the dusty haze. Alec left him the means for police persuasion should he need it to help gain access to Josh. Jennings was taken into custody yesterday for an investigative grilling in the hopes of a confession. It's unlikely they'll get an admission of guilt, for he is too coy and clever to give up information that easily. People who keep secrets well usually are.

Jennings's attorney mentioned the DIA; an anti-Mafia investigation department is involved with the crime. Since Benita could have a connection there, it's hard to know what kind of welcome to expect inside. Drake's next stop will be a check-in at the morgue to see what can be uncovered there. Watching a dissection of the human body can take some getting used to, but with any luck, Benita's autopsy is already complete. Drake is screwed if the medical examiner can't converse and isn't willing to translate the examination report.

Drake's shirt clings to his waist and arms like sausage casing. A familiar feeling he used to get before riding the fire truck to a four-alarm fire. This time it's a different kind of blaze that could take down a family dynasty.

He spots a pair of election signs showing two different men in uniform running against each other, surprised they allow politics so close to police headquarters. As Drake approaches the glass doors, he realizes he's left the cash and euro from Alec in the car. A lot of good they'll do him there. After consideration, he opts for the gold pieces hidden in his pants pocket. He'll take his chances that gold is more appetizing than paper.

Drake enters their sterile world of polished tile floors and rows of metal file cabinets. An out-of-place uniform in green military gear sits behind a counter, reading a battered auto magazine. Police in dark slacks and white shirts are seated randomly, surrounded by personal photos, paperweights, and patriotic flags of the police force groups. There are five national forces in Italy. Of note, women don't exist in this office. Radios are silent, barring an occasional static burst from keying a mike button. A funky odor of yeast and hot rubber soles, similar to a gymnasium in the last period of a basketball game, floats on the air.

"Excuse me."

The clerk in army green dog-ears his magazine.

"I'd like to see a recent detainee. He'll be in one of your interrogation rooms with his attorney. Josh Jennings."

In perfect English, he rolls his tongue around his mouth and says, "You're here about the murder."

"No."

"He's a suspect. You can't see him." The guy's brows lift.

"I'm investigating from the States."

"Ah, he's wanted in the United States?"

Curious stares follow the conversation that's taken an unexpected alley.

"Have you charged Mr. Jennings?" Drake asks.

A figure of a higher rank, dressed in navy, enters from a hallway, and things get more complicated.

"Does Mr. Jennings have a criminal history?" he asks. "What can you tell us about him?" The braid on the policeman's cap is glaring, and so are the many insignias on his uniform that's missing a name tag. "Will you come to my office?"

An order, not a request. Stress levels climb as Drake follows the leader to his cubicle.

"Please, sit down."

"I appreciate that you speak English. May I see Mr. Josh Jennings?"

Heart palpitations thump against his rib cage due to the reaction coming from across the desk. The high-ranking officer with jet-black hair and a super cleft in his chin is scribbling on a tablet with such force, it's certain the page will rip through at any minute. A half-eaten cake donut covered in white icing and sprinkles reminds him it's way past lunchtime.

The interrogation begins with, "Who are you, and why are you interested in him? What has he done in the United States?"

"Detective Bill Drake. I'm here on behalf of my client. He read news in a tabloid about his father." Drake leaves out the part about Pearce's death. Another one to explain would only complicate things more. "My client wishes to verify the story with Mr. Jennings."

"Do you have this tabloid with you?"

"Unfortunately, no."

The officer reaches for his donut and takes a bite, chewing with delight. "Would you like one? Best bakery in Lecce. Some say it's as old as the town." He raises what's left of his pastry and continues, "Your client's name?"

His demeanor is calculated but friendly. How many times has he practiced his routine?

"Alec Zavos. Pardon me." Drake pretends to scan the room for a clock and using his watch as a prop, says, "I have a flight soon. Is Mr. Jennings available?"

Officer no-name pauses, then leaves his chair and closes the door, drawing the vertical blinds.

Capture in a foreign country by police adds half a dozen reasons why detectives should study international law if they're planning to go abroad. Drake skipped that part. Questioning Josh seems harmless on its face, but Drake's caught by his imaginary tail. One wrong mention or move regarding the murder victim can take them down a rabbit hole of no return and possibly land him in a cell next to Josh. The urge to flee strikes and just as quickly subsides. He's being hidden from view of the office staff. Think.

Drake knew where this exercise was going. Best to be cool and wait for the officer.

"Before you go, would our friends from the West like to donate to the DIA?" He notices Drake's unemotional repose and frowns. "The police force against organized crime."

"Oh, I see." Alec's famous name prompts the ask for money, so it's Drake's turn to feign ignorance of the police coercion he's witnessed several times. "If you'll accept this for the DIA?"

A fistful of gold bullion coins clink across his blotter, and Drake receives a joyous smile as his reward and, with hope, a visitation with Josh. Their anti-Mafia investigation department is a joke. The hypocrisy shown by this man is hip deep, as organized crime is all around them.

"Accepted. Your name again. I forgot." The coins disappear into a desk drawer.

"Detective Drake."

"Detective, we are questioning Josh Jennings. His credit card was found in the victim's effects. Did you know her?" His eyes shift to the right, then straight ahead. He has to be aware the information hasn't been released to the public yet, so Drake ignores the ploy.

"Is he charged?" Drake asks, to take the focus back to Josh.

"Not yet."

The officer hits an intercom button and utters a word string in Italian.

"Si." The scratchy voice turns into a sneeze. *"Si."*

"We'll give you time with Mr. Jennings, but in case we need to, can we phone?"

"Of course." Drake flips out his wallet and hands him a card. "Call day or night. I'll pick up. May I ask who'll be calling?" His eyes fall to the blank area over the officer's breast pocket.

He touches his shirt and smiles. "Sorry, Bill. *Commissario Capo* Ortelle. Call me Salvatore."

Amazing how gold coins shared between men puts them on a first-name basis.

Salvatore gives Drake his official superintendent business card. "Down the hall to the right. CID will escort you. Good day."

A guard stands at the door of interrogation, chewing on a hangnail between hacking coughs. There's no chair, just him.

"I'm Detective Drake. Is Josh Jennings inside?"

Wordlessly, the guard in street clothes opens the door, and Drake slides in without touching anything. Josh's attorney is sitting next to him, and he nods from his own folding chair. Both of them are sweating profusely, and Josh has turned a minty shade of green since they last met.

"You're Mr. Zavos's friend, aren't you?" the attorney asks.

"Bill." The air inside this room is warmer than the hallway. Two nearly empty water bottles are the only items on the table. "How long have you been in here?"

"They called and wanted to question my client today. I'm Terrance Clark, by the way." He lights a cigarette, and smoke curls in a question mark near his face. "I handle legal affairs."

"Mr. Clark, may I speak with him in private, please?"

His smile gleams. "There's nothing private in this room, but if you'd like me to leave... Josh?" He waits for his acceptance that comes in the form of a one-shoul-dered shrug. "Are you sure? Fine, I'll wait outside." Clark whispers inaudibly in Josh's ear and departs.

"Why are you here again? I don't know any more."

"Don't or won't say?"

Josh expels a long sigh. "It's like this; when I opened the building, I went to my office and found Benita lying in blood in front of my desk. Tied to a chair." Josh's hand cups his brow. "I keep seeing her splayed out in a bloody puddle—her head bashed—blood spatters on the floor. Made me wanna puke."

"That's tough. I'm sorry for your loss, truly." Lame and unoriginal clichés seem to pop out when nothing else comes to mind. "I'd like to ask you about before that. Did you ask her to come to Lecce? When did you first speak to her?"

"She showed up unannounced a couple of days ago while I was eating lunch on the square. Came hold-ing the tabloid and said that reading it was homework. Hard to take Benita serious sometimes."

"She's an old girlfriend?" Drake asks.

"Yes."

"Have you seen that cover picture of Pearce before?"

"Can't be sure. He liked the camera. Photogenic celebrities typically do."

Envy tinged his statement. A perfect motive to take what isn't given by birthright or status, like money or power. Josh definitely has the personality of a killer who expects to get away with murder. Drake blows off trying to stereotype him and files it away in random thoughts. Many of the renowned serial killers brought to justice were actually quiet, timid-mannered people who could shift their personalities to rage on a whim.

"Did Ms. Alvarez give Pearce's racing photo to the tabloid? I assume she wasn't married."

"Not the marrying type." Josh chuckles. "How should I know if she was behind the photo? She does what she wants. Always has."

"Did she arrive on her own?"

Josh shrugs. "I assume so. What bleach do you use on your teeth? Man, they're blinding me."

Drake pulls out a notebook and feels Josh's gaze surveilling him. Getting answers more to his liking was going to be a chore; he's added no new information.

"You mentioned she was trying to extort money from you. Because of the tabloid article?"

"Yes. Thought she could use it against me."

"The story is about Alec's dad. Where do you come in?"

"Benita used to hang around the pits. You know, in with the pit crew at races. She's what you'd call a pit lizard. Pretty women who want a piece of the action, want to meet the drivers."

"Hook up with the drivers?" Drake asks with a good idea where he was going.

"It was a way for her to get a job inside the racing team, which she landed fairly easily. She's a savvy woman beyond her good looks." Josh shakes off what appears to be a shudder. "If that damned cat hadn't run off, I wouldn't be here."

"How do you know?"

"She would've walked out of the office with me; that's how I know. I left her behind; don't you get that? I hated how she was shaking me down, but I didn't want her dead. She wasn't a bad person, just hard up for cash."

"If Pearce were alive, would he want her... dispatched?"

"Dispatched? Wow. That's a word I haven't heard in a while. You'd have to ask him." Josh's smug smile follows. "Seriously though, Pearce was a great guy, a straight arrow. I've never known him to wish ill of anyone. When he raced, it was purely for the adrenaline rush. The team's fiercest competitors liked ol' Zavos the Greek."

Everything Josh said Drake already knew about Pearce because Alec was just like him: driven, smart, and with loads of charisma. When Alec had asked him to look into Signorile finance irregularities a few years ago, they'd uncovered nothing to implicate Pearce in any wrongdoing. Nothing that showed him in direct correlation with missing funds. Money had shuffled in and out of accounts to places unknown, but on paper, Alec's dad wasn't at the heart of it. Whoever supplied the tabloid with the article had intimate knowledge of the laundering scheme that began at the racing team or had a darn good idea of who was behind it. Drake didn't need to hear Josh admit his part. Pearce Zavos was the honorable man he'd studied at great length. The odd couple's headscratcher is Josh, unless he was acting on his own. It's doubtful Josh would offer proof of Pearce's innocence if asked, so Drake decides not to go there unless he gets an opening. The issue at hand now is the Mafia influence at the corporation, if any exists.

"Can you think of any reason someone might want to end this woman's life?" Drake asks.

"Tons. She's an irritant. I haven't seen Benita in years, but she whines, and she's immature. She doesn't like to drop a subject until you're harped into submission. She wants what she wants until she gets it. We ended our relationship when I moved to Italy at Pearce's request, but it was time anyway. Things had cooled off between us."

"Long-distance relationships. I understand." Drake writes seven years in the book since Pearce began Signorile around that time. "Can you give me the background on the cat? You said she belongs to the Manettis."

"I think she belongs to Joey; he's nuts for calicos. Must be some kind of fetish. Benita didn't mention his name, only that he was abusing the cat. I assumed it was him since she was running around with that hood." Josh makes a face showing his distaste.

"What does Joey Manetti do?" Drake asks.

"Joseph Leonardo Manetti. The head of a crime family in New York. One of many families with ties to the Cosa Nostra. He's the son of the big boss, Leo, who lives in Sicily on a plantation in Palermo, not far from the Signorile plant. I heard through the grapevine that Benita quit marketing for the Quicken team and went north with Manetti after I left for Signorile. Joey hangs out in his own territory: Staten Island and the Bronx. The Mafia has feelers long enough to pop someone here or in the States if they want to. Man, she shouldn't have taken his cat."

I uncross my ankles and lean on the table. "Josh, this is important. Do you know if Ms. Alvarez ever saw Pearce romantically?"

Josh drains the last drop of his water and caps the bottle. "No way. Generosa would've eaten him for lunch. Sure, he had eyes and noticed the chickies parading around, but no, he loved his wife and was loyal to her."

"Did Pearce ever ask you to find investors for Signorile's start-up?"

"He needed investors, so I loaned him the money, which he paid back with interest."

"How much was that?"

Josh squirms. "Look, you want to help Alec, but I don't owe him anything. We severed our ties completely a few months ago. I'd still be at Signorile instead of an Italian jail if Pearce were alive. Go and get my attorney."

"You have Alec's full support. Please understand his decisions were made in the best interest of the company." Drake tosses the support lie in there to set him at ease. "Alec came here because you asked him to. He didn't have to come at all."

"Yeah, and he's here because daddy's reputation is being dragged through the mud." Josh settles back and folds his arms comfortably over his chest.

Still defiant and free of bracelets; the officials haven't put him in cuffs yet. Whatever they find in the medical examiner's report will seal Josh's fate.

"Having Alec's support is good to know." Josh fondles the table like he's stroking a pet. "A little surprising, but I'll sleep easier tonight. Are they going to formally arrest me?"

"Your attorney is a better person to ask. At the office, you brought up protection for Signorile and Alec's mother. What does that mean exactly?"

"You're a smart guy; use your imagination." Josh demonstrates a sinister grin that's chilling. "Do your research on how the Cosa Nostra conducts business in Italy. You'll get your answers." He throws his head back and laughs. "Better yet, men die with their secrets and so did Pearce, but he swore me to secrecy about his precious Generosa. Bring back my attorney, and I'll tell you what Pearce told me. You may find it interesting."

Sitting in the parking spot at the detention center, Drake checks the time and autodials Alec at their bed-and-breakfast in Bari, then presses speakerphone.

"Morning, how's it going with Josh?" Alec asks.

"We concluded a few minutes ago, and I'm about to grab a sandwich. They haven't charged him yet, but he's been detained. The police superintendent wants a solid suspect, and Jennings lines up perfectly in their sights. I believe they have enough to hold him before a judge. Homicide is rare in Lecce, and a trial could take time while they gather evidence. It's not open-and-shut, but there's enough basis to make a case against him if they want to. I saw a few political signs outside the department too. It's an election year, so that works against Josh if his proverbial head is needed on the pike as an example of crime enforcement for constituents."

After a pregnant pause, Alec asks, "Did he kill Benita?"

"He's an ass but not a killer. I think the Alvarez woman wanted payment from him in exchange for her silence because she knew Josh laundered during his time with Quicken Racing. She might have had physical proof; we'll never know. The tabloid was her medium to frighten Josh into believing his secret could get exposed once the digging began with Pearce. Josh likes to feel important, so he could've told her at a weak moment about his plan to embezzle team money." Drake catches his breath. "It's my belief Josh was envious of your dad's influence and took the opportunity to play around with funds while he was CFO there and finally financial officer for Signorile, although he admitted nothing freely. I watched him for any dents in his armor, especially when he mentioned loaning your father the start-up money for Signorile."

"No kidding? I hadn't thought of that angle. Huh. Loaned Dad his dirty money in a clean agreement."

"Surprised me too. Josh's account is entirely plausible. Pearce asks his friend for the loan and pays him back, which he did. I didn't press Josh for nitty-gritty specifics, but it answers the big question how your dad got the bucks for a new business. If the money came to Jennings by dirty means, your dad is either diabolically evil or he didn't know."

Alec sighs. "We know the answer to that one. Why didn't Benita finger Josh in that article instead of Dad?"

"Pearce has the household name and star power to get people talking about a sensational conspiracy theory. If your dad was stealing from his own corporation, Josh would've said that since your dad is gone and couldn't refute it. Jennings had plenty of opportunities to blame someone other than Benita and the cat. Where's your mom right now?" Drake asks, as a more pressing issue pops into his head.

"She's resting at the estate for a few days. We thought it best to have her in the background and not at the gallery. Chase is handling things there."

Drake closes his eyes and thinks about what he said. "Alec, allow me to call an associate and send him over to Brookehaven right away. His name is Derrick Mason. As a precaution, I'd like you to double up on your estate security detail."

"Any relation to Perry?" Alec laughs nervously. "What's Mom have to do with Josh?"

Alec has no idea how serious his situation has become. Drake mulls over telling Alec everything Josh said versus keeping the story to himself until he can confirm details. Why worry him until Josh's account can be verified? Jennings could be taking advantage of Alec's generosity to save his hide while making up believable lies in order to do it.

"Josh divulged an incredible fantasy—told to him by your dad, *supposedly*. One I doubt you've heard or you would've said something. His story is way out there. It could be true, yet there's plausible deniability. Before I give you a possible made-up story, I should confirm the facts. I'm asking for your blessing to visit Staten Island to look up one of the Manettis." Alec's side of the conversation has been silent for a while. "You there?"

"I heard. Hang on a minute."

Breathing enters the earpiece replaced by the sounds of ocean waves.

"Sorry about that. I'm on my way to Annalisse. She got up early and took off for the beach without telling me."

"Is Brad with her?" Drake's trying to control his voice.

"No. Under the weather."

"Don't let her go anywhere unaccompanied."

"She knows better, but she's headstrong, and well, I don't have to say any more." Alec's tone softens. "If Anna knew Mom was in trouble, she'd beg me to go home. *Should* we go back to the States? Is it safer for Mom to have us there?"

Worry has finally joined the call, like an eavesdropper lying in wait for the appropriate time to spring. Drake considers his options to unveil all possibilities, truths, or lies. He decides Alec should settle it, so he lets it fly...

"Your mother may not be who you've been brought up to believe she is." Drake blurts it out and waits for the eruption.

"Jennings said that? What's he pulling?"

"A sick joke, perhaps, but don't you want the truth? I'd like to take the jet back to New York. It's the only way we can be sure. As far as you and Annalisse returning, your trip hasn't been made public. You guys need a few days away, right? Take them. Allow me to do the digging, and try to enjoy yourselves. Don't worry about Generosa. I have your back."

"Okay, I'll let the pilots know."

"I'd like them to stay where they are. When I'm done at the morgue, I'll drive to the Bari airport and drop off the car."

"It's a relief uncovering Dad's deal with Josh, but I still don't understand the connection between Mom and the Manettis. Find out what you can and never forget what I've heard; the Manettis are shrewd and dangerous on home turf. Be careful," Alec warns.

"I should mention one other thing. Members of their crime family may be lurking around Bari."

"When? Now?"

"Unknown. All Josh would say is their family vendettas have everyone on edge. Alec, they don't wear name tags or badges. These guys will not seem out of place or unusual. They won't be obvious goons wearing gangster *Godfather* hats like in the movies. You have firsthand knowledge of corrupt cops, so we can't trust the police to be on our side should we need help taking down someone in the Mob. How's Stella the cat?"

"Resting."

"What are you going to do with her?"

"We haven't gotten that far in discussions, why?"

"Don't tell *anyone* you've retrieved Stella from the investment office. I really have to go—due at the morgue in minutes. I'll call you when I have something to report."

Drake taps the call to a close. There's no way Alec's going to believe all of Josh's tale.

CHAPTER
SEVEN

Bari, Italy

I turn over in the chaise to view the aquamarine ocean a stone's throw from my feet, the waves rising and spilling onto coarse sand. The Bari beach isn't at all how I'd imagined it. Not the fine grains of flour sand like the travel brochures touted but more akin to tiny pebbles beneath a running creek. Aquamarine and water go together, soothing the heart and sending out its cooling effects on the body and mind. Gen raves about these four hundred nautical miles of Italy's coastline. It's easy to understand why. Amid the current turmoil, Bari is what Alec and I crave—a place to wind down, regroup, and discover our love and passion for each other again.

Tourists in Bari's off-season must be eating brunch because dozens of umbrella chairs are open and alone, awaiting sunbathers. At first glance, the greenish Adriatic mimics the color of the Aegean Sea surrounding Greece, with differences. In the fall, this sea is cooler, has fewer sailboats in the inlet, and smells more like a seafood stew. Shellfish, squid, and prawns are prized in these waters. Mollusks are best when harvested in the months that have an R in them, Gen says. I close my eyes behind a new pair of Vanni sunglasses and draw in a mouthful of humid air, tasting briny salt. Waves lapping the shore melt away cares temporarily. Josh Jennings, Pearce, Alec's business, and the blackbird references will hold for now. It's Gen and the old rosary beads that intrigue me. The verification of an antique's beginning and chronological ownership. What era they came from and who the religious prayer beads belonged to feel more important than the other problems combined. I watch the methodical surf for a time and pick up my tablet, scrolling through the photos taken of the rosary beads before we left for Italy. I like to have visual records saved on devices to refer back to. Alec stayed behind in our room this morning, and I couldn't wait to get outside to catch the sunrise's pink essence over the horizon, and now the serenity is the perfect time to study these pictures.

I enlarge the back of the Madonna medal, the section that connects the final string of the rosary above the cross, and notice the scratches.

"I remember this." A rush pulses new vitality into my quest for information. Lifting my dark glasses, I look at the image again with a different light on the screen. "What is that?"

Crude lines score the surface as an engraving would. The ancient metal is discolored and darkened at the stamped edges, but there are marks clearly etched by a rough tool with a sharp point like a nail or stylus. I dig through my tote resting next to the chair leg and lift out the very same beads, checking the center medal against the photo in the tablet, scrutinizing the real piece in my hand. Three separate etchings, but they're unclear. I touch the area gently to brighten the discoloration and see the letter *M*. The second and third letters are too faint in natural light.

"Is that a *C*? Can't be sure; it might be an *O*. I'll have to look at this inside."

Each bone bead is shaped like an olive pit, the links blackened with time, and the beads are worn to a smooth finish. Special carved black beads resembling roses next to tiny medals are stationed between each decade of beads. There are five sections of ten beads or decades that make up the rosary, which signals more of its origin. My first inclination in Gen's office had been correct. These prayer beads are designed for the Catholic faith following the Our Father and Apostle's Creed when they were added to the Hail Mary stations of the rosary. Gen's version would date between the late sixteenth century and the eighteenth. Possibly the nineteenth, but I doubt it was that modern due to the materials used and the Holy Mother medal's primitive workmanship. Picking through two hundred years for answers is going to take more time than I have on this beach. While Alec snoozes, I'll search for similarly styled prayer beads and narrow down the century.

"Magnificent."

It's hard to concentrate on a computer screen when surrounded by the sounds of gulls and pelicans and the largesse of Mother Nature. The seas—one of God's many miracles—weather cycles, oceans, and the sun are all intertwined in harmony. Astrology, transits and aspects of celestial bodies that go way beyond horoscopes and signs of the zodiac, were one of my favorite pastimes as a child. Gen, too, enjoys astronomy—what's beyond our planet far into the universe and other galaxies. Gen can lecture like an expert on the subject for hours if allowed to. She's a brilliant woman on many topics other than antiquities.

Setting the beads and tablet carefully inside my tote, I survey the long, golden strip of beach, my toes sunk deep in the warm sand. Heat moves through my feet, sending the sensation to my calves. On the right are brilliant blue umbrellas in retro swirls and dots that border the outer edges near plaster and brick hotels with conical-shaped roofs. Curving palms sway in the breeze, reaching their fronds toward the opaline waves. Truly a spectacular break for an occupied mind.

"Found you."

His soothing voice floats in, and I turn my attention to the main reason we're here. Alec is changed beyond his appearance. Freshly shaven, clean clothes, and an urgency—an uneasiness in his stride.

"I wish you'd waited for me or taken Brad with you." Alec scans the premises for unsavory criminals who may want to harm us. "I don't mind if you go out without me, but I'll feel better if you're not alone for long periods. Your safety is more important than anything else."

Laughing, I assure him. "It's deserted, see? You're sweet to worry about me, although I'm just an obscure antiquities dealer. You're the famous guy."

His strong arms caress and pull me into his scent of soap and aftershave. "Infamous, you mean? This part of the Adriatic is even more beautiful than I recall. We have to come back in the evening and check out the stars. Wish we had one of Mom's telescopes with us. We could've packed it on the plane." He lifts his shoulders, then relaxes them in an exhale.

"This is the first I've heard of Gen's telescopes. I know about that old collection of books on astronomy. Those ancient volumes in her office above her credenza? No wonder your mother is an expert on this wide subject. How did I miss that?"

He snickers. "She considers it a hobby of no consequence, but I'm surprised she hasn't brought you in on a conversation or two. She loves to talk about the planets. There's a kinship with the universe deep within her. I've felt it myself, like the grandeur of this place."

"Yes, it's almost mystical. Hard to pull my eyes away from the rhythm of the waves."

"Italy. We belong here. Wouldn't you like a home in Firenze or Tuscany, the gem of the Renaissance? A countryside you were made for. Misty mornings, tall cypress, Siena and its horseracing… suits us fine." He sighs. "Until now, I didn't see it before."

My breath catches. This is completely out of character for him. "Alec, are you serious?"

He pulls me to a chair and sits alongside, flinging arms about in the excitement of the moment. "We can find ourselves a vineyard with Sangiovese grapes and make our own signature wines. I've always wanted to do that."

"Do you know anything about winemaking? I hear it's an art." I try not to joke, wanting to join his daydream.

"No, but we can find people who do. I'm good at that." The genuine Zavos smile I fell in love with beams like the spotlight we've searched for these past few months. If he sells the corporation, his many aspirations can become a reality.

His short sleeves tickle, and I feel both giddy and cold. In my excitement to see the outdoors, I didn't bother bringing a sweater. Capri pants and a thin blouse suddenly aren't enough for the cloudy cast interrupting the sunshine.

"We can talk about this later; you're shivering. How long have you been on the beach?" Alec kisses me without two days' worth of stubble, and my body is flushed with warmth.

"Not long. Where are you hiding Brad? I expected to find the early riser here."

"I checked in with him. He's not feeling well."

"Oh no." Not a good way to start the Bari trip. "Let's walk, shall we? There's so much more to see on foot." I must have sighed without thinking.

"What's wrong? You're preoccupied," Alec asks.

"A little too engrossed in research when you arrived. Remind me to show you something later. I tried to on the plane but got sidetracked—*after* we browse the shops and find the locals who sell the little pasta. I'd like to visit churches too, one in particular. The Church of Saint Anne." Alec doesn't react. "Have you heard of that one?"

"You've planned our entire day, I see. Glad you're getting into the vacation spirit." His laughter is contagious, and I add mine. "Mom's old stomping grounds." Alec looks as if he's eaten a lemon drop. "I forgot about the time difference and gave her a call. I think I woke her out of a deep sleep."

"Six hours is early morning back home. Gen won't mind. Oh, I just thought of another stop for us. The farm where she and your grandfather lived."

Alec plucks a stray thread from my blouse. "We sold it after *Nonno* died in—"

"Prison?"

He starts, and his gaze meets mine. "You knew that?"

"I guessed from conversations overheard." Resting my chin on his shoulder, I add, "I'm sorry. A prison sentence must have been hard on everyone. What crime did he commit?"

"The entire incident was kept a secret. One day *Nonno* was home, and the next he's behind bars. I tried to dig into it a few times, but Mom shut me down."

"Your dad knew what happened?"

"He had to have known. When I asked, he'd leave the room, and Mom would clam up."

Without asking more, either my face or my silence unleashes a few extra details.

"I was a boy with a grandparent I barely knew. Prison talk was taboo, so the need to know died away and, in time, moved on when we bought the villa. All forgotten. Come to think of it, that was when *Nonno* entered prison."

"He went to jail, and your family moved to Greece."

"Yeah, around then. We were living in the States before we moved to Crete."

"And distancing you from Italy. Of course Gen would want to protect you from family embarrassment. What's your grandfather's last name?" Gen has never mentioned her maiden name. I've always been curious about it.

"DePalma. My middle name is his given one, Antonio. I'm named after Dad's father, Alec."

"If you told me that before, I don't remember. Beautiful names. They roll off the tongue—Alec Antonio Zavos."

"In the flesh." Alec spreads his arms and settles one across my shoulders. "Why don't we head to the room, pick up your camera, and see what we can find for lunch."

With that gesture, he studies me as his father had on the yacht. Laughing, bedroom eyes, and a mass of wavy hair impeccably styled—add the dimples and his old-fashioned manners, and he has more than his share of boyish charm. Drawn to him the night of the party, I fought my attraction to one of the most sought-after men on the planet. The irresistible Zavos men find it hard to escape notice in the papers, and here we are, fighting another media battle.

"I'm yours, Alec. Lead on."

His hand is slimmer in mine than it used to be, and he's grown pale since taking control of Signorile. When I met him, tender lines from sun worship creased the skin near his eyes when he smiled. He used to spend his days with Hank, the thoroughbred's trainer, the breeding operation and workout jockeys riding young colts around the barns or at the racetrack. The track is a place I've never been because Alec rarely spends time with Hank anymore. The carefree, fun-loving Alec who seduced me with opulence and his values has left on hiatus for Sports Cars Land and bottom lines. Now Alec shuttles to Pennsylvania on a private jet and meets in corporate boardrooms elsewhere, shaking hands and giving speeches. In the transition from vet training and four-legged animals to two-seat sports cars, he's lost his zest for savoring a golden existence. His mention of finding a home in Italy is a positive sign that he's about to be liberated.

My own questions about Kate leaving things undone between us ends here. Negativity ends here. My need to know Alec's past stops here. I'm responsible for me.

A puzzle piece snaps into place.

Alec wants what I want.

Walking barefoot in sand, my legs feel like weights. I'm so out of shape, it isn't funny to these sore muscles. In between hard breaths, I jump back into small talk.

"Your mom asked me to check on a Sister, or nun, who knew her in Bari."

"She's probably moved into another community or passed on by now."

"Gen said as much. She wants me to light a candle for Sister Mary Margaret. The least I can do is ask around for her whereabouts. Luck may be on our side; who knows?"

"We haven't been big on luck lately." Alec's phone rings, and we stop our walk on the beach.

"It's probably Brad," I say half-heartedly.

"No. He texts."

Alec reads the caller ID. Before he answers, he rubs one hand down his pant leg.

"Ian. How are things in Palermo?" Alec bites his lip, and a hand drifts through his hair.

A terrible signal.

Alec's side of the conversation involves pacing, listening, and shaking his head. It feels even worse when he steps out of earshot. He doesn't want me to overhear. Again, I'm being shut out.

After several minutes, I'm about to walk back to the bed-and-breakfast on my own when I see Alec stow his phone. His expression is dour.

"Whatever it is, we'll work through it." No sense in asking. If Alec wants me to know, he'll offer, and he does.

"Ian Craig is our primary attorney for Signorile. The corporation keeps several, but he's the lead sled dog. When Ian phones, it's serious. Lanny Quicken Racing has—"

"Seen the tabloid. That was quick, no pun intended. Go on."

"The media has already convicted Dad without a jury."

"It's how they roll these days."

"Anything goes. Lies, truth, anonymous sources, personal opinions are all considered facts. Ian knows Dad. Apparently, the team found fake invoices after we left South Carolina, similar to what I found at Signorile. Ian doubts that Lanny Quicken has proof Dad did anything, or they would have gone after him long ago, but *Reveal Reality* reopens the old wound and sticks a hot poker into it. When the media was kind enough to spill my parents' wealth last year, lawsuits are to be expected."

"Josh *knows* what happened to the Quicken Racing money. He may be the only one who does."

"Yep. Bill thinks so too."

"You've spoken to him since he met with Josh?" I ask.

Alec stops to check his watch, then informs me about the conversation he had with Bill. In actuality, it's good news for Pearce, even though Josh hasn't produced proof of innocence in either case—the suspected embezzlement or the woman's murder. Alec knows down deep that his dad didn't do the things he's accused of, but to convince buyers… that's a different story.

"Quicken Racing might have contacted your dad long ago and asked him about the missing money. He also might have cleared himself already. Isn't that possible?" I'm holding out a teeny bit of hope.

"If they did, it was a private discussion held with Dad. Ian said the money was never found."

"Mysteries all around us." I can't stop the headshake that follows.

"Most of us have secrets," he says bluntly.

"Really? Kept any from me lately?"

Alec smiles to keep me guessing. "That's a secret. If you need to know, don't worry, I'll tell you." He swats at my thigh, and when I jump out of reach, he misses his mark. Being flippant doesn't feel like a joke when it comes from a powerful man I trust.

"Gee, that's comforting. So, what's Ian say about the suit?"

"I have a Zoom call with him in thirty minutes. A strategy session to work out the best way forward— before we get lunch and sightsee, if that's okay. They're coming after us for millions. I told Ian I'm inclined to settle with the race team and get it out of the news fast. It's better than having Quicken own Signorile and have Dad go down this way."

We won't let that happen.

CHAPTER
EIGHT

The Zoom meeting is taking longer than Alec thought, and I'm getting weak from hunger. I convince him in hand gestures to allow me to pick up our lunch and find soup for Brad.

Alec had found Brad through London's chauffeur service. Because of the man's extraordinary skills, there's a nagging suspicion it's a fictitious background used as a coverup for anyone who asks, including me. Brad's main task is chauffeuring for Alec, with a secondary skill as his security when traveling. I have no idea what other abilities Brad could have in his repertoire, but nothing would be a surprise.

I hurry around the corridor near La Leccornia restaurant, and a tiny child with missing front teeth runs at me, latching onto my leg. She's dark in tan and dirt, wearing a thin peach-and-blue-striped pinafore dress to her ankles. Her sandals flap on the bottom when she runs, and she has either a crocheted or knitted red flower in her hair.

"Please." The sweet-faced child, maybe three or four, with big, sad eyes, holds out a paper cup with a few coins in the bottom. "Help *madre. Malata.*"

No matter the language, a cup in an outstretched hand is universal. My heart dissolves for the little thing begging for her mother. Reaching into my bag, I pour out a handful of change from my billfold, stretching out to drop coins into her cup.

"*Cosa fai!*" Someone realizes the child is missing and screams from the street. The warning sets her to flight, flapping tiny toes on the cobblestones. A woman flails her arms in an unpleasant manner, and her dark hair is bound with a loud red scarf that matches her tank dress. She may be her mother. She's mad at the child but seems more interested in me than the little one running toward her, as if she's sizing me up as a would-be abductor.

With my wallet safely zipped inside my bag, I smooth back my hair and continue toward the restaurant. Tourists are easy targets for grifters. Being a woman with a soft heart, I'm like most Americans drawn to children in need. My designer bag and Western clothing are like a flashing beacon to the less fortunate in the main square.

There are eyes on me.

Within the surrounding brick walls and ancient white stone buildings, people are seated in plastic chairs outside their homes, watching my situation. I've put myself in danger from pickpockets and thieves waiting to prey on the unaware. It's broad daylight, so there's some comfort in that if I move on quickly.

A nun in a traditional black habit stands behind a folding table, ladling out soup or a slushy stew from a large stainless pot. Ragtag people form lines in front of her, some with bowls, others holding utensils. She's quite a distance across the square, so I make a mental note not to bother her during lunch rush, thus interrupting her meal service. The Sister might have heard of Gen's Sister Mary Margaret. My spirits are lifted by the possibility of accomplishing one of our goals and running Gen's errand to find someone who may know about the rosary beads.

I have to come back here.

Opening the door to La Leccornia, I smell rosemary-garlic focaccia bread and the sweetest mussels beyond description.

I arrive at our room with heavy bags of takeout, minus the little taste of linguini and mussels I sampled—because it was impossible not to. Brad was apologetic and looked awful but accepted the minestrone soup and plain broth at his door with his typical coolish gratitude. He's an old-school Brit who's not warm even on his good days. I seem to make him uneasy for some reason, or it could be my overactive imagination. We all have a small microwave and fridge in our rooms, so when he feels like eating, it may bring some relief to settle his stomach.

Alec hasn't made a move in thirty minutes.

"Oh, Alec, how much longer?" I whisper with a sinking feeling that lunch will be on perpetual hold, and nothing exciting will happen today with Alec in business mode.

"Hey, Ian." Alec smiles my way. "Annalisse has arrived with lunch. When you have the figures and we're ready to present, touch base with me first. I'd like to see the final documentation ahead of the meeting. Thanks." Alec ends the call and closes his laptop. "Saved by the bags. Did you have any trouble? I was beginning to wonder about you." He sniffs. "Is that mussels... and cheese?"

"Good guess. Mussels in linguini and cream sauce, and for you, a large sandwich with every cold cut known to man with fresh sheep cheeses and peppers. The smells are heavenly."

It's best not to mention the mishap with the little girl near the restaurant in case he gets the idea to revoke my walking-around day pass. The Sister in front of the church stirs my curiosity, and I'd love to visit her, with or without Alec.

"Hungrier than I thought." He digs into the bags and sets out the to-go boxes. "Were you able to find something for Brad?"

"Two kinds of soup. You're right. He looks terrible."

"He'll pop out of it soon. He's a health nut and knows which supplements to take. I've been on many trips with him; he's quite amazing."

After we wolf down our spectacular meals and are contentedly full, the memory of the Sister at her soup kitchen is calling me. I explain my plan to visit her, and Alec agrees to the long walk across the square. Our first stop.

We observe no food line, and she's clearing her table.

"Is that her?" Alec points to the small church ahead. "There are other churches nearby if she can't help you."

"I wonder where the Church of Saint Anne is? This little place of worship among the shops can't be it."

We advance and get a bird's-eye view of the parishioner's menu at the Basilica di Augustina. The pot is gone, but there are loaves of round bread and a steam table with risotto and a broccoli dish. What appears to be sliced peaches and milk lurches my insides. "Too much to take in after a huge lunch," I announce too loudly.

"It's not much, but it's nourishing," the Sister answers.

Below her white coif and black veil, the nun breaks into an affectionate smile. Her voice is soft and pleasing to the ear, and her hearing is excellent. I'd like to run and hide in shame someplace far away.

"Your food is a godsend, Sister. Forgive me. My lunch isn't settling well."

"Would the gentleman like a plate? The risotto is still warm."

By our dress alone, she has to see us for who we are. Tourists wandering the town. Yet she offers a meal to us like any other from the neighborhood. It's easy to understand how Gen could single out a young novice to confide in. Catholicism and charity go hand in hand.

"Thank you, Sister. We finished a meal from the square." Alec jumps in and offers her a bright smile, saving me from more embarrassment.

"Is there something I can do for you?" Her English is impeccable with a tinge of an accent. She glances from me to Alec's jacket where he's hiding a firearm.

"May I donate to the church?" I ask.

"There's a box near the door. Bless you."

Before I can open my purse, Alec hands me euros from his wallet and whispers, "For both of us."

Feeling a slight guilt for his gesture when the donation was my idea, I accept his money and drop it inside the collection box.

The Sister roams the area, picking up litter and plastic utensils, dropping them into the can near the table, and then lifting what has to be a heavy bread platter.

"May I help you clear this away?" Alec unplugs the steam table, and she stops him with a flip of her wrist.

"Thank you, no. I have help from the kitchen. Enjoy our lovely city. It's such a beautiful day. No need to bus tables for an old Sister."

The youthful eyes and her apricot glow were anything but elderly. In fact, they were as young and vital as that of a thirty-year-old woman. How old could she be?

"I'm Annalisse. We're hoping for information about a Sister who lived in Bari many years ago. Do you know of Sister Mary Margaret from the Church of Saint Anne?"

She pauses, her brown eyes fixed on me, and places the bread plate back on the table.

I take it as a positive sign and jump in. "Is it possible to speak to her?"

"I haven't heard that name in ages," she begins. "My terrible manners. I'm Sister Mary Natalina. Where did you say you're from?"

A stall tactic and a polite ploy to get information. We didn't tell her anything about ourselves, and we're stirring her curiosity.

"New York. Have you been there?" I counter the invasion of privacy.

There's a flicker in her intensive stare for an instant, and she blushes. "Oh dear no. I've never known any place but Italy."

She knows more than she's letting on, especially with such superb English speech. She may be a local, but Mary Natalina has had some excellent private training in the American language.

"Where in New York, may I ask? I have relatives there on an island or somewhere close by." Sister Mary Natalina is trying to bring up a memory or purposely be evasive. Sisters don't do evasive, so it can't be that.

"New York is a big place." The smile Alec displays is the one he saves for close friends.

"Come." Sister Mary Natalina gestures me to an adjoining courtyard with olive trees and climbing bougainvillea growing out of brick planters. Numerous rust-colored doors center each wall, reminding me of another oil painting I tried to acquire for the gallery.

A colorful Italian villa near Positano by an unknown French artist. But as we enter the main archway, she stands in our way, folding her arms beneath a flap in the black habit. "This is the house of God. Guns are not permitted here." Her glare narrows on Alec.

His mouth tightens when he's caught off guard, and Alec passes me a long, thoughtful look. "I'll be outside, but stay where I can see you—and be cautious."

He knows how I dislike being cautious.

Turning away, odd sensations are pelting my legs with each step. Cold needles prick my skin, then, without warning, disappear into numbness, as if ice cubes have left their marks behind. Sister Mary Natalina has shorter legs and a faster gait, so I allow her more distance between us in case the tactile jabs are stemming from her person. She's sending out a strange aura that my intuition doesn't trust—not at all like the books and paintings where nuns are encircled by brilliant halos of light and rays of peace. Allowing more faith in instincts to guide us is the safer route while in Italy and inside this house of worship.

"We don't invite inquiries from strangers about the Order. What would you like to know about Mary Margaret?" She pivots and guides me over to a bench.

Should I excuse myself and leave? Her accusatory glare is a bit like being attacked physically as well as mentally. Since our arrival, Sister Mary Natalina has changed from pleasant to curt—and her new signals are far from friendly.

The rosary may help to calm her concerns.

Out from my pocket, the beads and crucifix over-fill my hands when presenting them to her. By her wide eyes and tiny gasp, the giant-size rosary is a surprise.

She claps her hands and crosses herself, whispering, "How wonderful. May I?" The Sister fondles the string lovingly, counting each bead as if they were made from precious gold. "We thought it lost forever. How did you come by them? It's a miracle."

We? "I'm desperate to know their story. Tell me what you can, please." The question is stowed to the back burner when movement catches my eye at the building.

Squeaks from a metal door on rusty hinges grate against the rustle in the olive trees. A white-haired priest in his collar with a wrinkled brow stands in the threshold.

"Is everything all right, Sister?" Out of nowhere, a gray fluff ball flash dances between his legs, making the priest skip aside, and a cat scampers toward the Sister, depositing long hair along her black tunic.

Sister Mary Natalina sends the priest an exuberant wave. "All's well, Father. Rejoice in His name. The table in front needs clearing from lunch. We had a good crowd today. Would you ask Vito to do it, please?"

The priest wipes his hands on a handkerchief and leaves us alone.

Alec is nervously moving about on the other side of the stone archway, pacing while on the telephone, making extreme gestures. A one-handed twist at the wrist, and poof, he's dueling with an unseen, unknown foe. Who this time? Heated discussions seem to be the norm with him until he sells his business. I feel his palpable frustration from here.

Mary Natalina pets the cat, flips over the cross carefully, and examines the details of the Madonna medal. She's beaming as she touches the scratches I found from my earlier audit.

"Valentino, you know you mustn't follow me outside." She pats the cat's head, bringing loud pleasure purrs as he weaves his body in a figure S against her clothing.

He has the cutest white mustache below his little nose. It reminds me of the mustache of Italian actor Rudolph Valentino. The white fur takes the same upturn on the ends. Valentino is the perfect description for him.

"What name do you go by?" Mary Natalina asks me. "Are you Sophia? We heard you disappeared many years ago."

"No, that's not me."

Sister Mary Natalina is way off track and bewildering.

"Sister, the beads were given to me by a dear friend, Generosa Zavos. She asked me to look for the novice who gave her the rosary. That novice would have taken her vows by now or have moved on to another community. Who is Sophia, and why do you think this rosary belongs to her?"

"I don't know Zavos." She holds the beads to her forehead. "I'm so overwhelmed I can't think. Do you have a photo of your friend Generosa's father? If you do, I'd like to see it."

The confusion is mounting by the minute. We're talking at cross purposes, mentioning people who have nothing to do with each other. She thinks Gen's father is synonymous with a set of rosary beads. Does it have something to do with the etching on the back of the medal?

"Are those someone's initials on the Madonna medal?" I ask.

"Yes. MCG." Her eyes glisten with a knowledge that I don't have and for some reason she's enjoying it.

"All right, we're getting somewhere. Thank you. Who is that?" I'm about to receive a big reveal. The true owner of the rosary is known by this Sister.

"Zavos is Generosa's married name, yes?" When I agree, she continues her teachings, because I'm totally lost by these snippets that don't match up in my mind. "Do you have Ms. Zavos's childhood name? Her maiden name. It will be helpful to you." She switches the subject away from the beads.

"Generosa DePalma, I believe. The man outside waiting is her son, Alec."

The Sister shakes her head in a strong protest. "That's not correct." She sighs. "It wouldn't be unusual to change the names. Yes, that must be what happened."

"Alec Antonio Zavos and Generosa DePalma, later Zavos. That's what Alec told me a short time ago."

Sister Mary Natalina pauses to daydream through the stone archway for a few moments, then returns to the present. "Annalisse, you've been told a little white lie. I don't blame you for not knowing. It's like the truths you uncover in mysteries—relics from civilizations long ago. I feel that drive in you. It's in your blood, isn't it? Figuring out origins from the past; artifacts are a specialty for you, aren't they? The young man who waits for you there." She points through the arch. "He doesn't know his true ancestry. You must help him find his lineage as you have discovered your own."

This is spooky.

"My family wants confirmation of this line too, so be careful. They will push anyone aside for this rosary." The Sister brings herself into the mystery.

Her family? My head is pounding from an elevated pressure and a case of the sweats. It's getting late, and I take a few calming breaths to focus on my goals with this Sister. She's given me new information about the beads to pursue, but I'd like more clarification.

"Since you seem familiar with this rosary, how old is it?"

"Try 1600. By century, that will be the closest date. You are a passionate woman when on a mission, Annalisse." She smiles insincerely, and it feels out of place. "Passion is the genesis of genius."

I've read that phrase somewhere and make a mental note to check that out as well. Every word from Sister Natalina feels like breadcrumbs leading us along.

"One more question, if you don't mind. The beads and crucifix are large for a standard rosary. Do you agree they were worn by someone, not carried, habitually worn daily by a priest or nun? I'm thinking a Sister might have owned them. A huge cross attached to prayer beads is unusual for a parishioner's personal use. It barely fits into my purse." It's my turn to smile. "May I have them back? I should go to Alec."

Sister Mary Natalina hesitates without an expression, weighing her options, I suspect.

"Did I say something wrong?" I ask.

"If my intuition is correct, your beads belonged to a nun—a very significant one." Sister Mary Natalina kisses the crucifix and places it in my hands. "You are special to Sophia, or she wouldn't have given the rosary to you." She accepts my clasped hands in her sandpaper palms and closes her eyes for what feels like an eternity. Her hands are warm at first, then explode into ice. When her eyes open, and she withdraws, she tells me, "You're waiting for someone who has left you. A woman perhaps? She's not here." Under her skin, Mary Natalina has a bluish birthmark in a heart shape near her thumb. "You must leave with Alec Antonio. Leave Bari. Leave Italy. Trouble remains if you stay."

Not again.

She adds, "I won't mention your visit to anyone who asks. I'm bound by God's oath before that of my own family." She pats my hand. "I'll pray for you."

"Sister, I don't understand. We don't know a Sophia, and what does she have to do with us?" At once, I'm stuck by dizziness.

"Study Marinagamba. Now, I must go to afternoon prayers. I would appreciate it if you'll add me to yours. Pray for safety and Mary's divine guidance. Be well and go with God."

Just like that, she picks up Valentino and leaves me at the bench.

Alec notices that I'm alone and helps me to my feet as the cruddy feeling ebbs away.

"I thought I was going to be ill a minute ago. That was so strange." Alec guides me by my elbow as we walk back to the square. "I'm okay, I think. It's probably the mussels acting up. I haven't eaten anything that rich in a long time."

"I liked watching you tear into them." Alec laughter is a strain, and he's perspiring in buckets. "Let's get you something cool to drink."

"You can use it too. I noticed you were having a heavy conversation while I was in the courtyard. Wish I'd had Bill's handy-dandy recording device from when we were in Massachusetts looking for Kate. Sister Mary Natalina gave me tons to research even though she held so much back."

"How do you know?"

"It felt like she was fighting with herself not to divulge everything. Like, when there are blanks that need filling in and she stops short of doing so. The Sister withheld information, and it's my job to figure out what's missing. I have to make notes before I forget any of it."

Alec must be shown his mom's beads. He may have the answers.

CHAPTER
NINE

Rushing off the starkly orange ferry at Saint George terminal with a dyed, shaggy hairstyle and a mustache, Bill Drake believes his own mother wouldn't recognize him. The disguise is necessary if he's going to blend into Staten Island's Little Italy, wearing a listening device. He's pursuing Joseph Manetti, the only son of Sicilian Mob boss Leo "Birdman" Manetti, at one of Joseph's favorite hangouts on his home turf. Asking questions in seedier places, he found good leads on Joey Manetti and his gang: where they meet, what they like to eat, and places they do their business. If Jennings is a link to Signorile Corporation involved in a protection racket with the Manetti family, Alec has to act soon.

Dan Chappell, Drake's assistant working in Connecticut, sent him a trove of photos for other members as well. Manetti has a few wardrobe quirks that include a pair of thick, dark glasses last seen in the Sixties. He never wears a hood or a ball cap over his shorter cropped hair and has the vivid blue eyes inherited from his father. The family is known for their stark eye coloration. Joey's other siblings are sisters, and all live in Italy on the mainland, covering their involvement in the family business while they make wines and run hotels. Manetti has built a reputation around New York for his strange calico cat fetish, so Jennings had been straight in the interrogation room. The Manettis take a low profile when conducting business; bottom-level mafiosi build their street cred by swindling judges, policemen, and politicians and end up on death squads in pursuit of the next victim. Murder is a prerequisite for installation into the Mafia.

If the information is correct from hearsay, and Jennings's past relationship with the victim Benita Alvarez is solid, Drake is walking the neighborhood to Manetti's Staten Island hangout and not down a tunnel without an exit. A lot of unknowns leave room for error with a half million residents on a fourteen-mile island. Is it as simple as Manetti ordering a hit on girlfriend Benita if she'd stolen his cat? The family has soldiers to carry it out, but Drake can't be sure there isn't more to it with the razor wire setup on Benita. It took the examiner hours to remove the wire from her body, apparently put there while she was still alive. Drake touches the pocket where his copy of the medical examiner's report lies.

After the twenty-five-minute ferry ride to the other side, it feels good to be on foot, scoping out the shortest distance to the two Italian restaurants that keep popping up on the radar. Lucky for him, they're both within walking distance from the terminal, with easy access on and off Staten Island to Manhattan. The old terminal clock, where time doesn't move, always shows ten minutes after ten, but he's sure it's the lunch hour because of his cranky stomach and the ferry patrons pouring onto the concrete pavers. Around here, he's known as Joey Calico and eats lunch at twelve thirty sharp every day during the week. He's older than his baby face appears, rubbing forty hard, and he likes to spend weekends with an entourage, picking up the ladies in Manhattan bars and dance clubs. It's Wednesday, so Drake's in the right place.

He adjusts the listening device and fluffs hair over both ears. The bionic ear picks up even the slightest whispers from conversations within ten feet, and in an enclosed room, the distance should double. First generations, like listening devices advertised on TV in the 1990s, weren't reliable, and the headphones were bulky unless the surveillance was done off-site. These devices opened the floodgates to amateur private investigators casting nets over cheating partners with mistresses or lonely housewives with lovers. Bill didn't take jobs like that because the work was too slimy.

Mustache glue burns his upper lip from too close a shave, but the sting is tolerable for a few hours. He considered leaving stubble to cover the jawline scars until the resulting natural beard turned out to be too weird for the new dye job. He lifts his shirt collar high just in case the burn scar draws attention.

He misses the ocean breezes in Lecce compared to the rotten landfills covered by Manhattan's garbage and fishy maple syrup from the pancake house somewhere close by. Living in a place surrounded by water is a novelty, but this ain't the spectacular Florida Keys—Drake couldn't see himself making an overpriced wasteland his home. He'd checked into commercial real estate here for the heck of it after finding Annalisse's Kate. Prices are out of sight in the nicer areas. On his left, he passes a freshly painted colonial two-story with a stoop and a For Sale sign. Drake's parents in New Hampshire own a similar colonial. He couldn't guess what they're asking for this one.

Places on his restaurant scavenger list include the Sicily Grill and Toscallina's Ristorante. Toscallina's is a block away, so he decides to make that stop first, then it dawns on him he's overdue to send Alec a text that he's made it to New York. It won't hurt to drop a text to Brad as well to see how he's feeling.

Jennings left Signorile unguarded when his CFO position wasn't backfilled immediately, and that makes Alec's business vulnerable to the money-grabbing protection ring. There's still the confirmation needed from Alec about the one-hundred-grand payout every month to the Manettis that Jennings initiated. He wants to hurt Alec for his firing, so he kept the premise for that payment to himself. Alec won't agree to continue paying it. If he doesn't, the Cosa Nostra will wipe out Alec and his mother without consideration of consequences because most of their murders go unpunished. Dan's research found that the Birdman takes action first, then disappears before the fallout.

It's half past twelve, and the guy who likes cats and doesn't mind a little homicide on the side should be sitting down to his meal. If he's anything like his father's reputation, this is the most dangerous situation Drake's allowed himself to wander into since becoming a private detective. Alec would do the same for him.

Before Drake enters the restaurant, he checks the position of his recorder hidden in his breast pocket. On the screened porch, a wedding shower is in progress; wrapped gifts in white bows are piled high, and toilet paper gowns are being constructed by several giggling women wearing gobs of makeup—scripted right out of a reality show. If Joey's here, he won't be eating outside today.

Drake's mouth is set for an authentic dish of ziti and meatballs. Toscallina's is bustling during the noon hour and strong in the aromas of marinara and garlic bread. Instrumental music, mostly accordion, leaches outside from the dining area. Jumbled voices and vibrations from the air-conditioning unit hit him, and he's bombarded by frigid air, cold enough to refreeze a melted ice cube. He'll have to adjust the volume to hear separate conversations in this noisy environment.

It's his lucky day, twice. First, sitting at a remote table from prying eyes, where seating capacity can't be more than twenty-five. White and gold coverings and dark chairs are the theme at each table, which reminds him of his grandmother's dining room and smells even better. Second, when he's shown to a seat, the server with big hair at another table namedrops Joey when he calls her over. Drake's focus will be on that table. This saves him the trouble of asking about a mobster or eyeballing the customers who match Manetti's description. Unless it's a different Joey, the foursome in black T-shirts near the bar is his target. Drake ignores their table for the moment to get a feel for the surroundings and condition himself to segmenting out the individual conversations.

Food must be good here, considering the overflow crowd. His table is one that teeters on the uneven brick every time he places his elbows down. He's sitting at the back of the room in the corner at a two-person hideaway near the kitchen. Plenty of distracting talk and banging dishes make great ambiance, but the racket is terrible to hear people talking.

During inquiries, he found out Joey is deaf in one ear from a car bomb blast that went awry while he lived in Sicily. Leo Manetti moved Joey to the States when he feared a rival Mafia head had ordered a hit on Leo's only son, the next possible don and leader of the Manetti crime family. Drake's been around elderly war veterans who are hard of hearing, and they tend to speak a few decibels louder. In this ruckus, raising a voice would give Drake an advantage to pull out more details. The dining hall is at capacity, barstools are occupied, and lunchtime is in full swing.

Josh Jennings is certain the young Manetti would send someone to follow Benita if she'd stolen his beloved cat; he loved his cat that much, but is Stella the same animal? Ordinarily, Drake wouldn't worry about Benita Alvarez's death and Jennings sitting in a Lecce jail for her murder, but since Stella is in the care of Alec and Annalisse, he has to consider Manetti for Alvarez's homicide and what lengths he'd go to for a missing cat.

"Do you need a menu?" The mini-skirted server recognizes a stranger.

"Can I get a plate of ziti and meatballs, please?"

"Sure. Salad with house dressing and a glass of wine?"

"Pass on both. Does it come with bread?"

"A full basket. Plain or Chef's famous garlic bread? We can do half and half to keep the girlfriend happy. Chef likes big garlic chunks."

She's grinning or laughing. Who can tell in this noise?

"Surprise me." He trumps her grin with his own.

She blushes. "Honestly, you have gorgeous teeth. Hey, Bennie." She swats the arm of a customer behind her. "Doesn't he have nice teeth?"

Crap. Thanks a lot.

Drake shuts his mouth and fiddles with his napkin so that no one sees them or looks in their direction.

With a sideways skirt tug, she sets the water glass in front of him and leaves with his menu.

His glance strays to the table with black T-shirts, and he quickly rearranges his napkin. The black shirts seem oblivious to everyone else in the restaurant. If Joey is a part of this group, so far, he doesn't see his thick glasses.

Pulling out his phone, Drake reviews Dan's email and studies each photo for marks, scars, tattoos, or any other characteristics that make them stand out in a crowd. There's not much to go on at the table other than a balding man who doesn't mix with the younger set. Talk is low while they twirl their spaghetti and drink from a house bottle of red wine without a label.

Drake sends a basic text to Alec and lets him know his status.

"Don't worry about things here, Joey," a random voice says.

His ears perk, zeroing in on the table. Drake leans back in the chair, folding his hands nonchalantly, taking a sip of water and pretending to pick up something from the floor.

"Man, this is a tough break. The big man upstairs has his own plans for your dad. Nicky takes over at the track. No sweat. Right, Nicky?" A slap on a back. "We got this. You'll come back to New York in no time. Did Geno tell you who's running in the third? Birdman. There's a horse called Birdman. Can you believe that?" Laughter. "The Birdman's racing with your dad on his back. It's an omen; that's what I think. He's a surefire winner."

Someone plants their fist into the table, stunning the entire restaurant into silence. The listening device gets a welcome reprieve from the din, and so do his ears. In moments, forks scrape their plates again, and the servers move from their at-attention positions.

"Rave, shut up."

This person hasn't spoken before. He has a different cadence, and the accent is more old-world, like someone who speaks Italian in the household. Joey Manetti must be the man with his back to Drake, but that's a guess at this point. Silverware clangs, and a plate slides to the middle of the men's table, causing everyone there to stop eating their spaghetti midbite. The men are sitting upright at the back of their chairs, attentively watching one man.

"I decide who goes where." The guy with his back to Drake leans onto the table and in a lower voice grumbles, "Rocco runs book, Nicky collects loans. The rest of you knuckleheads, especially Rave, don't make a stinkin' move until you hear from me, got it? You're out of the joint for a couple of weeks and you're running the place. Don't be a Guido. What a time for the ol' man to kick the bucket. I'm busy here, and that flight to Sicily sucks."

There doesn't seem to be any love for this family member. Is Leo Manetti aka the Birdman on his death-bed, or is it someone else?

The server arrives with Drake's ziti and bread bas-ket, scooting around faster than before. She looks over her shoulder at the Manetti table, drops the plate on the cloth in front of Drake without a word, and zips into the kitchen.

"Maybe the doctors got it wrong, Joey. Birdman's a strong guy."

"Not this time. Uncle Carlo says Doc told him Pop's on borrowed time. He's coughing up blood."

If anyone was still eating at that table and the sur-rounding ones, talking about blood put off a few ap-petites. It almost did his, but he's too hungry, and the pasta is incredible.

"What about the cat? What do we do about that?" someone asks.

Instinctively, Drake inches forward in his chair because he couldn't tell who had brought up the cat. Picking out separate voices is getting difficult again in the restaurant.

"Ask her."

An attractive brunette in a snug tank and even tighter jeans slides alongside the man with his back turned and gives him a peck on both cheeks. A few of the black shirts say "Hey" and "How's it goin'?"

"Sorellina, tell me something I don't know," Joey asks her and swats her backside like a parent would a young child.

His daughter? A girlfriend? They seem pretty chummy. Could be a Manetti cousin.

The server appears with a single chair and sets it down for the woman. She must be a regular.

"Did Rave tell you? We got shut out. No sign of Stella," the woman called Sorellina says.

A mouthful of pasta slid down sideways, and Drake quickly gulps water and clears his windpipe several times to avoid coughing. He's torn between being on the right track with Stella the cat and hoping against it for Alec's sake. Two people at that table were looking for something or someone named Stella. There are few coincidences.

"Get another one."

"Yeah, easy for you to say," the girl answers.

Drake can't tell who she's talking to.

"Everybody shut up. She's got rights." The guy with his back turned finishes it.

Joey seems to be sticking up for her. She's got pull with him.

"How did you get the name Rave anyway?" a new voice around the table asks.

"Yeah, we wondered about it."

"Scratched a guy's eye out with a tool I made. Left jagged claw marks. The guys on my block said they looked like raven tracks." The bald guy laughs. "They stopped razzing me after that. Glad to be out of there. Thanks again for springin' me, Joey." In a lowered voice he says, "The fake passport from Italy was a nice touch. I guess that makes me a *paisano* now."

"Terms of probation. Without it, you won't be able to fly."

Rave has a fake ID for boarding planes. Has he been to Lecce lately looking for Stella on Manetti's behalf? He had time to get down there and back, just like Drake.

"Are we done here? Joey, I need to talk to you. In private. It's important." Sorellina slides over to Manetti.

"Hear that? Lunch is over." The person who's taking the lead stands up, which cascades scooting chairs around the table.

"When do you take off?" someone asks.

"Tomorrow night. I'm on a red-eye, so I can get some sleep on the plane."

"Give the Birdman our best." With food left on their plates, three guys leave, and Manetti escorts the girl through a door behind the bar.

Drake never saw the man's blue eyes to confirm the identification.

Toscallina's meatballs are too huge to finish, but he takes a few small bites, giving the black shirts time to scatter. He shoves a piece of bread in his mouth, checks his phone for the time, and leaves the server cash for lunch and a healthy tip. Drake heard enough circumstantial evidence that ties the Manettis to a cat and a crime family. Did anyone at that table murder Alvarez? Could have, but Jennings had the better opportunity.

He'll recommend to Alec that he drop Stella at a shelter in the high probability that she belongs to Joey Manetti. Holes and missing pieces in cases aren't Drake's specialty; he'll leave that to his partner.

TEN

"When is Bill supposed to check in? He texted an hour ago." My anxiety level is hard to keep down. It would be less stressful to rule out Joseph Manetti as the owner of Stella before the hospital calls us to pick her up. Alec wants to haul her in a leg cast to a shelter, and it's a painful thought when we can give her the love she needs.

"We can't put this off any longer." Near the window, a green, oversized cushion in the chair where my purse is looks inviting. This is the ideal time to show Alec the rosary beads while we wait on Bill.

The Sister's story from the courtyard unfolds simply without fanfare. Alec is pensive and unfazed by either the age of the beads or his mom's story. A child of Gen, the eclectic collector extraordinaire, wouldn't be surprised.

"Why do you think Mom gave these to you, now of all times?" he asks.

"She must have had her reasons. When we figure out the meaning of MCG on the medal, that may give us the answers. Sister Mary Natalina saw the initials right away, deciphering it like a simple code with no effort. She's not going to give us more than initials though. It's up to us to figure out who owned them."

"You do love a good mystery." He weighs the black crucifix in his hand. "Large. I agree with the Sister. Designed for a Reverend Mother or a nun. I don't think a priest or someone ordained at a higher level like a bishop or cardinal would wear this style, but I could be wrong. It matches the photos I've seen throughout history for nuns—the fat beads and black cross. Mom doesn't usually keep religious articles in her safe. I would've recalled seeing these. She's either forgotten about them, or they're so precious she had to keep them hidden."

"For heaven's sake, why give them to me? I can't explain Gen hiding these from you if they're so important. For all we know, they could be a simple keepsake with only sentimental value." My thoughts reason the other way. "Then why did the Sister tell me to help you find your ancestry after handling this rosary?"

"How did Sister Mary Natalina know Mom and put that together just by seeing this?" Alec holds out the cross. "Is she a clairvoyant?"

"The original Mary Margaret was Gen's friend and a seer, but she didn't mention any other Sister with that gift. Unfortunately, Sister Natalina never got around to telling me anything about Mary Margaret, my entire reason for seeking her out. I could tell by her body language that she knows the name. We may never get another chance to return to Bari, so I'm digging in on the research during this trip."

Standing at the window to conceal my trembling chin, I watch the calm sea and the fishing boats, like a mini armada, all painted a cerulean blue, bobbing along the wakes. Water in motion is so cool…

"We can come back to Bari whenever you want, preferably when there isn't a scandal or a business to sell, or we aren't dragged into a crime." Alec's trying to be witty, but there is doubt in him. Alec and I may not be together forever.

"Nothing is easy with you, Zavos. As wonderful as an incognito vacation would be, you're way too high profile to hang with us peons. The public always finds you." A sigh escapes, and I'm instantly sorry. He might not have caught it. "We need some sea air. Are you ready for another stroll on the beach?" My eye waters, and I blink it away. In times like this, I wonder if he wouldn't be better off with someone who's used to the limelight and doesn't doubt herself continually. "Bring your cell so we won't miss Bill's call."

"Are you ashamed to be seen with me?" Alec's picking up my negative vibe.

I'm making the situation worse. "Never."

We sit together on the edge of the mattress, my hand in his, neither of us speaking the thoughts swirling in our heads. Stop being so truthful and showing him reasons to leave. He wants me with him, or I wouldn't be here pawing through his rubble that used to be a carefree existence before his dad left the earth. He was there for me with the Kate disaster. *Be here for him; he needs you.*

Alec's staring a hole in his phone.

"You can't will it to ring. Bill has to call soon. C'mon, let's talk strategy and go outside. You'll feel better."

"Doubt it."

"Then do it for me. I'll feel better. Beach atmosphere will clear your mind." I reach for him to get off the bed and stop sulking. We're turning into a couple of sad lumps in one of the most romantic places in Europe.

"Not with Brad under the weather and so much up in the air. I'm thinking of cutting our trip short."

Alarm hammers me to the floor. The negativity surrounding us is convincing him we shouldn't stay, and I've been a big contributor.

"Aw, you'd spoil this time alone for us. Please don't."

"I can't let anything happen to you and won't take that chance again, Anna." Alec springs from the mattress and gathers me in his arms. "Seriously, I'm afraid." His breath is warm in my ear. "Since Dad died, I'm helpless to solve problems, and it *scares the stuffing out of me,*" he mocks in laughter as it rumbles against my chest. "Mom's words. It seems the right metaphor to use. What if there's truth in what the Sister said, and we should leave? You're suggesting we ignore her for a few days' vacation?" He squeezes tighter and kisses my hair. A gesture he makes when he's worried, like the hair thing, but I doubt he realizes it.

Brad's voice filters through the south wall from our room.

"Brad's up. Who's he talking to?" I ask.

"No idea." He breaks from me, heads toward the adjoining wall, and halts. "Look at me, eavesdropping on a friend. I need a life."

"You have one of those. There's no room for another." My slow smile breaks Alec's stony facade. "Knock on his door, if for nothing else than to check on him."

Alec flexes his back, fluffs his shirt, and removes his pistol. "We'll leave this in the room while we're on the beach. It's wearing a sore on my spine. I don't have a permit for it, should anyone notice." He rummages through his partially empty suitcase and lays the revolver beneath folded clothes. "Brad can take that walk with us for the exercise. It'll do him good too."

We lock our door and arrive at Brad's. He's no longer talking to his caller and opens it on the first knock.

"Time to get some air. Come with us to the beach if you're up to it." I'm grateful Alec didn't mention it was my idea. Brad already thinks my ideas are *a little daft*, as he would put it.

"Yes. Very good. I'll be right out."

Brad practically slams the door in our faces, and I look at Alec.

"We've interrupted something." I'm regretting this plan. Bodyguards make things so complicated.

A short time later, Brad returns, rested and in better spirits since I brought him the soup. The three of us amble down the long tapestry runner on the floor. A tall man in a British-style herringbone beret comes out of a room at the end of the corridor near the exit, sees us, and waves gleefully at Alec. I think he's being a friendly guest, but his broad smile spells something more—recognition.

"Lad, nice to find you, yes indeed. Generosa said you were staying here." The man closes his door and extends his hand to Alec, shaking it like a pump handle priming for water. "We've spoken before. King, Oliver King from—"

"Yes, hello. I remember. Board of directors for Global Star Class. I'm sorry our trip to Florence was canceled in light of developments, but it's nice to see you. When did you get in?" Alec asks unsteadily, as mystified as I am by King's sudden appearance and his mention of Gen.

When did he speak to her? Did Gen get the Signorile sale back on track?

"Got in a few hours ago. Splendid that you haven't left yet." His reddish brows quirk up. "I haven't had the pleasure." The woolly hand came for mine. "This must be your lovely lass, Anna…"

"Annalisse. Hello, Mr. King." I help the conversation move along, hoping he divulges more details to the many questions we have.

"Out for a stroll, are ye?" King has such a strong Scottish or Welsh brogue, he's hard to understand.

"On the beach. It's a beautiful night." Alec shifts me a bewildering glance, then asks King, "Would you like to join us?"

"I'm after a biscuit and cuppa. Meet you out there. Save an umbrella." He looks my way and walks past us down the terracotta tiles.

With Brad in our space, I zip my lips and wait until we're away from the bed-and-breakfast before I launch a hundred questions at Alec. The night air near dusk is a brisk sixty degrees, but it's refreshing on my skin. Alec and I walk hand in hand after removing our shoes. The rough sand is still warm from the day and is toasty, oozing through each toe. I've heard it called Puglia, between the sea and the sky. The perfect description of this beach; a sandy window opens to the turquoise Adriatic where it meets the salty air and pale blue horizon. Tonight the firmament encasing our atmosphere slowly changes over to a light gray from the approaching storm as the sun goes down. Bari is a magical place, and I can't wait to see more of it from the picturesque Town Square where the real residents live.

"Can't help it, Alec. It's been years since I felt like a carefree kid." I kick up sand and build up speed, racing toward the surf on a desolate peninsula.

"Not too far out, Anna. We have cloud cover tonight. I don't want to lose sight of you," Alec says loudly from behind.

When I finally turn to acknowledge him, he's forgotten me entirely and taken up a discussion with Brad. I have no idea if Brad's met Oliver King before, but it's entirely possible he has. There are pelicans milling around on shore, but few people are using the umbrellas this late in the day. The incredible seafood restaurants have seduced most visitors to come in and savor their brightly colored catch from the ocean. In the distance, a lone fisherman slaps his octopus on the rocks to tenderize it. I heard this plopping earlier, and there's no mistaking the repetitious sound. Visualizing this, I won't be adding octopus to my menu anytime soon. Using simple tools and bare hands are the preferred methods in old-world Bari.

Alec's phone rings, and I run back to catch up, hooking his arm with mine.

"Hi, Bill, we're on the beach, not in our room. I want Anna in on this too." He ushers me to a distant section of beach and signals a cross gesture to Brad, who stays a few paces away. "Can you hear this?" he asks me.

"Hey, we're dying to know what happened in New York. Where are you?" I ask.

"On the way to Connecticut to meet Dan."

"Any more on the victim in Josh's office?" Alec asks.

"Yes, but you'll find this more interesting. Josh's attorney sent over the loan document between your dad and Jennings. We have the proof that Pearce borrowed the start-up Signorile funds and didn't embezzle the money himself."

"That's not irrefutable, but it's a good beginning." Alec can't seem to find anything positive. "The racing team could say they set up the papers to cover Dad."

"Sure, but it's more logical that the CFO in charge of accounts would have better access to embezzle without Pearce's part in it. Alec, we've checked years of billing, and I found nothing to implicate your father. You should be happy. Cheer up, man. Quicken Racing must have checked into your dad from their end, came up dry, and wrote the whole thing off."

"Is Josh formally charged in the Alvarez homicide?" I ask, getting back to Alec's original question before Bill heads into already-covered territory.

"I don't know."

There's an uncomfortable silence on both ends of the phone.

"What did you find out in New York? Is Stella a Mob cat?" I ask.

"I found who I think is Joey Manetti at one of his Italian restaurant hangouts. That's where I texted Alec earlier."

"What happened?" Alec asks.

"Joey's name came out at a table with four guys. There's a lot of people named Joe or Joey in Little Italy, so I couldn't be sure I had the right guy until they mentioned a Birdman. Birdman is a Manetti and the big Mob boss in Sicily—he's also Joey's father. The kid is going to Sicily tomorrow night because something's wrong with his old man." Bill takes a breath. "While I ate lunch, a gal shows up in tight red gear and schmoozes with Manetti. Couldn't tell if she was a sister or girlfriend. He had a pet name for her, sorie something, can't remember it. I'll review the tape and write it down."

"What did she say, Drake?" When Alec calls him by a last name, he's annoyed.

"She announced that they didn't find the cat."

"That doesn't mean Stella. Could be any cat." Indignant me wants another option.

"She said Stella."

The other me is speechless.

"Sorry, guys. I think she, this sorie person, might have been in Lecce looking for Stella. She was looking for a cat by the same name, possibly with one of the black-shirted guys sitting at the table. One of 'em talked about fake IDs and flying after leaving jail. She had enough time to get to Italy and back. I don't know which one at the table owns Stella, but I got the feeling one of them does."

"Benita could've set up a goose chase to a place other than Lecce?" I toss in a last hope.

"A chase that ends in her death in Lecce. It's likely they found Benita and tortured her for the cat that was hiding in the conference room, but would they kill Alvarez without finding the cat? Losing any chance of finding Stella?" Alec asks. "It's hard to believe anyone would go to the trouble to torture this woman with razor wire for a cat. The reason must be more sinister, more personal."

"Any reason is good enough for the Mob, unless Jennings actually murdered her and told us the cat story to finger Manetti. The woman shook him down for money, after all. It's a tell that he turned green, reciting the gore around Benita after she was tortured. A killer who commits the act typically doesn't turn colors and shake uncontrollably while recounting it, unless multiple personalities are involved. Had a case like that once."

"I've not seen that in Josh," Alec says. "We can rule it out."

"Agreed. We're dealing with a calculating man in charge of his faculties. Benita took the tabloid to get cash from Josh; that's it. It's that simple. He chose an unfortunate place to meet with her, too close to home. If she'd been in a hotel, they might have found his credit card, which they did, but the other evidence wouldn't be so damning. Lecce authorities want a quick conviction that shows Josh was with the victim long enough to murder her. Speaking of which, I confirmed the protection payments he was making. He's laid an ugly trap for you."

"The protection monies are for real?" Alec asks.

"Josh made the payment to the Mob per Pearce's recommendation. How long has it been since you let him go?" Bill asks.

"April."

"Josh believes you're seven hundred grand in arrears. I'm surprised someone hasn't come for it yet."

I gasped. To what lengths would the Mafia go to get that money from Alec?

"They might have tried to get payment, but I haven't heard about it yet. One of our lead accountants has taken over for Josh temporarily. I left the preliminary CFO interviews to him before I take over the process. A Mafia bill collector wouldn't know who to go to for that kind of money... other than me." Alec unhooks my arm and rubs his forehead furiously. "That's a sizable amount to ignore. I wonder why I wasn't approached?"

"No one is paying the bill," I say bluntly. "How long before some goon puts a gun to your head or a knife at your throat? You'll need a battery of security guards before you set foot in Palermo again. They may be following us right now."

Brad steps in stealthily, but I notice his casual movement.

"I have to finish this talk later, Alec, but there's one more thing to mention. Josh passed along something Pearce told him in complete secrecy. I got the impression that if Pearce were alive, Josh wouldn't have told me this. I don't know if I believe him because it's so far-fetched."

"Let's hear it." Alec is focusing like a laser on Bill's next words.

"What I alluded to about your mother earlier. Josh said her real name was something else, not Generosa."

Alec looks at me as if he wants my confirmation, so I mouth the word *no*.

"Bill, that's absurd. Did he offer more than that?" Alec asks.

"Your grandfather's name is Antonio."

"Correct."

"Antonio Giambruno."

"Granddad is Antonio DePalma. Josh must have mixed up the names."

Bill pauses. "Josh said before your mom met Pearce, her family changed names to keep your mom's true heritage a secret. Antonio did this when she was very young. She might have told you she was a DePalma to—"

"C'mon. Why would he hide their last name? Wait a second. Alec isn't who he thinks he is, like what Kate did to me? No way." I'm trying to dial back the emotions for Alec's sake. This story is getting too bizarre and too familiar.

"Not in the same way. Alec is the son of Pearce and Generosa, but Generosa's true birth name is supposedly Sophia Giambruno. Annalisse, this is your department; it should be easy to check heritage and verify Josh's story. Ancestry websites may have photos of Alec's grandparents, cousins, et cetera, so you can see for yourselves. Hey, guys, I really gotta go. I'm sitting at a truck stop, and it's swamped at the pumps. Keep Brad close by. I'll check in tomorrow."

"Sophia. The Sister's Sophia?" I whisper, recalling her reference to it.

"We'll check on that, Bill. Call us back when you can." Alec stashes the phone in a jacket pocket and says, "I know that look. You forgot to tell me something."

"Sister Mary Natalina mentioned a woman and asked about Gen's maiden name. She also thought the DePalma surname was incorrect, and she asked to see a photo of your grandfather, which I don't have."

"What reason would Granddad and Mom have to change their names?"

"Her father might have been in serious trouble. The same trouble that landed him in prison would be my guess. Suppose your grandfather wanted your mother as far from Bari as possible. Gen told me she can never come back here. I didn't understand what she meant at the time, but name changes fit the arrangement to stay out of sight. Antonio might have informed Pearce because he married into the DePalma or Giambruno family, whichever it is. You said each time you brought up prison and your grandfather together, your parents clammed up. They were protecting you like Antonio did Gen."

Giambruno should be easy to remember. "Let's hurry back to the room so I can begin a few searches. Oh, sorry, Alec, I've jumped ahead. You do want to know the truth, don't you?"

Alec is quiet, and his lips are twitching as he muses over my question. He wants the truth, and he doesn't.

I'm allowing my enthusiasm for history and solving riddles to get out in front of him. It's his choice how deeply we dig into his mother's past.

"Granddad wasn't Sicilian, so that keeps him out of the Cosa Nostra." Alec swipes away a no-see-um bug in the descending sunset. "Now I understand how you felt with Kate, not knowing the difference between the stories she told and the truth she hides. We've gone this far, may as well discover what's myth. Start with both sets of last names and trace them; see if Mom pops up anyplace. You have my blessing."

The simpler solution would be to come right out and ask Gen directly. The approach I would use, but Alec has the scars of being shut down about his grandfather before. Questions over the telephone would make stalling too easy for Gen.

"Brilliant, you're here." Oliver King comes into view at the top of the beach, waving with the enthusiasm of a child about to romp in the ocean.

He makes his way down to Alec as a new man with a lighter step. Mr. King must have located a great batch of tea at the bed-and-breakfast. As he nears, he's changed his clothes to Bermuda shorts and a polo, and he's wearing strange over-the-toe sandals with big buckles.

"I usually run before bed, but I forgot my joggers. A walk will have to do. Have a pleasant night. We'll chat tomorrow, I'm sure." King turns, with an arm taking flight above his head.

We watch him get smaller at the edge of the surf for a minute or two, and I snuggle toward Alec's sweet heat. Every muscle in my body is collapsing under my weight. This has been such an uneven day, starting with learning about Gen's love of telescopes this morning. I'm ready to fall into bed and sleep for eight hours so that we can process the deluge of new events with clearer minds.

A jogger out for a run, wearing a black hoodie and gray sweatpants with a white stripe down the sides, doesn't acknowledge us as he passes, splashing ocean water in Oliver King's earlier path. It's almost dark and silent except for the lapping waves washing onshore. We're the only human beings left strolling on a moonless night.

"Have you had enough beach for one day, babe?" Alec asks with a sideways hug. "I'd like to scribble a few things down while I can hold my eyes open." He stoops to put on his shoes.

"Just thinking the same thing. Meeting Mr. King in Bari was a surprise."

"Yeah. A good one. I'll phone Oliver in the morning and set up a meeting after lunch. That'll give me time to talk strategy with Mom beforehand. She's arranged this impromptu meeting. It has her fingerprints all over it."

"That's my feeling too. Gen is in New York, yet she's here with us. Operating like she does at the gallery. I love your mother's sneaky, behind-the-scenes moxie." I slip my shoes back on and approach Brad, who's watching a place in the surf.

Alec pivots and stares that way.

"What's up?" I ask.

"Shh." Alec's hand cups my mouth and shields me with his body.

Figures surround a lump near the water, but all I can make out are fuzzy shadows and an occasional flashlight at this distance.

Brad takes out his weapon and steps ahead of Alec, then changes his mind and holsters his pistol.

"Is that a knife in a person's back? Don't move, Anna." Alec blocks my view. "This doesn't look good."

CHAPTER
ELEVEN

I'm rooted in place as if I'm a tree rising from the sandy landscape. It's none of our business if there's been a knifing on the beach, so why are we still here, gawking at the spectacle? We're at least a hundred yards from the splayed limbs, now fully aglow in shining beams at all angles. A car and a pair of Vespas illuminate what appears to be a collapsed or dead form in the wet sand.

"I'll escort you to your room now, Ms. Drury, Alec. When you're inside, lock the door and your windows, please," Brad says quietly in a monotone.

"We aren't leaving your side, Brad. Anyone seen Oliver? He didn't come back this way." Alec isn't about to leave with the commotion around us. "Stay behind me, Anna."

Hair prickles my arms as we creep together in a tight cluster. I feel the tenseness in Alec's and Brad's discomfort without a weapon drawn. On a public beach in a foreign country, it's a wise decision to keep firearms hidden.

Blaring police whistles from behind get our attention, and we turn in unison. Two, maybe three cops are blowing loudly to stop our progression to the scene.

"Arresto!" I know what that means and stop dead, hanging on to Alec's arm.

A uniformed officer approaches Brad first, and he accepts the wallet Brad offers. They converse in Italian for a time before Brad is asked to remove a slip of paper. He then flaps open his jacket for a view of his leather harness and pistol. The policeman glares at what I suspect is Brad's permit, looks at Alec, and finally frisks Brad's legs and waist, looking for more small arms. Another, perhaps his partner, searches us for hidden weapons. Thank goodness Alec had the foresight to leave his illegal gun in the room. Without a permit, he surely would've been taken to jail or held for the crime on the beach. In this low light, it's hard to discern any signals from the dark-haired officer quizzing Brad. He's answering in Italian as if it were his native language, something I didn't know about him. I have to assume Brad explained his status as bodyguard to Alec during the exchange. We were quite a distance away from the crime scene, which will be in our favor. The more details Brad can relate to him, the better the alibi for all of us.

"How long have you been on the beach tonight?" the officer asks Brad in English, prompting yet another lengthy explanation.

"Mr. Alec Zavos, what can you tell me about the victim?" The officer points down the beach. "Do you work with him?"

Alec breaks into his own Italian spiel and says in English, "Who is it? I can't make him out from here."

My eyes sharpen and focus on the form lying, facedown wearing Bermuda shorts, a polo shirt, and funny sandals—with a knife handle sticking out of his back.

"My God, Alec, Oliver King. That has to be him." Words are wedging past my gasps. "I… I recognize his funny sandals."

"Explain, *signorina*." The officer switches his attention to me.

"He changed his clothes." I pick at my own blouse. "Different from when we met him there." Pointing to the building, I add, "He's an acquaintance only. How do you say that in Italian, Alec?"

"Conoscenza casuale."

He nods, and in a cop's mechanical cadence, he follows up. "Did he seem nervous?"

"No, not at all. There was this jogger, a runner, not far behind Mr. King, but…" I give him a description, and Alec translates as the policeman records everything in a notebook. "Nothing weird about his running suit, but he didn't make eye contact, so I can't tell you what he looked like. Is Mr. King dead?"

He's silent and avoids eye contact.

My heart sinks for Oliver King but also for Alec. King might have been the last hope to resurrect a sale for Signorile. Who would want King out of the picture?

When the officers exhausted all their questions, we were released from the beach but told not to go near the scene or tell anyone what happened until family notifications. The policeman questioning us asked to meet in the morning at our bed-and-breakfast once they run our background checks and gather more on Mr. King. Law enforcement quizzed Alec relentlessly on what he knew about Oliver King's possible affiliations with the Mafia and child trafficking. That last one turns my stomach. Traffickers are the lowest of lowlifes. To me, King didn't fit that profile, but I've read about celebs doing awful things with child actors. I hope Mr. King wasn't involved in such things.

Alec has been long on thought and short on talk during most of the interrogation. His mind is calculating something, I know it. When he sulks, he's making alternative plans. The sale of Signorile Corporation is an anchor around his waist, dead weight, and sinking fast into the Adriatic Ocean.

I didn't get ten minutes of sleep; it's doubtful Alec slept much more than that himself. He got up to use the bathroom twice that I know of and turned over to check the time repeatedly. Our early beach stroll and quiet night in our room has been anything but, when we spent two hours near the homicide scene with Bari *polizia* and the carabinieri, their national military. It wasn't until one of the police recognized Alec that interrogations lightened up and our situation improved. There's lots to be said against being in the wrong place at the wrong time—that was us at six forty-five last night.

After I slept on what happened to us, other than poor Mr. King, it turns out Brad endured the worst of it, explaining why he carries a pistol and why he needs a weapon on the beach. I was uncomfortable watching Brad squirm under interrogation, conversing in Italian, telling his story again and again a little differently each time. Alec came to his rescue on numerous occasions when Brad's explanations seemed more incriminating than helpful. Shame on me for wanting that look at the calm sea last night. What a terrible idea. The police wouldn't admit King's true condition, but we're sure he didn't make it.

A quick tap on our door.

It's Brad's polite knuckles barely making a sound.

Alec rolls out of bed and hits the tile in a barefooted *splat*. He jumps into his jeans. "Yes?"

"It's Bradley, Mr. Zavos."

"Mr. Zavos?" I haven't heard Brad be so formal with Alec in a while.

"Apologies for the early call. I have something you should see. It can't wait."

My robe is near the bed, and I slip into it and a pair of slippers, nodding to Alec.

Standing in the threshold, Brad looks rested and in better shape than yesterday. He's in a fresh blue button-down and holds a newspaper, unfolded. The only thing I'm able to read is *La Gazzetta*. The local Bari gazette we haven't had time to scan since we arrived. I'm good for the colorful photos and nothing else. Brad speaks Italian so well; he must also read the language.

Alec reaches for the paper. "What page?"

"It's yesterday's gazette. Page two."

"Good morning, how're you feeling?" I ask.

"Well, thank you, Ms. Drury. That spot of soup helped."

"What is it, Alec?" I'm watching him skim an article while chewing a fingernail.

"Why wasn't I told about this? Who'd do this?" He gives me the newspaper, like I'm going to understand a foreign language, and I notice Signorile's name in the tallest headline.

"What does it say about Signorile?" I ask.

"Someone let it out that Global Star Class is in talks to buy us."

"Weren't talks in secret? Would Serge tell others?" I ask Alec.

"Since the deal is dead, maybe, although there's nothing to gain by it."

Dropping into the armchair at the window, I groan reflexively, bringing round, expressive eyes from Brad.

"Are you all right, Miss?"

"I'm fine. In order for the sale to go through, Global Star needs a unanimous decision from its board members, right?" I bring Alec into a more in-depth conversation.

"Yes. If there are any holdouts, the sale is vetoed. That's what Mom's been working on. Oliver King might have been the lone holdout. I'm only guessing."

"Or he's an ally to Serge, who's on your side—who also likes your mother."

Alec raises a brow.

"Not romantically—admires, respects; you know what I mean. Mr. King was too personable not to be on board with the sale. Perhaps he wanted the meeting with you to get an assurance that Pearce didn't embezzle the start-up money for Signorile. Then he could go back to any board member against the sale—or on the fence—and convince them to approve with proof from you or simply your word to Oliver."

"With King removed, the board will be in disarray. Shelving the acquisition until they find a replacement for King and can take up that business again." Alec rubs his chin, pondering the theory. "It's a logical assumption. Too bad we'll never know for sure."

"Feels more like a leaker to the media is trying to stop the sale of Signorile. The article could've been a signal for the hit on Oliver King." Sister Mary Natalina's words of caution hit my brain. "Need I mention the Sister warned me about staying in Bari. The only other person on that deserted beach with us was the jogger. I didn't get a good look at him. Why didn't I look more closely?"

"It doesn't matter. If he stabbed Oliver, he may be a contractor, covering the real person who paid the killer. That's the way they do things around here." Alec's frown shifts to the night table. He must have turned on his notifications because his phone is blowing up with different tones. "Word must be out about Oliver."

"Would you like me to pick up today's paper, sir?" Brad asks.

"The bed-and-breakfast may have them downstairs, gratis," I offer.

"We stay together. Don't go anywhere without us, Brad. Last night's knifing is big news in town. With our luck, Oliver's picture may be on the front page." Alec checks his phone, nodding at the screen. "Yep. Word's out on everything. Oliver, the sale... Sorry, babe. I've gotta dampen down these fires. I'll take care of business while you start the research."

"We have a meeting with the police downstairs, remember? All of us. Nine sharp. In the dining room."

"Aw, that's right. I don't know what more we can tell them."

"What time is it back home?" I ask, running the hours backward in my head. "Shoot. Too early to call Gen."

"It's the middle of the night. Does Mom pick up her texts?"

"Better to call her. Put it off for a few hours and let her sleep. News of Oliver's death might—"

"I'll wait outside." Brad turns the door handle. "Lock behind me and keep windows locked. Take your time." He slips out, and I point to the bathroom.

"No time for using the laptop. I'll jump in the shower first. Please hurry. We have an hour before we need to be downstairs." I'm talking to myself while Alec paces.

My research on the beads and Alec's family is urgent now that more people are dying. Two homicides in the space of a few days—and both have a tether to Alec and Signorile.

In a calming nook featuring hutches and wall coverings in tonal beiges, I'm sipping a cappuccino strong enough to eat the glaze off the cup. I take the last bite of the flakiest, most melt-in-your-mouth croissant in memory and chew slowly, savoring the butter. My fingertips glisten, and I stop myself from sticking them in my mouth, remembering Brad is with us, so a napkin will do instead. The food in this town is heavenly, albeit simple with few ingredients in most dishes. Tomatoes, garlic, basil, and olive oil are the most appreciated, and bread. Never forget the bread with pasta noodles and pecorino, a sharp sheep's milk cheese made in large wheels. Bari shellfish is like no seafood cuisine on the East Coast. Manhattan fish houses can't compare to those on Italy's south shore.

Alec and Brad have finished their eggs and deli meat breakfast, heavy on the brioche with lots of homemade fruit preserves. Both of them love their sweets. They're quietly chatting about cars and the latest technology, which doesn't interest me in the least, other than I like observing Alec wind down in the comfort of a trusted friend. He's sporting his outdoorsy, rugged look since he didn't shave and only towel-dried his wet hair. He carries it off well, with the exception of the worry lines fixed in his forehead. Picking up his messages and placing so many callbacks, he barely got his shower in before breakfast.

I take another sip of coffee and ponder last night's stolen glances at him by other women waiting for Alec to make eye contact. His steely bedroom eyes can make one imagine sinful acts. He must see it, or it's likely he gets the once-over treatment so often he doesn't notice. I wish I didn't. His European good looks naturally fit into the scenery here. I'm with Alec and shouldn't worry about such things, but the nagging question *Am I good enough?* rears its head again.

I'm content to hit a shop or two before we have to leave, but with each passing hour, that's less likely. I vow to at least give my camera some air in the square while we check out the orecchiette pasta ladies that we've heard so much about. If we see her, Sister Mary Natalina must know where the Church of Saint Anne is. Absolutely, I have to light a candle for Gen's Sister Mary Margaret before we go home.

The police are late for our meeting by twenty minutes, and I'm getting anxious to pull out my laptop for research. Wish I'd brought it down with us but also glad it's still in our room, considering the snooping through our backgrounds. They could ask to see the hard drive and view my visual records of Gen's priceless gallery merchandise. As corrupt as some law enforcement agencies are, it's best not to display more of the Zavos wealth. The laptop agenda can wait.

A pair of new guests wander into the dining area. I hope they aren't also meeting with the police. She's much younger than her escort of maybe fifty years. He's trim and has rock-solid thighs and biceps. His studious, round glasses and peppered hair are contradictory to his muscle-bound physique, unless he works out in order to attract a younger woman or owns a gym. She's blonde and busty, wearing a plunging neckline dress, carrying a straw hat, and hanging on his arm demurely. It's easy to picture them as a shallow trope made for a Hollywood production. They appear to be from the States, but it's hard to know without a conversation. Unmarried—no wedding rings. They're definitely having a fling: her pink glow and constant glances at him tell the story. They're as startled at seeing guests in the dining room as we are.

Alec stands and scrapes a chair across the tile. "Please, have a seat."

A round of how-do-you-dos fall loosely like dominoes.

Then three of Bari's finest in dark glasses and full uniform strut in, dumping a frigid breeze on our comfortable room temperature.

Like racing from a fire, the guests from Virginia make their excuses about being late for a breakfast meeting and scurry away. Who could blame them? Meeting cops first thing in the morning isn't the kind of day they had in mind for a fun-filled vacation at the inn.

Brad stands as guard beside Alec with the same rigid stance he had last night.

"I'm sorry your friends ran off," one of them dryly jokes in a throaty voice. He raises his glasses to the top of his head and exposes the tan lines from the aviator rims.

The sky-blue color in his short-sleeved shirt seems pale in comparison to his cool, iridescent eyes. I've noticed so many blue-eyed Italian men in Bari. He has a head start on Alec with his beard over hollowed cheeks. The five-day-stubble look is sexy and popular in Italy. This one is following my actions with great interest.

They take off their official black caps with plumes on the front, and Alec glides to the side of my chair.

"Have you found the man who killed Mr. King?" Alec asks.

"How do you know it's a man? May we?" Officer Blue Eyes has a heavy accent that's difficult to translate. He adjusts the white belt on an angle across his chest and sits down. The other two follow suit. "Do you know if Mr. King... how you say... has hot spray... ah, *pepe?*"

"I met King one other time. If he jogs, he may carry pepper spray. I've heard some use it as protection. Last night, I didn't notice." Alec finishes with a slight shrug.

Alec's short answers in English trigger an annoyance from the three officers. Two of them keep checking their watches. The one from the carabinieri with the most elaborate medallions on his uniform is quizzing Alec as if Brad and I aren't there. They're wearing the typical attire of the military police: blue shirt, a white suspender belt, and skintight black pants with red stripes, stuffed inside their tall boots. Collectively, they reek of masculine sweat, leather, and aftershave lotion, which is curious since none have had a recent shave. No showers for these boys in a while.

"How well does Mrs. Zavos know Mr. King?" He gazes at Alec, not me.

He's assuming a lot, and I stiffen at what he's implying.

Setting my cup down with tightening lips, I dare a glance upward toward Alec.

He draws the chair out next to mine. His smile is broad without a show of teeth, and it's certain he's considering a sarcastic comeback. *Please don't, Alec.*

"*Ms.* Drury is right here. Ask her."

It might have been better to just ignore the marital status part. The officer may be making a lame attempt to confirm my status with Alec, or he's used to talking to men and not women. A quick check of our naked left hands should say plenty, unless he wants to see how we writhe from the inquiry.

Three pairs of eyes shift on me. The one with the earlier smirk fidgets with a fork, clearly embarrassed by his mistake. He removes the glasses from his head and sets them on the table.

"I see." He lowers his gaze briefly before turning his scary attention to me. The man's eyes are startling. "Are you a friend of Mr. King's?"

"How did you arrive at that?" Alec's fuse is shortening. "She's no friend of his."

"It's okay, Alec." I pat his hand and see no point in provoking hostility across the table. "I didn't know him, Officer."

"Il Capitano."

"Captain, why are you asking about pepper spray? No one mentioned it last night," I ask.

"Capsaicin was found on his clothing." Another officer speaks in sharper English, bringing a grunt from his captain.

"Most who run carry Mace or pepper spray. I do. Not all the time, only when traveling alone on the street," I lie, too late to stop another avenue of questioning.

Did I take the spray off my key chain before we left? Are my keys with me?

"May we search your handbag, Miss Drury?"

I turn in time to watch Alec close his eyes.

Too much information falls out of my mouth at inopportune times like this one. Kate's gift of gab I inherited is a curse on me.

"We already told you. There are two witnesses who corroborate our location on the beach when Mr. King jogged away. He ran from us, not toward us." *That probably didn't help.*

The captain's teardrop glasses spring back on his head. "Your friends could be protecting you. Mr. King might have harassed a beautiful woman like yourself, and you—"

"Pepper spray is legal in Italy, is it not?" Brad asks.

"Yes."

"Women in Manhattan… New York City, expect the unexpected. Ms. Drury is a professional woman who owns an exclusive art gallery. She doesn't make a habit of spraying bystanders with noxious ingredients." Brad folds his napkin precisely and settles it next to his plate.

My heart flutters, and a small weight lifts from my chest.

"Have you ever used pepper spray in self-defense?" The captain's pinpoint stare is meant to unsettle me. He has all the body language and charisma of an IRS auditor. They don't scare me, and my shoulders snap back to indignant.

Alec's hand on mine under the table is comforting to my nerves.

"When I travel, I don't go *anywhere* alone, Captain. It's safer in groups. Last night, I was in the best hands, surrounded by two capable men. I don't need the false security a can of pepper brings. Don't they leak?" My voice is shrill on purpose. "Handbags are too expensive to risk smelly pepper juice spilling out. Ugh." I openly shudder, trying my darndest to come off as a snooty, privileged American with more means than the captain has.

He stands, having lost that round and with not enough grounds to search my belongings.

"You've already checked into our backgrounds." Alec brings a smile from Blue Eyes. "We were all on the beach together, and unfortunately, Oliver King was alone, the length of a football field away from us. We didn't know he was in any danger. Have your men watch the beach for the jogger we described to you. Now, if you'll excuse us, we have an appointment with the church."

Church? I smile sweetly at the three men, and Brad is stone-faced, showing his contempt for their questioning.

"Unfortunately for Mr. King, he wasn't completely alone. Someone came calling." The captain couldn't help but contradict Alec. With the sparring brings another broad smile. "Watch yourselves while you're in Bari. Stay in our city in case we have more questions for you. We will let you know when you can leave."

Alec hesitates. "We have the rooms through Friday and leave the next day. Please capture the killer before

we check out on Saturday. We'll help you with anything until then. Good day." Alec turns, and the police
leave us.

Our itinerary has an earlier departure. He's decided that a longer stay is too risky, given King's death. We
climb the stairs to our room, Alec asking Brad to join
us there. Other than that, not another word is spoken
between us as we formulate separate opinions of the
authorities' case. They keep to inquiries, so there's thin
evidence against us, beyond my use of pepper spray,
thanks to a blunder.

"I don't know what possessed me to mention the
spray. It just fell out. What happens when they uncover
my encounter with Peter at the gallery? It's going to in-
criminate me, isn't it?" I sink into the armchair cushion
and stare at the brocade on the wall.

"Don't sweat it. You covered yourself well. After
that performance, no one would suspect you'd dirty
your purse with pepper spray." Alec laughs. "I wanted to cheer your acting prowess. We didn't file against
Peter Gregory, remember? The district attorney wanted
to bring him up on assault, but you chose not to press
charges. Unless he's been included in the latest prison release, Gregory is still in jail for laundering money
and stealing artwork from Westinn Gallery. That's what
closed the gallery, not what he tried to do to you." He
addresses Brad. "We appreciate what you said to the
police on Annalisse's behalf. It made the officer question himself for asking. Nice work."

"But Alec, isn't there a record of my using an entire
container of pepper spray on Peter? Detective Mooney

took my statement. Won't the Bari police be able to dig that up?"

Brad began to pace. He must be recalling what I said on the plane about where I'd actually used the spray on an attacker a year ago.

"Do you still keep it on your key ring?" Alec asks.

"I've never taken it off. I replaced it after my encounter with Peter."

"I'd get it off the ring and dispose of it in a community trash bin."

"What if the police are watching us?" Brad asks. "Wouldn't it look like Ms. Drury is throwing away pepper spray evidence?"

"It would. Alec, I can't do that. If I brought my keys with me, it stays in my purse—along with the rosary. The container is full. Anyone can see I've never depressed the nozzle."

"Wouldn't you have time to dispose of the one used on the beach if they were inclined to believe it?" Brad's revelation isn't a comfort.

"The captain wasn't pleased with our departure date. I don't blame you for leaving sooner." I toss that in there with a pang of disappointment.

"I didn't plan the earlier flight. I should've spoken to you about it first instead of springing it on you like that. I didn't like the way he ordered us to stick around."

"It's okay. Every additional day we're here is like we're tempting fate somehow. The last time I felt this kind of uncertainty was on Crete last year."

Alec nods. "And we know how that turned out."

"Can the police keep us here if the killer's at large?" I ask.

"I don't see how. We didn't witness the act; we just happened to be on the same beach at the time of the knifing. I'd be out of here today if—"

Alec's phone rings, and he picks up.

"Morning, Bill. Not getting much sleep, I see. What is it, five back home?" He switches to speakerphone and sets it down on the armoire. "You're on speaker with Anna and Brad."

"I saw something cross the AP. Knifed on a beach in Bari. How long after we talked, and how close to you did it happen?" Bill asks.

I wait for Alec to answer, and he's strangely quiet.

"Alec?" Bill tries again.

"Quite a distance away. We spoke to Oliver King minutes before. Mom might have sent him, but I won't know that until we talk to her. No suspects other than a jogger on the beach."

"Is everybody okay? Do you need an attorney?"

"I hope not. No. I don't think it'll come to that. I'll handle it if we need one. We're all fine."

"Let me know if I can help in any way. I want to give you the medical examiner's report on the Alvarez case. He's determined her cause of death."

"Wow, that's great. You aren't part of that case officially, so how did you get that out of him?" I ask.

"As fortune would have it, I worked with Enrico on a missing person's case in Florida once. Since then, he's relocated to Italy with his wife who happens to be from Lecce. We were insanely lucky on this one." I could imagine Bill buffing his fingernails on his shirt.

"What did he say?" Alec asks.

"Benita Alvarez's official cause of death is head trauma with a heavy object like the baseball bat found at the scene. They're making a DNA match on a longer, lighter hair found on the victim's clothing. Blood other than Alvarez's own was obtained from the wire barbs. The assailant or assailants might have stuck themselves trying to coil it around the girl. That type of barbed tape nicks the skin on the barb points, not the razor's edge. The metal bat has prints also, but none match any of the locals in their database. Interpol is checking through AFIS and will let me know if anything pops up. No one has been able to determine the significance of why the concertina wire was used to bind her. Alvarez had a drug in her system, GHB, gamma-hydroxybutyrate. The drowsy effects have a short-term life of three to six hours and can easily be dosed in a drink. A liquid with juniper berries was found in her hair, probably from a martini or another gin drink. Stomach contents showed some alcohol present."

"So, after Josh left Benita alone looking for Stella, she was drugged, tied in his office, and beaten with a bat, and then someone poured a drink on her? Over the top, isn't it?" Alec asks Bill.

"Yeah, one other thing. Her wrists were clawed up so deeply that she bled out the entire time. The claw marks don't match with the concertina wire. Enrico believes she was clawed prior to wrapping her in the barbed tape."

I scrunch my neck into my shoulders and look at Alec. "That poor woman's last moments must have been excruciating. Someone really hated her to go to that much trouble. It's personal. Would Josh do this?"

"Jennings has been released because prints and blood are not his," Bill adds. "His attorney convinced the police he wasn't a flight risk, but his passport was confiscated. His story checks out from the adjoining buildings surveillance tapes, but they've attached a leg monitor to him, just in case he gets any ideas."

I consider the bat left behind at the scene. A pro wouldn't have made that mistake unless they wanted it found.

"Did surveillance pick up the killer entering the building?" Alec asks.

"I don't know that. The security system was disabled in Josh's building."

"Bill, can you think of any reason Oliver King's death and Benita Alvarez's death may be related?" Alec asks.

"Both involve persons with indirect ties to your dad or his business." Brad answers before Bill has a chance to. "Mr. Jennings used to be CFO and knew Ms. Alvarez because of their past relationship. Mr. King was tied to the company in talks with Signorile."

"Nicely summed up, Brad." There's clicking on Bill's end of the phone. "I'm making notes while we speak. The clawed wrists brought up something I just remembered. I heard one of Joey Calico's men talk about fashioning a claw device and using it to scratch out a prisoner's eye."

"Then Alvarez's killer may not be looking for Stella the cat," I say with some hope.

"That's still a question. I'd like to put the cat in the clear, but we can't yet. For all we know, Alvarez's murder could still involve the missing cat. *Sorellina* mentioned Stella. I listened to the tape again. Joey called the woman *Sorellina*. It means little sister or kid sister. Have you ever heard that term used by anyone?"

I scan the room, and we're all shaking our heads.

"No, we haven't. Mom doesn't use it either. Did anyone at Manetti's table mention being in Bari this week?" Alec asks.

"That didn't come up. Joey's due to arrive today or tonight in Sicily, and he's not happy about it. Like I mentioned before, his old man is sick."

"Too bad. That would've nailed a Manetti family member on the beach and available to order a Mob hit, but it still doesn't explain why anyone would want Oliver killed. Maybe it's random after all. Who knew he was here?" Alec asks. "Frankly, I think staying in this country is a big mistake."

Alec reads the I-told-you-so in my eyes and looks away.

"Bill, if anything comes up from our end, I'll let you know."

"Watch your backs, my friends. Stay aware and hang tough. I don't want to read about any of you on the wires."

"Will do. Be careful digging. We aren't sure if our actions were monitored before, but they are now, by police. Our Bari vacation might have gotten Oliver killed." Alec fires a pitiful look at me.

More like it was Oliver King's misfortune to follow us that got him murdered.

CHAPTER
TWELVE

Joey Manetti knows this trip is going to cramp his style. The old man picked a piss-poor time to get sick. It's stupid leaving New York to the boys when business is cranking on high and he's making a lot of money in trafficking. He prefers the drugs because he can't put a face on them, but a few kids here and there; once in a while, he'll turn his back. His Uncle Carlo knows the business, and he's closer to his dad's age, so he can handle things in Sicily. If Joey finds Pop in a good mood, he'll give him the figures and remind him how profitable they are in Staten Island.

He turns the hall corner and puffs out his chest in the bathroom mirror, the one that used to be his mom's. No matter what his dad says, he plans to do what's right for his part in the family. He's not taking over in Sicily when his uncle is capable.

"Still got it, Manetti." Running water, he drags a comb through the stream and smooths down the cowlick from the airplane seat made for tiny people wanting a backache by the time the flight is over. His eyes are bloodshot and scratchy, and his polo shirt's tight from extra pounds, but in a dark room, he knows his dad won't see the weight he put on from too much pasta. His papa doesn't care if he gets enough sleep on the godforsaken long flights. All he cares about are his sisters' wineries and hotel. He says they make money, and he doesn't.

His mom's makeup and hair crap stand against the wall on the vanity in formation like lint-covered toy soldiers. Joey doesn't understand why it's all still here when she's dead and never plans to use it again. He imagines his dad's bedroom still looks the same. Same crocheted quilt, same pictures on the wall, same smell of his mom's perfume and mothballs in the closet. Uncle Carlo mentioned he's bedridden. It's hard to look forward to the raunchy smell in that room.

His breakfast jumps to his throat, and his hands are sweating like they always do when he's summoned to the palace. In the Birdman's presence, the man changes from a father into this mythical creature who sees everything and finds fault in anything.

"Face it, Joey. You're here now. Rip off the Band-Aid and find out what the ol' man wants," he mutters.

Joey stands outside his bedroom at the end of the hall, looking at the closed sage-green door painted in the eighties. It's never been closed before. Maybe he's passed, on and the chance to talk has slipped away.

The floorboard squeaks when he shifts his weight.

"Who's there?" the presumed dead speaks.

"It's me, Pops. You got time? I can come back if you're taking a nap."

"What nap? I live in this bed. Why would I be napping when my favorite son is here? Come in, come in, please."

His only son is a favorite? He must be ready to kick off.

Joey doesn't remember the last time the great Mafia don said please. Running his tongue over his teeth to clear any remnants of the spinach-and-egg frittata he ate on the plane, he straightens the horn on his necklace and slowly turns the handle, preparing himself for what he'll see in the bed.

Uncle Carlo opens the door and gives Joey his snaggletooth grin, left to him by a rival family Geep in a territory war.

"Hey, Joey boy. Lookin' good." He grabs him in the usual bear hug and lays a couple of wet ones on the cheeks. "Have a good flight? What can I get you? Coffee, wine, or maybe..." He lifts his arm and makes the motion for drinking a shot.

"Carlo, stop mothering him, for the love of my dear departed Lina."

"I'm good, Uncle Carlo. Maybe later."

Carlo turns his attention to Pops, who's sitting against a stack of pillows behind his shoulders. "Leo, you doin' all right?"

His eyes are smaller and beady, sunken deep into their sockets. He's little more than a skeleton with skin stretching over his bones. Since February, when Joey last saw him, he's a shrunken shell of himself.

"Aren't you eating?" Joey asks his dad.

"Now it's your turn? Carlo feeds me well enough. The *stomaco* don't hold as much these days." He taps his belly. "Pull up a chair and talk to me."

Joey does as he asks and plops his aching butt into the flat paisley cushion.

"What? No kiss for me?"

He creeps to the bedside and kisses his papa's cheeks, no more than bones.

"You haven't missed any meals, Joseph. They must have good cooks in New York. Once you get a gut full of Carlo's bland dishes, you'll drop the weight in a few months. Heh, heh." His papa jerks the crocheted quilt higher on his chest.

"Did the groves make a good crop? Where's Uncle Mario? I didn't see him."

His dad looks through him, squinting the black beads that used to be a soft brown gaze, while spinning the bird in amber around his finger joint.

"How's Aunt Gina? Why didn't she come? I thought she'd visit after your mother passed."

The chitchat isn't getting to the point.

"Auntie's fine. She has her hands full with Bella's girls and keeping up with the bakery. Tell me what Doc Rinaldi said. How long before you're up and around?" Joey asks, louder than intended.

"Don't raise your voice to me. I haven't lost my hearing." His raspy breaths turn into a round of croupy coughs. He points to the tissues, holding one to his mouth. Blood soaks into a corner, and he balls the tissue in his hand.

His lungs are bad off. The cancer's more advanced than Joey knew. "Take it easy. What do you need, Papa? I'll get it for you."

He rests his balding head back on the pillow and sighs. "What I need is this tumor out of my chest, but Doc says if they cut it out, I won't be able to breathe, so here it is, growing by the day. Can't breathe with it, can't without it." He digs his index finger into his chest. The last few words are a mere whisper.

"Don't talk now. Rest." Joey starts for the door, and his pop motions him to sit down again. "I should unpack. You rest."

"I'll be resting permanently soon. Don't rush me." He coughs once and clears phlegm from his throat in another tissue. "Here's the deal. The business requires you to come home for good."

"What did you say?" His good ear muffles the words.

The great Leo Manetti repeats himself.

"Aw, Pops. Can't Carlo or Mario take over here? I'm too busy."

"Get over here." He slaps the bed. "Respect. *Uncle* Carlo and *Uncle* Mario have enough to do. Since when are you too busy for family? You're my only son, *ingrato* piece of…" Coughing stops his tirade.

His uncle sweeps into the room with a glass of water and an evil eye for Joey, giving the glass to Pops.

"We'll talk later." This time Joey jumps up in a feat of defiance, spotting his mama's embroidered sampler on the wall. Nothing changes.

Leo beckons Joey to his side. He watches in horror, waiting to be struck by his hand or God above. Instead, his papa slides the bird ring off and puts it on Joey's middle finger. The weight of the gold is as heavy as the burden it brings.

"Yours now." He coughs, then turns his head. "Go away and come back when you can show respect."

Walking around to the other side of the bed, Uncle Carlo is following Joey like a tailgating car. He hates tailgaters and wishes he could apply the brakes and have his uncle bump into him to learn a lesson not to follow so closely. The walls are closing in, and Joey needs to be outside in the groves, so he lengthens his steps. When he can't feel any smaller, he looks at his pitiful dad—Leo waves him over. The fist is coming, and he winces for what awaits him, in case he's strong enough to deliver. The good Lord knows how many times Joey's been hit in rage by family members.

"Joey, I'm depending on you to get back what Giambruno stole from us. He had no right to take it. I don't care if it belonged to his Gamba ancestors. It's been in the Manetti family for two hundred years and has given us prosperity. Nothing but bad has happened since Giambruno took it away. Ask your cousin. She's in Bari now. Sister Mary Natalina. She's the last one to see it. Wear the bird ring as a reminder. Use its strength and make me proud." He wipes his mouth. "And remember, no Siggies or Primitives. They're no good. Don't trust 'em like I did. Look what happened."

"Okay, I promise. No outsiders. What is this thing he took?"

There's no proof Tony the Terror took anything from them thirty-two years ago, before he was born, but Pops insists, so Joey humors him.

His papa ignores the question and closes his eyes.

CHAPTER

THIRTEEN

Our old-world Tuscan bedroom with arched windows and a cathedral ceiling is silent except for the faint whooshing waves talking in the language of sweet nothings and... *What's that sound?* Somewhere outside, a reedy organ and several tambourines jangle on a current of air. Straining at the window to learn the tune, I recognize an accordion playing a tarantella, the native folk dance of southern Italy. Envisioning dancers in costumes of red, green, and white, performing in the square or on the beach, I long to join them in celebration, but we can't celebrate yet. Not until we unravel several mysteries and at least one anomaly. It's so easy to get distracted in this beautiful place, so I sniff the salt breezes a final time and wander to my laptop near pages of notes spread out on the desk. Brad doesn't need to know about the window cracked open, and I don't plan to tell him. We're in romantic Italy on the Adriatic, after all.

Alec and Brad are giving me space to research a list of topics that's grown longer in the past twenty-four hours. Topics that may change Alec's future. Our future. Brad's stationed in the hall at his post, while Alec wanders the grounds, taking calls and waiting to phone his mother in an earlier time zone. They have lots to discuss about Oliver King. Breaking the bad news to Gen himself is the only decent way to notify her of his death in case the two had a longtime, personal friendship.

Occasionally I catch a pacing, paranoid Alec walking the beach not far from our room. With so much turmoil in our lane this week, I'm keenly aware of Alec's concerns for my safety. He has a loving heart like his mother, and these past few days are a huge reminder of why I'm totally in love with him. He requires my help, and it's time to focus, but first, I have something to do...

The bedroom door squeals a little when I peek outside and down the hallway. Brad's there sitting on a chair, reading a hardbound book through a pair of half-moon readers.

"Are you in need of something, Miss Drury?" He lowers the glasses farther down his nose and looks above them. He reminds me of a wise owl sitting on a limb, surveying the forest.

"I want to thank you for your friendship with Alec, your dedication to him—and looking out for me. I'm glad he has you."

He removes his glasses as a slow pink tinge enters his cheeks.

"It's what I do." Brad passes me a smile. "Thank you... Annalisse. I would give my life in order to keep Alec from harm, and you too."

The puff to my ego was the adrenaline supercharge I needed. "Enjoy your book."

Brad squares his shoulders and adjusts his frames in place, dropping his eyes to the book once again.

So far, the ancestry websites and random searches have led me down paths to dead ends while pulling up entries for Generosa DePalma from Bari, Italy. The name is attached to two women from the region in the past fifty years, but none were recorded with a father named Antonio. I uncovered a mere two black-and-white photos online to cross-reference the family trees, finding the whole process fruitless, yielding no connections. One woman came from Sicily, where another was born in the inland section of the northeast in Vincenza. Neither picture was Gen's likeness, nor were their relatives. It's as if she doesn't exist at all—until she marries Pearce and becomes a Zavos. Gen's marriage certificate shows her using the DePalma maiden name, but that's the only record I've found of hers with any certainty. Unless she wasn't born in Bari? That's ridiculous. If hiding a real name, it's always best to supply the most facts so that there are fewer lies to tell later. Generosa Zavos doesn't lie about anything. If she's created a falsehood surrounding her original surname and made up a given name, she has good reason to do it.

The dull ache at the back of my eyes lets me know I'm on the verge of defeat. I don't like losing. Names and places tug me down the only logical avenue left, to seek out her possible alias, Sophia Giambruno. I so wanted to discount Josh's mention of a false identity for Alec's sake. He has enough worries without wondering what his family has done in their pasts. Pearce Zavos, the Greek from the isle of Crete, seems solid from my discoveries, but my friend as a DePalma doesn't exist. If only Pearce were here to explain away the dilemma of Gen and the beads. In the wake of his death, Alec's father left such a mess of Swiss cheese behind. So many holes to fill in.

Samantha was great at this kind of research. Where would you go from here? I miss your spirit around me.

What was that word? I pore through scribbled notes for the name Sister Mary Natalina mentioned as I was leaving. She said it so quickly, it never fully registered. Another page shuffled, and there it is. Marinara gamba. Is it a sauce? Can't be. I must have been hungry for pasta when writing this. Typing in the name exactly as I wrote it, the search engine page brings up a Galileo Project and a woman named Marina Gamba. Could the Sister have meant for me to see this? Reading further, the article talks about Marina moving to Padua with Galileo and having three children by him. All illegitimate. This fits the time period of the beads mentioned by the Sister. I reach over and arrange the rosary beads in front of me, flipping the larger Madonna medal to expose the etching. MCG. The article goes on to mention the children, Virginia, Livia, and Vincenzio, the youngest. Because his daughters were illegitimate and had no chance of marrying well, Galileo took both daughters from Gamba and put them into—a convent. Ah. A religious order where they have prayer beads. His daughters were then known as Sister Maria Celeste and Sister Arcangela. Vincenzio was four years old when his sisters were taken from the home, and Galileo eventually made the boy legitimate many years later.

Vincenzio Gamba became Vincenzio Galilei, married, and had a family of his own. Virginia and Livia died in their service to God.

"Some of the wandering fits." I lean back against the chair and touch my lips in thought. The beads' age ties well to when the Gamba girls became nuns. "Sister Maria Celeste, SMC. Sister Maria Celeste Gamba, SMCG. MCG. Of course." My heart leaps inside my chest. With a racing pulse, I reread the online text. Could the rosary belong to Galileo's daughter? How does the rosary tie back to Gen? Or does it? Did Sister Mary Margaret acquire the beads and find out about their intrinsic value to Galileo and make a connection to Gen by using the Catholic Church's records? The rosary is a wonderful artifact by itself, but is it more than that, like Gen's interest in astronomy, is it a stretch too far?

With renewed enthusiasm, I pull up another website and glance at the clock. It's close to eleven, and I'm far from journey's end. Sophia Giambruno may be the key to unlocking one of our big mysteries. If Gen's in the database, the Giambruno modern family tree in the twentieth century will uncover her.

I drop into the best and most thorough ancestry websites and attack the Giambruno name with everything I have on Alec's mother. Some of the Giambruno family members came over on ships, so those entries were instantly ignored because Gen's father stayed in Italy. A few years and family trees later, a younger version of Alec's mother appears in a faded picture with a much older, reed-thin, and leathery man with a hoe in one hand and an arm over the girl's shoulder—her father, Antonio, based on Sophia's birthdate, which matches Gen's exactly. There's mention of her mother, Sophie, who died from a childbirth infection shortly after Sophia was born, so the girl never knew her mother. I hurt with sadness and lay down the pen in my hand. Luckily for me, I had two mothers watching over me but didn't understand it at the time. A young girl running the household with only her father to raise her must have been a hard life to endure. If Sophia Giambruno is Gen Zavos, she turned out pretty darn well.

A sigh from the back of my throat fills the room. Do I search through four hundred years of records to find a link to the nun from the San Matteo convent? The Gamba girls did not marry or have children, so it leaves Vincenzio, the son, to carry on Galileo's line.

It's not long before I realize that Italian Medieval genealogy is limited to the Napoleonic Civil Records beginning at the year 1809. Italian Catholic Church directories began at 1500, but many are written in Latin or Italian and are obtained by special request. If the photo I found is correct, they lived in a province called Bittrito; it's inland from the coastline but still considered part of Bari. In order to start a search from 1600 forward, I would need a translator beyond what Brad can do, and that's impossible when we needed the records yesterday.

Galileo's son had three children, all boys, and if Gen is related, she's on one of those family trees, either on the direct line from Vincenzio's offspring or an offshoot by marriage via their wives. There are four plus main generations to search through.

My head is swimming with dates and names. I massage my eyelids and consider the options. Making one last stab at Generosa DePalma using the town Bittrito instead of birthplace Bari, I come up with zilch. From here on, we stick with the Giambruno name.

A growl rumbles from my stomach.

"That's it then." If I show Alec the man standing with the hoe and he verifies his grandfather, we have that much of our answer. This will confirm the Giambruno lineage is his, and Gen is really Sophia.

Alec is talking to Brad on the other side of the door, so I quickly stack my notes into a neat pile. It's easier for me to think when pages are strewn about, but it makes Alec wig out. He's so tidy, with objects on his desk and paperwork organized in a bin. My workspace at the gallery looks as if a tornado came through, sprinkling cookie crumbs, gum wrappers, and yellow sticky notes like confetti. If it's possible to be both excited and apprehensive, that's me. It's a pleasure to uncover new facts to confirm one's existence, but will Alec be happy about his mother's and grandfather's secret?

"Hey, babe." Alec clicks the door shut. "Make any headway?" His arm scoops me at the waist, and he crouches at the laptop beside me.

He smells good. Sea air and sandalwood mix well together.

"Did you call your mom?"

"Can't reach her. My calls go straight to her mailbox."

"No telling what she's doing."

"Don't worry, our contingency plans are in place," he says.

"What plans?" That's new information. I swivel and wait for him to explain.

"I don't want to talk about Signorile right now; show me what you have." He points to the screen.

"We're making progress."

I recite my trips into the ancestry sites and end with my theories on Gen and recommendations on where to go from here. Through it all, Alec is cool and distant. Not once did he interrupt me for a clarification or ask any questions.

"Are you okay?" I ask.

He walks over to the Victorian armchair and sinks down, making the bones of the chair creak. "I tend to agree with the findings. Josh has nothing to gain by making up stories about Mom. We'll ask her to explain. She gets the last word."

"That may not be true. I almost forgot. Found this." Scrolling the site to an earlier screen, I pull up the man standing with a gardening tool. "What do you think? Anyone familiar?"

Both sides of Alec's mouth turn upward. "I do recognize her. That's Mom. She can't be more than ten or twelve."

"Is that your grandfather Antonio?"

"Yes. He hasn't changed much from when I saw him last."

"Alec, in the records he's listed as Antonio Giambruno, and Sophia is in his line."

"What are they hiding from?" His platinum eyes are watering. "Do you have any theories? I'd like to hear them."

"She stored the beads because they're precious. Sister Mary Natalina recognized the rosary, as if she has a personal stake in them. She told me how old the beads were, not from a guess but from actual knowledge. If we can get the Sister to open up about them, then we find out if the beads were responsible for Gen's name change. Families stay together in small communities. There may be people living in Bittrito who know the truth—why your grandfather went to prison. Possibly the Sister knows. We should ask her."

"Are you hungry? Let's grab Brad and stretch our legs." He helps me to my feet and groans.

"Watch out, you'll give a girl a complex."

"It's not you. I don't know why that came out."

"You're mentally exhausted. We'll make this a short outing so that you can take a power nap."

"I've been the worst travel host, Anna." He kisses my nose. "Where would you like to go for lunch? Then I have a much better idea how we'll spend some quiet time together, and it doesn't include napping. Are you up for it?"

Feeling a renewal coming on, I laugh. "You know the answer. Count me in, with one caveat. Allow me to wipe off the camera dust and locate the famous orecchiette Pasta Ladies of Bari. I'm dying to take their pictures or record a short video if they don't mind. Wouldn't it be a nice touch of authenticity to play this video for the gallery as a promo? For the Southern Italy Renaissance art on the upper level. I'm sure Chase can figure out how to activate it when someone enters the upstairs area."

"Hmm. You'll have to convince Mom. She's not big on noise in the gallery."

"She'll love it because you're going to be the leading man." My arms gently fold around Alec's neck, and I plant a kiss on him that almost makes us forget about lunch.

CHAPTER
FOURTEEN

Forgoing the seafood pasta for a deli lunch of rustic homemade breads filled with salty prosciutto, mushrooms, and local cheeses, our trio visits a section of Bari called the old quarter. Alec with his phone in his ear, Brad between us, surveying each corridor as we enter, and me, looking every bit the visitor with my Nikon dangling on its patriotic strap. I'm determined to get pictures today since our plans can change at any moment. Oliver King's gloomy death hovers over us, and I wonder about his real reason for showing up at our bed-and-breakfast. I feel the power and aura of the rosary beads through the leather as we walk. Alec's trying to stay upbeat, but he's finding that simple task a chore with Brad a constant reminder that we aren't alone on a carefree vacation.

This is the oldest part of the city where traditions are alive, and the people are busy forming orecchiette pasta in the narrow aisleways between their cinderblock homes. The aroma of a bitter vegetable called broccoli rabe drifts through the streets, along with the earthy semolina flour, as if everyone is cooking from the same menu. Sometimes the women work in pairs, while others sit solo behind stacks of wire-screened trays layered with drying pasta. Most are quietly using small knives to form the thick pasta ears from ropes of dough handmade inside their small homes and basements. Ahead, a woman uses a mop and a rag to wash down the shiny pavers as we pass under an archway that opens to a neighborhood of grandmas in sleeveless dresses. Mothers and their young daughters help roll and scrape the signature pasta ears with their fingers.

I take a few photos and wave at the ladies to get their attention while we amble past their tables beneath balconies with laundry dripping high above us. Most residents have doors, but some use sheers as a means of dividing the street from their homes. I wonder how their operation functions during the winter months or if thieves are a concern. The close-knit environment seems to trust bystanders.

We arrive at a station piled with half a dozen pasta trays at angles to allow the air to circulate around each sheet. On the table, dried pasta is sorted into bags for the local stores and the public to buy. Alec speaks Italian to the woman at the first station, her silver hair severely fashioned in a barrette, and is rewarded with her smile, one bottom tooth missing. She carries a subtle recognition on her face, but it's possible I'm imagining it; he's a handsome man who turns most females into mush. Having Alec pictured as a witness to a murder on the front page of Bari's newspaper hasn't helped. They converse a few seconds, she grins my way, and Alec returns with clear sacks of her little pasta ears.

"I couldn't resist. Mom loves these." His genuine joy is infectious as he stuffs them inside my tote. "I told the woman they're your favorite."

A step backward, and I take a quick video of Alec beaming in full-out dimples, talking to the woman using her hands in the dough. I haven't seen him this happy since we made plans to be in Florence, our original destination. It's unlikely anyone in this old-town community knows who Alec is. A place where we can make the best of the last few days in Bari. I turn off the camera and take Alec's hand.

Two scooters motor by us in single file, causing Brad to move to our outside, closest to the men wearing helmets.

Brad whispers something to Alec, and we're on the march once again, out from tall walls and a blind alley.

"Brad thinks we should move on. The guys on bikes got too close." Alec glances at a bank of shops, not exactly enthusiastic at the prospect of going inside. Using an arm gesture, he asks me, "Are you ready to come on down?"

I can't help but laugh. "Later. Let's stick to pictures and a video today." I'm watching a nun approach us from the walkway. "Is that who I think it is?" *Saves us the trouble to find her.* "She's out of her neighborhood."

As the Sister navigates the cobblestones in flats, I verify Sister Mary Natalina's short steps and small feet. She's coming at us at a good clip.

"*Buongiorno,* Sister," Alec says. "Nice to see you."

"*Buongiorno,* Mr. Zavos. Annalisse." She greets me by taking my hand. "I had hoped you returned to the United States. Did you hear about the man on the beach?"

"He was an associate." Alec winces a little.

"I see." The Sister tsks, shaking her head. "May I look at your hand, Alec, is it?"

I try to pull mine away, but she holds it steadfast, with Alec's hand grasped in the other. She's studying his palm like a palm reader would.

"What is it?" Alec asks. "What's wrong?"

Sister Mary Natalina switches to my palm, letting Alec go.

"May I see the rosary again? Do you have it?" Her heart birthmark is darker today.

I gather the cross and beads and cup them in both hands.

She lovingly kisses the crucifix and says two verses of the Lord's Prayer with the first two beads.

We could be here all day if she goes through the entire rosary.

"Sister, we hate to rush, but we have questions about the prayer beads. I did as you asked and found Marina Gamba. What can you tell us about Galileo and this rosary? Does it belong to Galileo's daughter?" I glance at Brad's sudden movements around our perimeter.

The Sister turns to Alec and knits her brows. "Bari is not good for you. I can't stress this enough." She's shaking her finger and glaring at him.

"Do the beads have anything to do with last night's murder? If you know, it will be a help." Alec is trying his level best to ignore her sidetracks.

Sister Mary Natalina looks at me and then at Alec. "There are those who wish to do you great harm. If you stay, they will win. It's a game to them."

"Who?" Icy air blows past my neck, and I swat at it. "Are they Italian or American?"

"Your mother needs you. Sophia needs you now." Mary Natalina's gaze holds Alec's with an expression that's menacing and full of venom. Traits one doesn't see every day in Catholic nuns.

When she stares at me, her youthful complexion turns gray, imagined or real, I can't be certain. Glacial fingers play down my spine, and I reach for the prayer beads in Sister Natalina's death grip. At this point, I don't care if I'm rough or rude. Where the beads touch, my fingers thaw, even though I'm shivering hard enough to chatter the teeth from my mouth.

"Why did a young novice, Sister Mary Margaret, give them to Alec's mother before she married Pearce?"

The Sister scans the square, shifting her eyes side to side. She grabs my forearm and directs us to an alcove, whispering, "The beads were a family possession. Antonio stole them from my great uncle. You will be hunted by bad men as long as you have them."

"Give us a name, Sister. Who wants them back?" Alec has no patience for her riddles.

"Uncle Leo and Carlo—Manetti. I should take them from you myself, and I almost did, but I prayed to God for guidance, and it's not my place. God's will be done." She crosses herself. "The Galilei line is yours, Alec. Yours and Sophia's. It does not include the Manettis. Where the senses fail us, reason must step in. Now go. Please."

Gen said that to me in her office.

"Did my grandfather go to prison for stealing?"

"He turned on my family and led the police… many arrests. Antonio is known as a snitch."

"Mafia, Alec." I lower my voice. "Your grandfather was an informant."

This is bad for Alec. The protection money hasn't been paid, now this.

The sinking feeling is back, and my thoughts travel to Gen. Was she an informant on the Mafia too? If Antonio took the prayer beads, it's easy to understand why he gave them to the novice in his church. Sister Mary Margaret would keep them safe until she had an opportunity to give them to his daughter, Sophia, or she could hide them forever. It's plausible and so is the identity change for a daughter Antonio wanted to conceal from the Mafia. Once Antonio Giambruno went to prison, he could no longer protect his only child. He had to change her name and send her away.

"Alec, let's go. I'm cold." My back is to the nun as I shove the rosary in a side pocket.

Alec's helping me stow the beads.

"Did you feel the frozen air? Where did it come from, and where did the Sister go?" I ask, checking out the landscape.

Brad jogs over, scratching his head. "Is everything all right?"

I rest my cold cheeks against the closest thing for warmth, Alec's shirt, and notice our audience standing on the sidewalk. The women from old town left their pasta stations to watch us.

"We seem to be a spectacle." I step from Alec and straighten out hair that he ran his hands through as he held me. There's no sign of the Sister's black garb. "Did either of you see her leave?"

"I wasn't paying attention. Brad?" Alec asks, receiving a head shake.

We walk to the concrete where the group has formed, as if they've just witnessed a hit-and-run accident.

"Alec, ask if Sister Mary Natalina went back to her church."

In Italian, he asks twice, and one person answers in a few words.

"Anna, they've never heard of Mary Natalina."

He tries again and receives a lot of shrugs.

I point toward the church, and the pasta lady we bought from gives us the church name; Basilica de Augustina is what I read on the wall.

"Please find out which sisters are from that church. I'm sure they know them."

They give him three that mean nothing to me.

"I don't like this," I whisper to Alec and turn to the pasta lady on a hunch. "Sister Mary Margaret?"

"Si." She nods slowly.

"Where... did... she... go?" I speak slowly, but the woman doesn't understand and wrinkles her nose.

"Dove e andata?" Alec asks. "Sister Mary Margaret."

"E morta."

He turns to me with sorrow written on his face. "They say she's dead."

"Grazie." I smile and wave, pulling Alec aside. "The Sister has virtually vanished. How is it they've

never heard of Sister Mary Natalina? Would she go by an alias because of her Mafia family? Gen's novice friend has passed, and we have confirmation on the beads."

"Good enough. We pack up and fly out in the morning, but first, there's a place I know you'll want to see, Anna. It's a short drive from here. On the way, we'll check out the national park."

Brad wanders closer to us with genuine interest. Short of our excitement on the beach, I think he's ready for a change in scenery.

"Only if it's safe, Alec. Out in the open may not be the best move for us. I still have to light that candle for Gen and then an extra one for us before we leave. I think we're gonna need it."

CHAPTER
FIFTEEN

Silently, I pray for Sister Mary Margaret while the three of us drive around Bari to the province of Alberobello. The Trulli limestone and cone-shaped roofs, similar to those around our bed-and-breakfast, are commonplace in southern Italy. Building houses without mortar is an old technique saved and preserved from the prehistoric era, even though most of these homes were built around the sixteenth century. Our surroundings are too unique not to record them in pictures.

From our high vantage point, the homes resemble small versions of fairy-tale castles with sandstone balls at the pinnacle. The only missing objects to make them perfect are tiny flags flying from rooftop spires. Still, my heart doesn't care as much about the historic Puglia scenery as it once did. I'm a foreign object surrounded by so much splendor. I wish Gen were here to lighten our heavy atmosphere that's hard to cut through. Alec brought me to Bari for the history, and all I can think about is going home. Bad enough, I turned Alec away from the excursion to the archaeological museum tour in old town. I'm so ready to leave this country and all its Mafia ties behind. If Samantha were here, she'd kick me in the butt for wasting precious time and ignoring the beauty around us.

Back in the square once more, we're lounging in an indoor-outdoor pub, observing tourists as they wander the stores, carrying shopping bags, while others flaunt their skimpy swimsuits on the beach. Alec has been watching me since the nun episode, casting glances when he thinks I don't notice, as Brad calmly drinks his afternoon tea.

While I fixate on the empty tables and sort out the random, unrelated events, the checkered cloths blur together in blotchy green and white. Their flag colors show up in every aspect of Italian living. The people in Bari are warm and welcoming, like coming home for a Christmas holiday, and it saddens me to leave it so soon. I'm torn between leaving and staying.

Oliver King on the beach might have been a random killing after all. Sister Mary Natalina is a made-up name, apparently. Is she even a nun? Come to think of it, her place in the square at the Basilica fits; then again it doesn't. The priest who spoke to her in the courtyard didn't call her by name. I wish he had. No one but Gen knows she gave the beads to me before we left, so how can the Sister have so much knowledge about the old prayer beads and be related to the Manettis? Was she a plant? She drops into our Bari trip and drops out, just that fast. As Gen would say, *It smells like the head of a fish left in the sun to rot.* A few similarities I buy, but not this many.

I reach into my tote and unzip the compartment where the rosary hides. A sweet aroma lingers from the leather pocket. Vintage has a great scent.

"I'm trying to imagine what it must have been like in the 1600s for a nun in a sacred order. Young women like Maria Celeste had a hard, brief life. Her biological sister was an alcoholic and died of dysentery. Can you imagine? In a convent too. Ugh, the whole idea makes me ill. Galileo was a brilliant teacher but not a wealthy man. Alec, what if it's true? How does it feel to have this noted astronomer in your family?"

Alec and Brad are studying me.

"It hasn't sunk in yet." He's apprehensive, as he should be.

"This rosary is off the charts for historical value if they belonged to Galileo's daughter. That's it." I smack my head with the heel of my hand. "That's what the sister and Gen said. They recited a famous line from Galileo: 'Where the senses fail us, reason must step in.' I'm ninety-five percent certain they go back to Galileo from the provenance we've exposed. Without the inscription and Sister Mary Natalina, or whatever she calls herself, I'd be less sure. Since Catholic artifacts are not my strong suit, a museum or a curator who specializes in Catholic relics would be an excellent resource. When we get back to the room, this goes into my suitcase. It's too much treasure to carry around."

"What is that?" Brad points to a black key that fell onto the table.

"I forgot I still had it." I hold up the key to Alec. "Look familiar?"

His quirky smile touches me. "It's a good thing the guys checking the plane for weapons didn't figure it out when they searched. Looks like a harmless key, doesn't it, Brad?" Alec's face is serious when he turns his steady gaze on me. "My ribs still hurt when I think about Matt."

"That could've been you, and it almost was. Brad, I'm sure Alec didn't tell you he was kicked by the same guy who shot him at my brownstone, then tried to finish the job in Turkey with those steel-toed boots of his. I'm glad Luciana's father—what was his name?—Cremal, a waste of humanity, was taken out."

Alec rubs the spot near his neck where the bullet entered and exited. "Last year feels like a lifetime ago. I had a good nurse—hardly a scar." He squeezes my fingers, and I'm taken back to his drawing room, dressing his wound and attempting to keep my mind on changing the shoulder bandage—his muscles tensing when touched—with trembling hands and a longing about to burst from my chest.

I flip aside the key's long end and out pops a tiny knife.

"May I see that?" Brad surveys the key knife for himself, turning it over between his fingers, checking the blade's sharpness. "Brilliant."

"My own James Bond tool. It helped me out of a few scrapes in Turkey. I was drugged when the man who killed Pearce on the boat tricked me with a recording of Alec's mother begging me to help her. I stupidly went outside the hotel. I regained consciousness on the floor of the Italian Tower at Bodrum Castle, tied and bound with sticky tape. I didn't have my purse or anything with me, but I remembered Matt's small knife I'd stashed away. The duct tape at my wrists was easy enough to break with the right downward jolt, and the knife helped with the rest. Our adventure in Turkey is a long story." I squeeze Alec's hand across the table.

"We make a good team," he says with conviction. "Sometimes she needs reminding."

I hold my palm out to Brad for the key.

He snaps the knife portion shut and hands it back.

"This little guy is a lifesaver. It's small enough to hide anyplace." I tap my leather belt when the tool is safely hiding behind it. "No one's the wiser."

Alec strokes my hand underneath the table. "I'm happy you kept the knife and saved Mom, even though the risks you both took were crazy. We lost a lot of brave people on our side that day."

"Good people," I add.

"What happened to your friend Matt?" Brad asks Alec.

"He was hurt worse than me, but at the time, we didn't know it. Our liaison killed our captor who was about to grind me into more hamburger with his boot. She got him before he could put a bullet through my head."

"We didn't know several members of a European group were after the necklace at that point, including Luciana, the Zavos villa maid. She actually masterminded the entire pursuit when she saw the necklace on Crete."

"Khazarian Mafia?" Brad's question comes from left field.

"A different Mafia. Matt was injured by Luciana's father. At the amphitheater in Turkey, we piled Matt into a vehicle, but he succumbed to internal injuries at the hospital. A damn shame too," Alec says with regret.

"I wish I'd been there to help." Brad looks down and sets his cup on the saucer. "Dealing with crime families isn't a game for the untrained."

"After the death of her boss, I took Annalisse to Greece to meet Dad and spend time at the villa. Simple, right?" He taps the table. "A nice getaway from the stresses of New York. I ended up dumping her into the den of thieves. Anna had feelings of dread the entire time, and I ignored it." Alec's words choke off while he gathers his composure.

"I did meet your dad; your gift to me." I want to spring into Alec's lap and give him a hug and assure him not to blame himself. If we were alone in the pub, I would have. Instead, I gently caress Alec's knee.

Stretching from his chair, he kisses me with such desire it takes my breath. *This is the Alec I've missed on this trip.*

"Mom's alive because of you. I love you, Anna."

My remaining breath hitches, and my ego lifts. He said that in front of Brad. A first.

I, with my sham past and pretend parents, have no right to criticize Alec for any misgivings he has about that horrible yacht incident. I may never know my biological father, and my mother lied so many times to cover a multitude of sins. Alec's parents *are* his mother and father.

As if he's read my mind, Alec changes the subject. "I wanted to be there for you when you visited Ted

Walker. What happened when you went? Unless you'd rather not talk about it."

Uncle Ted is the biggest lie of all. But since Kate admitted she's my true mother, it leaves Ted in no man's land, a territory that I hope devours him whole. There's no way I could ever claim the sicko awaiting trial as my stepfather.

"Anna?" Alec asks.

"Nothing to tell. Ted refuses to see me."

Alec exhales a gush of air. "I'm relieved. You didn't hear him on that tape from the spa—how he spoke to Kate. The hatred he harbors for her and you…"

"I'll never understand why he didn't confront his wife when he found out about the affair. Why check out of the marriage without any showdown, especially the way he did it?" I ask. "He had options."

"When love leaves a relationship, all bets are off." Alec glances around the room and says under his breath, "I'd kill Ted myself if he *ever* tried to hurt you."

We pivot toward the crying outside the pub. A little dark-haired girl is being chewed out by her mother or guardian. *Swat.* The crack echoes the stone walls. Whatever her role, she's responsible for the red handprint left on the poor kid's arm.

It's hard to listen to her screaming and stamping her feet in an all-out meltdown, worse for me than grating fingernails along a chalkboard.

The woman, in her twenties, doubles down and strikes the little girl across the face.

I'm shocked into a recognition more powerful. The sound hits a chord like a guillotine's snap as it severs a neck exposed to the block. My palms flatten on the table, and in two seconds, I'm on my feet, sprinting toward the blubbering child. It's none of my business, but someone has to help the little person.

The girl is pounding her legs with fists but is oddly not tearstained when I reach her. There's a daisy in her stringy hair, and she bears a striking similarity to the gypsy beggar who crossed my path, only this one is wearing a yellow pinafore over short capris—what Kate would call pedal pushers. There must be an army of poor people in this area, sending children out to solicit the tourists.

Crouching to her level, I ask, "Are you hurt, sweetie?"

For my trouble, she socks me in the gut with something hard and blows a Scotland Yard-type whistle in my ears until they ring. It's impossible to know when my hearing will return to normal. The force behind her punch is shocking for her pint size.

There's a rock in her hand.

I'm flustered, sitting on my bottom and looking up at her while she screeches words that are unclear, jumbled Italian from a frightened little girl. Behind me, Alec and Brad are running on the cobblestones.

"Anna!"

An unusual cycle with fenders and saddlebags motors up, carrying a driver in carabinieri military uniform. I struggle to my full height and dust myself off. The officer motions me to get on behind him. What?

"No! Take c-c-care of the girl." I'm still reeling from the tiny person attack.

The child points me out and rattles more in Italian, but unfortunately, who knows what she's saying to the police?

"I tried to help. What's she telling you?"

From out of nowhere, a pair of hands manhandle me onto the scooter's seat, shoving me against the man's sweaty back. Leather and cologne singe my nose and turn my aching stomach.

Was he at the bed-and-breakfast this morning?

"Hey, Anna…" Alec's voice is fading away as the girl skips off into the side street we pass.

Helpless to do anything but clutch the driver with both arms, my gut goes cold. Alec and Brad are chasing us on foot, shouting. I'm numb from my brain to my ears and don't particularly feel like jumping off a moving motorcycle, so I hang on to think of a plan. We have to stop sometime, and when we do, I'll run back to Alec on foot if I can.

CHAPTER
SIXTEEN

"What did I do wrong?" I'm hollering close to the officer's earpiece, with chattering teeth from the bumpy pavement. "I didn't hurt that little girl. Stop this bike and let me off. I've broken no law here."

No matter how much I plead, he's ignoring me. The cycle picks up speed; the engine revving is all around us, which isn't helping, and it's entirely possible the officer doesn't speak a word of English. He's not wearing his cop helmet and has on the same dark glasses the officers wore this morning.

My nails sink into his fleshy side.

He shoves my hand away and swerves his powder-blue cycle into a side alley made of wall-to-wall bricks mortared long ago.

"Hey, where are we going?"

"Safe house," he booms in a gruff accent.

"What?" I don't need a safe house, but I do need to get off this bike.

He slows and then stops at three steps that lead to a concrete stoop.

The officer peels my arm away like an unwanted parasite and wrenches me from his vehicle.

"In there." He levels his arm toward the arching door at the top. "Go inside."

My gritty hands slide down my thighs, wiping grime away. "Not until you tell me why."

The officer gets off and slams down the kickstand.

As I'm backing up, his thin lips and second-skin uniform are all that I notice. No redeeming qualities stand out. He looks like every other carabinieri in Bari, short-cropped hair, blue-and-black uniform, and signature cavalier boots.

"Where are we?" The empty road shows no signs of Alec or Brad.

He drops his shoulder and sighs. "Please, *signorina*. I help you."

"I had two men back there to help, and you took me away." When I break into a run for the street, he snags my arm, scratching me. "Ow."

"Don't." He shakes his head, and in his snug grip, we begin our walk to the steps. "Help inside."

Once I realize I left my purse and ID at the pub, I get an old-fashioned case of the sweats. I want to flee, but he's determined not to let me to do so.

Blood pulses at my temples. Slow, steady breaths.

I have to go through the door, wait until he leaves, then get the hell out of here. A minute or two, what harm can a delay be? The wood door is solid with no windows. He won't see me waiting...

"What is this place?" I ask again. "Tell me where we are, and I'll go."

"Ristorante." His hand covers the pistol handle at his waist.

If that's true, this place must be their back alley. Lots of people inside means that Alec can find me in the square when I exit the front. This cop wouldn't drop me at a restaurant for an easy getaway. Alec must be beside himself looking for me.

I don't get the safe house bit.

There is no safe house.

Nodding, I climb the steps and slide the latch. The door opens with ease, but it's dark inside. I won't close it all the way. The Italian Tower escape flashes through my head—how dark it was before I was able to work the door hinges loose.

A wave and a fake smile later, I open the door and enter. Per my plan, I hold the door from shutting all the way and survey my surroundings. I'm at a brick staircase that leads to a basement or cellar. The temperature is better in here, cooling the sweat on my brow. Burnt wood, maybe oak, and an acid like vinegar tickles my nose, making my mouth pucker. Am I in a wine cellar? It can't be the main floor of a restaurant, can it?

There's no engine noise from a motorcycle leaving. *Where is he?*

Just as I sneak a peek at the alley, the door slams in my face and locks from the outside with a solid metal click. No matter what I do to the handle on my side, it's secure and going nowhere.

"Hey." I back my shoulder into the door, but it doesn't budge. There's no going out this way without a battering ram, so I smash my fists against the wood and make as much noise as possible. "I can't stay in here."

The air around me is dense as dirt and smells like it too. Some bright idea I had.

The jerk locks me inside to be safe from whom?

"I've got to get to Alec."

A whimpering downstairs in the blackness activates my antennae.

"Who's there?" I skip two steps at a time until I reach the bottom. "Don't leave." I halt in the semidarkness.

The noise goes away.

"Hello?" Blinking doesn't make my eyes adjust to the low light any faster.

A slight girl in a white apron and inky dress rounds the corner, wiping her face with a tissue. She sniffs and snorts like she's been crying awhile. Actually crying, from her stained, puffy face.

"Why are you here?" The brunette with a wisp of pastel hair stays in the shadows where I can't see her features. She may be embarrassed about her tears.

"Came from up there." I point to the brick stairwell, and a thought strikes me. "You speak English well. Tell me how I get out of here."

"You can't."

"How did you get in here then?"

"I work here. Uh, I used to work here." She blows her nose. "I was fired. They told me to put myself together before I left, so they locked me with the booze."

My enthusiasm for a quick solution is short lived.

"Locked you here? If we bang on that door, will someone come?" I ask. "Show me where the other door is."

She hesitates. "We're in the cellar. There're no customers in the restaurant. It's too early."

It has to be after four. Surely there are people eating by now in a resort town with hungry tourists. My second sense detects flaws in her story just like the officer's. They're working together. I observe the wine barrels and dusty bottles for something heavy or useful to break the lock on the alley door. Wood and glass won't work unless there's a baseball bat down here.

"Are there tools or anything metal like an ax or pry bar? Something we can use as a crowbar to wedge the door?"

"Go ahead and look." The girl makes no move herself and shrugs. "Only wine is kept here."

"Don't you care about being locked in a cellar? I'd scream and kick until someone let me out. Show me the door you came through. If you won't try, I will. I have to leave."

"There's no one here. Go ahead." The woman backs deeper into a corner and directs me down the hall with one dim light bulb. "On your right."

A black metal door without a handle isn't much help when it opens from the other side. Anyone could get locked in down here.

I pound the door with both hands until they sting, yelling at the top of my lungs to be let out of the cellar. It's silent on the other side. No clanging dishes in the kitchen or talking restaurant patrons like those heard at booths or around tables. I seriously doubt this building houses a restaurant of any kind. There are no cooking aromas, frying, baking, or otherwise. It feels more like a residential cellar or off-site storage for a shop owner or a private home. The girl could be a household maid, but I doubt it; she's lying about her position here.

"How do you plan to get out?"

She meets my question with a blank stare.

Hairs rise on the back of my neck when my common sense kicks in. I was driven here to be with this strange woman. We've paid off law enforcement ourselves to get what we wanted, and somebody paid off that motorcycle cop, or he's impersonating the carabinieri.

I rush toward the girl and shake her. "Who are you, and who is doing this?"

She whirls away from my grip and starts a crying fit.

Her face isn't fully visible, and the emotional voice isn't familiar. I don't think we've crossed paths with her in Bari this week—and I'm sweating again.

Running for the bottom of the original staircase where I entered, I plant my backside on the last step. Alec has no idea where I've been taken, or he would've come for me by now. It's doubtful that law enforcement is willing to help him figure it out if they're all in on this chess game featuring us as sacrificed pawns.

The brunette walks out of the shadows with big eyes, looking like a scared hamster abused in its cage.

"You're bleeding." She touches my arm with her tissue where the officer grabbed me and does the strangest thing. She dabs it on her tongue and licks the blood. If that isn't weird enough, her breathing is labored as if the taste excites her. Is she a sanguinarian? Does she have a blood fetish?

I'm down here with a vampire. Great.

Hanging out in a place like this with my current companion isn't for me. It's time to figure out a way to leave. "What do you want?"

"Let me help you wipe off the blood before it dries." Her tongue strays over her lips.

Stepping aside, I continue the chitchat. "Have you ever been to New York?" It's as good a place to start as any. I've backed myself against the wall and take another stair upward.

"Where's your purse? I thought all rich people carry fancy bags." She removes her apron and pitches it onto a cask, exposing her wide lizard belt with greenish bumps all around. Not lizard. Reptilian in nature. A mock belt. The real deal is too gross to imagine, so I have to believe it's a fake.

"That's an unusual lizard belt. Where did you find such a, uh… lifelike accessory?" I ask.

"Honestly, you don't know very much. It's crocodile, stupid."

"No need to get nasty. Looks like a print from here." I chide her to buy time while I work things out. She's losing her composure, so I push harder. "If you know so much about that belt, what kind of a crocodile is it? Bet you don't know."

"Ha. I do so."

"Are you some expert?" I show her my brightest smile. "Do they call you the Croc Lady?"

"You mock me. I wouldn't if I were you."

Another step backward toward the door as I home in on her personally. "Why so touchy? You know who brought us together, don't you?"

"I thought you were interested in the belt?" Her lips twist into a snarl.

Another step up. By my recollection, there are about ten more to get to the door. At the top of the stairs, I'll have more leverage if she tries to rush me. Different self-defense techniques play out in my head, and I hope that any move she uses I can counter.

She adjusts her belt and smooths down her dress. "I *am* an expert, if you must know."

One more step backward.

She ascends three.

Another stair under my heel for me.

Folding her arms, she prods me. "There's no way out. You're as captive as this dumb croc I'm wearing. He got caught." The pat on her belt is as if the leather's an old friend. Perhaps it was.

Her dark eyes come into view for the first time, and gem jewelry glints on her nostril. Painted red nails—too perfect and plastic to be real. Not the hands of a working server or housekeeper. She has birds in her ears, blackbird earrings that dangle and flutter when she moves. Dark speckles in the leather along her waist are also prevalent now that my vision has adjusted to the low light. The olive-green croc belt may be real after all; it's the buckle that looks off.

"There must be *hundreds* of crocodile species. How could you know what group of reptiles you're wearing?" I ask.

"Thirteen species, and this one is the most endangered of all," she announces smugly.

"If it's endangered, then you've poached and broken the law." I struck a nerve because she's slinging her hair back in a grimace.

"You're a self-righteous one. My family raises crocodiles."

"For food?" I advance one more step up.

"Honestly, what a *stupida*. For the skins."

The voice deepens, and it's familiar, but I can't place where…

A pendant on a cord at her neck is almost visible. I dip a little lower for more light, and the view crystalizes. Heliotrope. Bloodstone pendant.

Crap, crap, crap.

She's Tie Dye Gwendolyn from the gallery. How did she know we were in Italy? Nate?

I scrape my ankle against the next stair, my eyes fixed on her, waiting for any sudden move. The brass buckle on her belt is a cat, a freaking cat with red stones on its collar. My stomach muscles tense, and my calves ache from mechanically stepping backward in such a straight posture. Her evil glare is daring me to turn my back and run. How many stairs to the top? Five? Four? Alec could be anywhere, several buildings or blocks away.

I'm stuck here.

Not if I can help it.

I hear male voices outside. Their words are faint, but people *are* on the street, not far from the door.

Tearing up the staircase, I couldn't care less if she tries to charge me. "Help! I'm locked inside." My fists hit the door hard. "Help me."

Something sharp nicks my skin, and I smack a palm over my neck. I don't dare move in case I'm bleeding.

She's standing behind me, her breath hot against my fingers.

"Turn around or I'll cut your head off." Staten Island girl places her shiny pocket knife in my line of sight, holding me and my breath as hostages.

I grab a gulp of fresh air, banging my head against the door, using the sole of my shoe to stamp it, attempting to make as much noise as possible.

Her knife blade whizzes past my jaw, and I barely feel it, but I know that I'm cut.

The hand I used on my neck clamps over the facial wound that's much deeper. Her blade is so sharp, and the gash may be long.

"What's your problem?" My groan is loud on purpose as I strike out to grab a handful of her hair.

The knife swishes past my arm.

"Shut up. Don't be a spaz. I hate yous people." She moves aside, pointing the knife tip at my nose. I'm gazing cross-eyed at my red blood, afraid to shift my head an inch. I can't get leverage from here.

My sweaty left hand is covering the cut, and it burns like fire from the salt. I don't know if she's nicked a major artery at the jawline or not. I sure hope she didn't, or I'll bleed out right here. At this awkward angle, with her pressed at my side, I can't get a leg or knee out to force her down the stairs. She'd surely kill me once she returns upstairs. It's too dangerous to jostle her around without an escape plan since she has no qualms about using that knife, and the next cut she makes could be fatal. Do I run past her down the steps, or stay where I am, near the door?

"Where's Stella?" She spits the question at me.

The reason I'm here; the darn cat.

My heart stutters the next few beats. If I say anything wrong, she'll jab me. Through my teeth, I exhale slowly, buying a few extra seconds to clear my fuzzy brain.

She hisses and shoves me hard against the bricks. "Did you hear what I said?"

My throat closes on a dry heave, and the hand covering the cut slips a little.

Her laughter sickens me, but it takes my thoughts from the sticky blood dripping between my fingers. There's a smell of copper that surrounds us, and I know what that means…

"Good, you're afraid of me." She runs a finger through the blood and sucks on it.

I close my eyes and shudder.

Thoughts of Alec, my purse left behind, the crucifix, and Gen spin slow-motion circles in my mind. Sister Mary Natalina's warning to leave. Then I recall showing Brad the key knife from Matt. I slid it beneath my belt at the pub. Please, let it be there. I need a distraction, something she's waiting to hear, but what? Words must be exact because she's not letting me out of here without the right ones.

Bill mentioned the *sorellina* person on Staten Island might have been looking for Stella. Was she in Lecce and watched us leave the building with the cat? We passed a woman with big sunglasses in front of

Josh's building. The timing in my head seems off. She couldn't be in two countries at one time.

She's grinning at me. "You're hurting, aren't you? That'll teach you for turning me in to the police. I didn't steal that damn diamond. I got in a lot of trouble for that."

"Stella the person, or Stella the cat?" is all I can think to ask.

"What Stella person? You know I mean the *caaatt*, you ditz." Her jaw hangs down in an ugly way when she refers to the cat. She's not Stella's owner, but I'd believe she would abuse her.

It's a logical gamble this is Sorellina, the same one Bill came across in the restaurant while he was surveilling Manetti's gang.

Gamble number two. "We never saw any cat, *Sorellina.*"

She hops backward and glowers with piercing daggers in her eyes. "How do you know this?"

Keeping my hand against my jaw, I wonder if the pressure has slowed the bleeding. I matter-of-factly swipe the unoccupied hand through my hair and straighten my shoulders like I'm naturally stretching. My thumb lands and hooks the device behind the leather belt. *Good.* The key hasn't shifted.

A tiny knife is no match to her four-inch blade, but at least it's a weapon that will inflict a painful flesh wound. If I can figure out how to put her out of commission temporarily, I might steal some needed time.

The brunette with pink hair spikes studies me through a glassy haze. She pauses several more seconds and holds out the knife again. Her wrist shakes ever so slightly, so her confidence is waning. She's calculating how much I know about her.

I cautiously slide my thumb and take the key with it. "Look, I know the real truth about you and the crime family you're with and won't make anything up to save my life. Save your threats because they won't work on me."

Sorellina's face is livid and darkening at her sudden loss of total control. The heat in her glare intensifies while she weighs her options and whether I'm valuable enough to keep alive.

At present, she has no idea if we took the cat or if I'm working with the Manettis as an ally. I'm playing a risky bluff this close to my broken neck at the bottom of the staircase.

CHAPTER
SEVENTEEN

Alec and Brad have been down every alley near the pub and find no sign of the motorcycle or Annalisse. Resting against the wall on a deserted street, catching his breath, Alec waits on Brad's door-to-door inquiries, trying hard not to lose hope they'll find the girl and she'll lead them to Annalisse. Brad's Italian is fluent, so he was given the harder job of questioning residents in the area. It was a dogfight to get Brad to leave Alec's side, but street coverage is greater this way. It's their best guess that the crying girl entered one of the row houses. They're making little headway in their search. He should've protected Anna and kept her from going to the street alone without a chaperone while a murderer was loose. The gypsy girl may be part of a crime ring, and the carabinieri are on constant watch for visitors who get shaken down.

And drive her away?

Alec can't stand the mugginess any longer and steps out into dead air to capture stray currents from the snapping laundry on the terraces. The police close their eyes to crime in this section of town, the locals told Brad. The guy on the motorcycle must have been a paid player in an abduction scheme. He may not be police at all and stole a uniform so as not to draw attention. He wasn't wearing the usual helmet, which sends red flags zooming up the pole for Alec. Cycle cops always wear helmets when they ride. There's no question their activities have been watched from the time they entered Bari and checked into the bed-and-breakfast.

Brad leaves the next block over, jogging from the last house. "I've asked everyone who will speak to me. There are many children who match the description. None are the right girl."

"We've looked in this entire section. Do we go to the police and report her missing, last seen speeding away on the back of a police motorcycle?" The straps to Annalisse's tote with her camera inside are cutting Alec's shoulder.

"I don't see another option."

Alec backs against cooler walls and rests his head. "If it's money, why not take me instead?"

"Ms. Drury is most gullible. She's attractive, and beautiful women are noticed."

On Alec's left, a door squeaks, and a brown-haired girl no older than five skips outside in tennis shoes and shorts.

She glances their way and runs at top speed in the opposite direction.

Before Alec can motivate his legs to move, Brad is behind her with his hand on her shoulder. He's marching her to the cinder blocks as the crying act she tried earlier begins. She's a superb actress, but they aren't falling for her performance a second time.

An adult woman exits her house, notices them, and retreats indoors, leaving the girl in Brad's custody.

The child, who matches the description from outside the pub, cries and blubbers so that all the neighborhood can hear, so Brad has no choice but to shush her by cupping her mouth.

Alec's a few feet away, unsure he's doing the right thing by standing guard, watching for her irate mother or the police if they've been called to the scene.

"Hurry, man. We can't hold her like this for long."

From the girl's freakish eyes, she gets Brad's message.

He asks her about Annalisse in a methodical way and in a friendly tone.

She stops squirming.

He slowly loosens his hand from her mouth but not his firm grip.

Alec watches the house the girl came from, out of sight by keeping a distance from it. Other than a change in clothes, Brad's captive is the same girl in the yellow dress. Kids who run from adults are usually covering up for something.

In a surprise gesture, she accepts Brad's hand and tugs him toward the street. As they pass, he whispers, *"Dalle i soldi."*

Give her money.

Drawing a clip from his pants pocket, Alec peels off bills, hurrying to catch Brad and the girl, yet some distance away, to keep from spooking her. They cross two main arteries and two alleyways, taking a right turn down another. The aggregate walls are beefed up with modern masonry in this part of Bari. The streets, too, have changed from cobblestone to used brick.

Brad looks over his shoulder, and Alec flashes a few euros, stashing them quickly should anyone observe them from a window.

She's guided them to the middle of the long, bare expanse of concrete stoops. This place is commercial in nature, clean and void of people moving about. She indicates three steps at the foot of an arched door that mimics the medieval era—a solid wood carving on top and a sliding lock with two door knocker-style rings in the center. Alec's had experience with these massive entrances; the Bodrum towers have doors like these.

He's near the girl in seconds.

She hangs on to Brad's legs, hiding behind him as her protector.

"Is this where Anna is?" Alec crouches to her level. "We have to find her."

Her small finger points to the door, then smiles a toothless grin at the money in his hand.

"*Sei sicuro*. Are you sure?" Alec palms the bills in front of her eyes but hasn't given them to her. "Don't let her go yet, Brad. I'll try the door." He runs up the steps and bangs on the door with both hands. "Anna! It's Alec!"

My head's buzzing and sweat stings my eyes. Time stands still for what feels like a century, then I faintly catch my name. *Alec?* I'm so desperate I'm believing what isn't there.

The whites of Sorellina's eyes shift.

She hears it too.

Shoes scuff the roadway.

Where?

Through the big door I'm resting against, voices are dull. How far away is the noise?

"I never saw a cat." Slithering to the center of the door, my pulse is soaring along with my hopes, but amplified heartbeats thrum in my ears, blocking the ability to pick out sounds clearly.

There's enough room to lift my knee.

"Describe the cat for me; maybe we've seen her." I sound puny to my ears and would rather yell out loud for someone to hear, but she'll jab me with the switch-blade—not until there's a window for escape. Against my jeans, with my thumb, I flick open the key to the small blade waiting in my palm.

Her knife isn't as close to me as it once was.

She's planning her next move.

But a fist from outside plasters the wood behind me.

Sorellina jumps, the knife blade pressing against her chest.

"Anna! Yell out if you're in there."

By the time Alec utters my name, Sorellina's slamming the stairwell wall, thanks to my kick to her stomach.

211

She tumbles down the dozen or so steps and lands at the bottom, groaning.

Spinning around, I lunge forward with both hands, screaming, "Alec, get the door open. Fast!"

Metal stutters, and the darkness cracks into a haze, then a bright light. Covering my eyes at the brilliance, Alec is waiting for me, arms outstretched.

"Close it. She's down there. Don't let her escape." I slip the key knife into my pocket and vow never to go anywhere again without it. It's my good-luck charm.

Brad holds the door from closing and hands me his handkerchief. "Apply pressure." He disappears into the darkness with his Glock drawn.

I glance down to find that my jaw has bled onto Alec's shirt. "I'm so sorry. Your polo's ruined." The tears I've held back flow down my cheeks from a spigot of hot emotion. He's here, and by some miracle they figured out which building I was in. I'm elated, drained, and nauseous at the same time.

"Shh." The warmth of Alec's fingers touches my face. "How bad? Let's see, babe."

I allow him to remove the kerchief, and he flinches, quickly covering the cut with the cloth.

"Are you hurt anywhere else?"

"Not badly." I resume the pressure to my jaw. "I know her."

"Come here." He gathers me close.

Brad enters the light and closes the door, locking it.

"Did you see her?" Alec asks.

With a shake of his head, Brad holsters his gun.

"She escaped? Don't tell us that she's gone." If there was a way out, she hid it from me. A secret passage that Sorellina knew about. It's possible.

"Ms. Drury, can you walk?"

"What about Sorellina? We have to find her."

"Not to worry; she's dead." Brad adjusts his jacket and steps ahead of us as we make our way down the street.

"Brad, how can that be? She was very much alive when I kicked her, and she fell down the steps." I might have committed a murder in a foreign country. If the police find out, I'm going to prison; that's a fact. I've heard of the long trials for American suspects in Italy. It's my word against a dead body's; they don't tend to say much.

Alec is moving us along faster, and my jaw is hurting like hell. The adrenaline surge has worn off, and the pain is real for the first time since the blade slashed my skin.

"Alec, my fingerprints are in the cellar. When they find her body, they'll know I killed her. But I didn't kill her. She fell."

"I took the liberty of wiping the doors and flat surfaces clean," Brad offers. "The knife is in her chest with her hand on it."

She was moving on the floor. Did Brad finish the job?
"But Brad, she was kicked, not stabbed."

"It was in her chest." He turns away, shutting me down.

"We should look for an emergency room and get you stitched up," Alec breaks in.

213

Brad stops and pivots around. "May I differ… A knife wound at the hospital will have to be reported to authorities."

"I'm open for suggestions. Anna's jaw needs attention." Alec's gaze is watery, and he's biting his lip.

The cut must look bad for Alec, who's a surgeon, to show this side of himself—or he's not thrilled about hanging out with a murderer.

An ice bucket dumps its contents on my lungs, and I wince. We're in an extremely bad situation without many good options.

"Pardon me." Brad carefully pulls back the handkerchief, nods, and replaces it. "Hold that tight, Ms. Drury. If you'll allow me, I have combat experience as a medic and keep a first aid kit for surgery needs."

Alec sighs. "Forgot that. I should do it myself, but I can't on Annalisse. I'm no cosmetologist and couldn't bear to leave a scar. Brad, your expertise is appreciated, thank you." Alec's shame in admitting his fear is written in his clenching jaw and lowered eyes. "Beautiful, tender skin isn't the same as animal hide. I trust you to take exceptional care with Anna." Alec squeezes my hand.

"Shouldn't we go back and do something with the body?" I ask, with her image etched on me like a tattoo. That's when I realize my pink blouse is so crimson it's purple and sticking to me.

"Guys, I look like I've survived a massacre. Alec too. Someone might turn us in. We can't explain this much blood at the police station without them investigating the cellar."

Alec sends hand gestures to Brad. Whatever it means, it's immediately understood.

"One moment." Brad whips off his jacket, unsnaps his holster, and inserts his weapon at his waistband, fluffing his shirt over it. He places the weight of his leather jacket on my shoulders, hiding the bloodstains entirely.

"That goes triple for me. The sun's going down. Time to move." Alec looks my way. "Stay close. Are you good?"

"Will be once this hole under my jaw mends. Any chance of getting something to deaden the pain while you stitch?" I'm laughing at Brad to keep my thoughts off how large a wound I've got and the battle scar that awaits me when this is over. "Where did you learn how to sew people up?"

"Gulf War."

What a pleasure it will be to see this day finally end, get off our feet, and stop bleeding to death. Sorellina chose the wrong place to give us a hard time, but I'm still confused why she lost her life, stabbed with her own knife. Did she fall on it, or was it helped into her chest by Brad? I'm sure I don't want to know—that'll be a discussion for later. What matters is the three of us are still alive. Stella has a role in our mysteries after all, which brings me to the conclusion that Italian pet rescues are everywhere, and she may need to stay in one.

CHAPTER
EIGHTEEN

The old man rests with the Holy Father in heaven.

Joey sips his drink and wipes the bottom of the glass on his mom's favorite blue-and-yellow tablecloth. He thought the cord that tied him to Sicily would snap when Pop died. So many times, Joey prayed to God he'd go and leave the family business. Be careful what you wish for, Joseph.

Uncle Carlo isn't taking over, you are.

Some cruel joke.

Pop spared Joey's sisters from seeing him cough up the black blood, but *he* had to watch the man wither to his grave. *They* got the kid-gloves treatment, his kisses, and the cash infusions whenever they asked the old man, and Joey had to beg for leftovers. Pop favored the girls; or he hated Joey. It felt more like he never measured up to his sisters. His uncles were waiting on him for the rosary and funeral plans. That's woman's work. His sisters should be home to take care of it. What did he know about death arrangements? It's dangerous for too many family members to attend the rosary—easy pickings for rivals. The whole thing is giving him a bellyache.

Carlo said he worried about a new flu virus spreading through Europe, killing people. How will the family say their goodbyes and show respect to the Birdman without showing up in person? Through video calls online? No way. Families pay their respects when the Don passes, especially Don Leo Manetti. They'll show up because that's what Pop would want. Just like they did for his mom, may she rest in peace. Carlo thinks a private viewing for immediate family, then a short graveside service, with masks in the mausoleum for the public. Spread out the family in different places.

Swarming flies bite and itch his sweaty arms. He's a pincushion for the ugly *mosca*.

"It's hot as hell on the patio, and this humidity stinks."

Wiping his forehead with one of Carlo's handkerchiefs, he stares into the smudge. No one uses these back home. Who takes time to wash hankies? *Hanky.* He hasn't thought about that word since he was a kid. Every Sicilian boy gets a new pack of hankies for their birthday and one for Christmas. Sometimes they're monogrammed, most times not. It's silly to throw them out when more always show up in their place. While Joey laughs to himself, he checks the awesome Piaget that Benita gave him last year when she was making good dough. He marvels at the quality diamonds around the square face to keep thoughts off the time. Neither Rave back home nor Gwen nor Nicky have checked in yet. He should've heard word by now if his

217

cousin's information was fact and not a bunch of bull. Nuns always tell the truth because a lie would be a sin.

Tingles race down his arms through the sweat, and a shiver follows. Stop worrying. Sorellina's polished and light-fingered. She's in and out before you know you've been robbed.

Joey downs the last bitter drop of scotch and wipes his mouth. It's anything but smooth and tastes like the rotgut Uncle Mario tried to make once. He looks into the sea; not even the ocean is calm enough to take a dip today. Gray blob meets black line where a sunset should be. He imagines the whitecaps as pitchforks in bird crap, and smelly seaweed rolls over the beach instead of waves. The forks pierce his belly, and nothing comes out. Joey's drained of energy and life and fears he'll never have fun again if he stays in Sicily.

The villa belongs to Joey unless Uncle Carlo talked Pop into giving it to him. Joey doesn't want the twenty-six rooms and seven baths where zero have been updated beyond the 1970 disco days. The stupid glitter ball still hangs in the dance hall, used for weddings, christenings, and Holy Communion parties. Manetti's Ali D'Angelo on Cefalu Beach used to be a hoppin' place when they were younger—ancient history. He'll take the States and New York any day of the week over Palermo's heat and bugs.

Villa Ali D'Angelo is worth a mint.

Any real estate agent would jump at the chance to list the villa on the market for a fat commission. The income from the vineyard and orange groves alone are a good selling point. Rivals would die to get their hands on the Birdman's place, but set the price too high, and they won't be able to afford it. Does he want to be stuck with the plantation? Sell, don't sell… He'll figure it out after the funeral. The chair squeals when Joey leans back and rests his heels on the table, a taboo gesture when his parents were alive. He could sink the sale money into some great digs on Staten Island or a casino bigger than Mohegan Sun.

Joey's little orange spot walks along the tile, looking for attention. "*Piccolo.* Who let you out?" Savina, his cat, jumps in his lap. "This isn't home. No ending up like Stella. Benita was stupid to take off with her." Savina's soft fur tickles his palm as she curls her tail around a black-and-white section on her body.

"Hey, Joey. Still playin' with… your, uh, cat?" Uncle Mario's getting better about his stuttering. When Joey lived at home, Mario barely got a sentence out. Uncle Carlo helped him with speech training for as long as he could remember. Mario has the mind of a twelve-year-old and the body of a middle-aged man, a man who's needed protection his entire life. Joey loves his special uncle like a brother. No one hurts his favorite uncle.

"Uncle Mario, *you* should get a cat. She makes me feel good."

"I can come up with better ways… ta… to feel good." His sideways grin is more information than Joey'd like to know.

He's gotten older since Mom passed. More gray at his temples, and the deep cracks near his mouth make him look more like *Nonno* Manetti. Joey's not sure if he understands his brother is gone and not coming back. Carlo can handle that situation.

Joey wasn't up for the talk.

"Savina, time to get you into the bedroom. I don't trust you out here." She hangs on to his shoulder by digging in with her claws, purring. "Let's make sure no one opens the door this time, right, Uncle Mario?"

"Sorry. Carlo needs you in the library. Gotta mm... minute to talk?"

"Jesus, he's quizzing me about Pop's rosary again. I'll get to it. Carlo, so help me, I'm gonna—"

"What?" Uncle Carlo walks in. "Get over it." His older uncle's face is round like a donut, and his eyes are glassy from too much drinking. He's taken the Birdman's death hard.

For talking out of line, he backhands Joey in the head.

"Stop taking the Lord's name in vain and show some respect, or I'll remind you how." Carlo adds, "Mario, bring us some limoncello. We'll sit outside instead."

Until now, Joey hadn't noticed how much Carlo sounds like his Pop when he orders people around. He gives Savina to his uncle Mario. "Take her to the spare room where her crate is. I'd appreciate it if you would shut her door."

Savina meows when she leaves him. *I shouldn't have given Stella to Rave. She was good company for her mother.* He feels his uncle's eyes on him. Carlo's *brutta* stare is following every move, trying to find fault he can use against him later.

Carlo sets two journals on the table and folds his hands on them. "We should talk finances. There are a few problems."

"Like what?"

"Revenues are down, and since the Birdman's been out of the picture for months convalescing, some clients are using it as leverage. They all have the same excuses. Business is slow. Times are tough. They promise to pay up later. You know the drill." He waves the air. "Some will, but most need encouragement."

"I'm pullin' my weight in New York; you handle it."

"New York is a tiny slice of the pie."

A minor gnat circling the pie, according to Uncle Carlo. His slam is so typical.

"Let me see." Joey slides the top book in front of him and flips pages. "Income looks all right to me except for that one at the top. Signorile. I thought Pop took that car company last year. Their payments stopped in April. Is that when Pop got really bad?" he asks Carlo.

"Got nothing to do with the Birdman getting sick. We don't know why they quit paying—they got the money. Nobody's talking to us or knows anything about the protection payments. The kid, Alec, runs Signorile the way he wants, and no one's seen him lately. He's no Pearce Zavos, I can tell you that. We could deal with that Greek. They owe three-quarters of a mil in greenbacks. This was Leo's deal—he told me to look the other way and stay out of it. Why? I dunno." He wipes his dripping nose on his sleeve. "I need you to dig into it and find out what's going on. I think we should dial up the protection fee, make up for lost revenue."

"The factory is near the groves—since Pop didn't take it, I want the business. We can expand the trees.

As far as I'm concerned, the Manettis *own* Signorile Corporation for money owed us. No pay, no business. Zavos the kid, as CEO, is a placeholder until we figure things out." *What was Carlo thinking? Stupido.*

"Joey, business ain't like that here. Do *you* know how to run a car company? *They* do the work, and *we* collect the money. *Capiche?* We don't buy anything. We extend the offer, and the people pay us to stay open."

"You don't hear me. Nicky and Gwen are working him from another angle anyway. It'll be freakin' awesome to drive around in a slick handmade car. A red one that looks like glass speeding down the highway."

"But, Joey…"

"For now, add a crapload of interest or double it if Signorile don't pay us by next month. Collecting is *your* job now." Joey straightens his back and folds his arms. Power feels good. "What's the other book for?" He gestures to the one in front of Carlo.

"We keep two sets. One ledger we show for business, and one we keep for our records with actual figures."

"I don't get it."

Carlo widens his eyes. "No one explained this? Joey, there's a ledger with the right numbers, and the one we show for IRES. You have the right one, the legit one for our use. You want *me* to collect?"

It took him long enough for his new job description to sink in.

"Tell me about Giambruno. How much money did he steal?" Joey asks.

Carlo shakes his head. "Giambruno's dead. You don't know nothing. Why Leo left the business to you—"

"I'm his son, that's why."

"You don't even want it."

"I'll grow into it."

Carlo grunts. "He took something out of my safe."

"Pops?"

"No." He slaps the table. "Tony the Terror. How you gonna do this if you don't wanna listen to me?"

Carlo swats at Joey's head, missing the mark when his wrist is caught in the air by Joey.

"Hey, cool it. I'm no punk kid you can bash anytime you want. You're so big on respect; why disrespect me, head of the family? I demand *your* respect, Uncle." He lets his wrist go, and the blackbird ring clacks the edge of the table.

Uncle Carlo sees its significance and lowers his eyes. "We aren't talkin' lira or euros, Joey. The Terror stole something priceless. It's been in our family for centuries, even before our clan in Sicily was invaded by Arabs and the French."

"Go on." Joey's losing patience in his roundabout way of getting to the point. He imagines rare gold coins worth millions.

Carlo pauses. "Keep this to yourself. It belonged to Galileo. A relative of his."

His uncle's shaking hand is curious.

"Tony was my good friend. A trusted ally, and I read him wrong. I convinced Leo he would be a loyal friend to us, and he broke the omerta," Carlo says.

"Giambruno ratted us out?"

He nods. "That's why the heat is always on. We're bleeding moles in and out. We never know who's working with the cops or other mafiosi. Giambruno almost broke us, Joey. Every day is a danger to our survival. Our luck has turned bad, real bad. We lost your mother and father, and the business is sinking into a hole. Since the beads left, the evil eye is upon us."

"What did Tony say to the cops?"

"They don't know about the rosary beads."

"Oh that. I heard about it already."

"Tony also took the ancient rendering out of the safe with Sister Maria Celeste holding these beads, the proof they're authentic. Her story is in a book from my safe. Tony stole our good fortune, and we want it back."

Tony used to read to Joey—tall tales of knights fighting to save their kingdoms from evil queens in neighboring lands. He made the stories sound realistic when he spoke through his crooked teeth, minus the big one on the side. He could tease him without any backlash, and that made Joey feel important, not worthless like Pop did.

"Didn't Tony have kids? I thought he had a couple."

"Only one. A girl. He raised her without her mama after his wife died. Best we could figure, she left the country as a teenager when Tony went to prison. Leo felt sorry for the kid. You know his big heart for the little ones. Anyway, he didn't want to bring Giambruno into the family, but I talked him into it." Carlo sips his limoncello and sighs. "What a putz I was to trust a Barese. He's been a curse on the Manettis."

"Where is she? Tony's girl," he asks.

"Don't do no good digging on her. We thought of that already. Sophia Giambruno doesn't exist. For all we know, she's dead too."

"Someone has to know." Joey gets a text from Rave. "About time. Excuse me." He reads and rereads the words, but they don't sink in.

"What's wrong? You look like you've seen the Holy Mother herself."

"Business in New York. I need to make a call." As hot as he is, Joey has goose bumps. "Can we finish this later?"

"Sure. Go ahead. I'll sit here and finish my drink."

Jumping off the patio onto the sandy beach, he hits autodial for Rave, and the line opens. He must've been sitting on the phone.

"Joey, you won't believe it. I didn't do it, so don't blame me. My setup was perfect."

"Stop blabberin' and give me the skinny. Did she meet the girl?"

"Yeah, I think so, but when Nicky went into the basement to let Gwen out, she was dead with her own switchblade in her chest."

"Gwen's dead?"

"Yeah, as a doornail. The cellar was locked from the outside. Someone helped busybody Ann out of there... I bet it's... *sss*... the boyfriend, Zavos... *sss*." The phone crackles with static.

"Talk slow so I can hear. Anyone listening to this call?" Joey asks.

"I'm sitting in a boat off the dock. Just me."

"Where's little sister now? Still in the cellar?"

"He had to move her; she was smelling bad."

Joey's lunch rolls over. If Zavos's girlfriend knows anything, they'll never know what she told Gwen. He hadn't thought of that. Pop would go ape—

An air horn blasts Joey's ear.

"Jesus, what was that?" He squeegees out the ear with his index finger.

"Some smart guy with a new horn, I guess. What do you want me to do?" Rave asks.

"I'll call the Russo and see what he says. We didn't count on losing Benita and her sister in this. It shouldn't have escalated like that."

"Okay." Rave sniffs.

Gwen and Rave; he forgot they had a thing.

"Hey, man. I'm sorry about Gwen. I know you were tight with her."

"Yeah, story of my life. The goodies get swiped away at the last minute. No money, no cat, and no girl. Speaking about; any chance of getting access to the vault?"

"Why?" Joey asks with a smile. "Are you missing the old life?"

"A looksee once in a while keeps me focused on my goal."

"We'll talk about it when I get back. Pops didn't make it, so there's a lot to do here."

"Aw, I didn't know. That's too bad, Joey. My condolences to you and the family."

"Thanks."

Joey stores the phone in his pocket. Zavos again. That's twice he's messed with them.

CHAPTER
NINETEEN

Brad has a light touch and a skilled hand, whipping the needle along sure and swift.

"That's beautiful work." Alec hasn't recovered from turning my surgery over to Brad. I can feel his anguish and embarrassment.

Brad pierces the needle into my skin, but I can't feel it, thanks to an anesthetic he keeps.

"The last stitch," Brad assures me.

I notice his slight tug on the filament, then he makes a knot in the last of many stitches. "Would you like to see what it looks like?" Alec offers a mirror from the dresser, and Brad hands it to me. "How does it feel, Ms. Drury?"

"Numb. Am I allowed to touch it?" My hand zeros in on the jaw.

His flashing eyes and stern warning come quickly. "Look only. Don't touch."

It's so Brad.

Alec squeezes my shoulder as he makes his way around the chair that Brad recommended I sit on, and he steps next to my surgeon. From driver to bodyguard to medic, Brad's diverse training amazes me. I recall the first time Alec introduced his driver, Bradley, to me. The small man came across as so stereotypical in his navy uniform and quirky driver's cap. Brad is so much more than a chauffeur and is handy to have around in emergencies.

Alec studies Brad's handiwork with a critical eye and purses his lips. "Tiny stitches. An excellent result. I *could not* have done it better. And you've saved me from having nightmares about scarring this gorgeous lady for life. Thank you, Brad." Alec turns from him and rakes fingers gracefully through my hair this time. "You look great. Can I get you anything?"

I pat his hand. "Don't worry about me. I'll live."

Stitches in a row about two inches long neatly line up beneath my jawbone. Around the incision is hot and swollen. When the painkiller wears off, ibuprofen should be enough to take the edge off, I hope.

"Keep the area clean with soap and water but use nothing strong like peroxide. The cut isn't as deep as it looked, so it will heal quickly. Would you like me to cover the stitches with a bandage now?" Brad asks Alec.

Alec and I both nod.

"How long before the stitches come out?" I take a closer look at the tiny sutures near the hollow of my throat. Blood loss made the cut appear worse than it actually was. The scary part of this bizarre meeting— she could've killed me easily if she wanted me out of the picture. Brad remarked how clean the cut was. I hope the blade hadn't been used on anyone or anything prior to sinking it into my flesh. A raging infection will complicate things.

"I did the best I could around the slight nick to the masseter muscle. You shouldn't have any permanent damage to worry about, but you'll experience a tightness when you chew until it mends. Take care when eating on the left side. Dissolving sutures are the only type I keep with me in my travel kit. They're made of animal proteins your body will absorb as you heal."

"Anna likes being close to animals." Alec smiles.

"That's really bad, hon. Ugh, I'm so stiff." Standing slowly, I waver, losing my balance, and seize the back of the chair with one hand. "Wow. Light-headed."

"Easy, babe." Alec helps me to the seat. "Sit there a minute. You've been through surgery."

"And lost a bit of blood. Sip some orange juice. That might help," Brad adds.

"Okay, boys. There's a gigantic elephant in the room that we have to address. What do we do about the woman in the cellar, and shouldn't we report the policeman who kidnapped me?"

Brad is looking at my forearm. "I didn't see this before. Did she graze you with her knife?" He motions to the scratch.

"It's nothing. When I got off the motorcycle, I tried to run, but he caught me with his fingernails. I'll go and wash."

"No." Alec looks at my upper arm. "The cop touched you with his bare hands. No gloves?"

"Bare."

"Your arm is loaded with DNA. Do you remember if the woman with the knife touched you there?"

229

"I don't think so... Wait. She dabbed the scratch with a tissue and put it in her mouth."

Alec's grimace sours his lips. "Why?"

"For the same reason she ran her finger through blood dripping from my jaw."

"That's super gross." Alec grimaces.

"Sanguinarian, or blood worship. I've heard of that but never witnessed it." Brad observes my skin and nods. "We might be able to use this to turn in the cyclist."

"Without the cellar discovery." Alec's eyes glitter, and he says to Brad, "I have to ask even though I think it's a long shot, do you carry a fingerprint kit with you?"

"No."

"Gwen, the woman in the cellar, came into the gallery the day you brought the tabloid in. She's the same girl from Staten Island. Nate caught her trying to steal the red diamond out of the case."

"Are you sure it's her?" Alec asks.

"Without question. She called herself Tie Dye, but her real name is Gwendolyn on her license. While we were in the cellar, she asked me about Stella. She freaked out over the *Sorellina* name Bill mentioned when I called her that. Did you hear from him again?"

Alec scrolls his phone. "Yep. His missed call. I'd better return it, then we'll get something to eat downstairs when your numbness wears off. Put some energy back into ya." His smile is put on for my benefit.

"Hello," Bill Drake answers on speakerphone. "Where've you guys been?"

Alec and I huddle together near his cell.

"Before you get alarmed, I forgot to tell you we took your mom's phone away as a precautionary measure until you return."

Alec sits on the bed and crosses his ankles. "That's why I can't reach her. Is your guy Mason there?"

"Nothing abnormal to report from the estate. But... I... uh. I couldn't get you, so I took the liberty and placed a call to Bari police and the local carabinieri."

Alec and I exchange glances.

"What about?" Alec's lips flatten.

"Be expecting a call from Giuseppe Bruno. Where are you now?"

"Back at the bed-and-breakfast." The steam is rolling out of Alec's ears, and he's unhappy. "Calling the police was rotten timing, Drake. You have no idea what we've been through. Anna's still recovering and—"

"From what?" Bill's voice is an octave higher. "What happened?"

Alec explains the events from seeing the nun and my encounter with the child to the wild ride on the cycle.

"Things got dicey in the cellar, Bill. *Sorellina* from New York was there waiting for me." I shift my jaw and almost touched the stitches because my face is beginning to ache.

"Ms. Drury. Be careful of the sutures." Brad must be watching me.

"Sutures? Did I hear that right?" It's Bill's turn to breathe hard into the phone. "Annalisse, stay clear of that woman. How could she be there already? Are you okay?"

"Anna's much better now, but if the police swarm— Why is Bruno calling?" Alec scoots next to me. "From the top."

"Too much to go into here."

"Make time. The woman in the cellar is dead," Alec blurts.

Waiting through Bill's long silence was horrible.

"Did you report it?" he eventually asks.

"Are you kidding?" Alec swipes a hand over one ear. "And tell them Anna was in a knife fight? We're still being looked at for Oliver's murder. When we found Anna and took her out of the cellar, Brad went down and saw Sorellina lying at the bottom of the staircase. The knife she'd used on Anna was buried in her chest."

"Annalisse didn't..."

"No, Bill. I didn't kill her, but I was with her before she tumbled down the steps. I kicked her in the stomach, and she—"

Bill gushed a lot of air. "You guys left a crime scene. Let me think."

Alec jumps in. "What about this?" He explains my arm scratch. "Anna's arm has the proof which officer grabbed her."

"Ask for prints and DNA?" Bill mumbles something inaudible. "I don't know. Why would they care with the rampant corruption? How would you go about it; walk into the police station and offer Annalisse's arm to their crime unit? They may see her as an American author creating juicy narratives for her next novel. What you've told me is quite a tale of intrigue. Law enforcement protects their own, and that code covers cops worldwide."

"It's the only idea we've come up with, short of escorting the police to the cellar door," Alec says.

Another uncomfortable pause from Bill. "Does anyone know you were in the cellar?"

"The little girl outside the pub. She showed us where the cop took Anna, but she pointed out the wrong door. The cellar was actually twenty yards away."

"So, she wasn't sure?" Bill asks.

"No. We think she was the ruse to get Anna outside the pub."

"Are Annalisse's prints on the door or on anything in the cellar?" Bill asks.

"It's Bradley here. I took it upon myself to use an apron to wipe two entrances and exit doors and every smooth surface, including the woman's arms and legs in case Ms. Drury might have touched her in a tussle. The switchblade knife has a bone handle and has also been carefully wiped. When I left, the deceased had her hand on the knife."

"You think I killed her?" I glare at Brad, aghast. "That's *not* what happened."

"Brad, where's the apron now?" Alec asks.

A cynical smile plays on his lips. "It took a little doing, but I managed to remove the bung hole plug on a cask and push the fabric through the hole until it disappeared inside. I replaced the bung plug." Brad shrugs. "It's lost until it clogs the spigot. Could be years."

Nervous laughter erupts all around.

"Ouch." I catch myself in time from rubbing the sutures.

"One more thing. Anna says the girl in the cellar was in Zavos Gallery. They caught her trying to steal a diamond." Alec stops and asks me, "Did Mom get any identification from her?"

"Colum Mooney will have a copy of her license. Nate sent her to the station courtesy of a patrol car." I'm grinning and have no idea why. There's nothing funny about our situation. "Oh, I just thought of something else. Remember that black feather and the bird pin we found in my tote? Sorellina had blackbirds dangling from her earlobes. They could be connected somehow."

"Noted. I'll call the First Precinct and see what the girl told them," Bill says.

"She lives in Staten Island. I read that on her license, plus her slang fits the area. She's Gwendolyn something."

"She may carry a fake ID. I'll verify that with the detective."

"You said earlier that you didn't know she was *already* here. Did you know she was coming to Bari?" Alec asks.

"That's Bruno's department. They have a truckload of information on the Manettis and need your help, Alec. He only wants to speak to you. If Annalisse has injuries from her encounter with Sorellina, I'd lay low. Annalisse would have to answer a battery of direct questions, and... uh... that *won't* go well."

The way he said it is more hurtful than his words.

"I'll talk too much, is that it?"

"Careful, Drake." Alec narrows his eyes.

"Look, I'm sorry. I don't mean to offend you or Annalisse. This is a hairy position to be in, and you guys seem to be in places where dead bodies are found. It's easy to inadvertently say the wrong words without meaning to. Americans involved in homicide cases take years to unravel with the best attorneys, even if the woman in the cellar isn't a local. Add in the Zavos name and money, and it'll be the international scandal of the century. Attorneys and the Italian government are the only winners. The sooner you're out of Italy, the better."

This is my fault. I should have ignored the girl and stayed inside the pub.

"Guys, I'll stress this again. Get in Leo Manetti's way, and you'll be erased as quickly as Oliver King," Bill says.

"You've confirmed King's death was a Mob hit?" Alec asks.

"Unknown. I used him as an example to make my point. The Birdman has terminal lung cancer, but he's still in charge. Police worry that the Sicilian Mafia syndicate will blow up into a power war when the Birdman dies. Factions are making plans and waiting to fill the vacuum left behind. These men don't just roam around Sicily; their nets stretch across Italy provinces, all the way to the US Eastern Seaboard. Birdman's son Joey is a young, single, and ruthless dude. I'm hearing that he has no scruples."

"Officer Bruno plans to put Alec in the middle of this Mafia war?" I join Alec on the bed. "That's not acceptable, Bill. What if we say no and leave now, before they discover the body?"

"Alec has to work with the police, for his mother's sake. Bruno can explain this better than I can."

"Mom again." Alec rubs his forehead and glances at me. "People are looking for her, aren't they? Anna, tell him what your research uncovered."

We spent the next several minutes going over the Giambruno legacy, including the prayer beads. He didn't seem surprised by any of it.

"By your silence, you agree with Anna's findings?" Alec asks Bill.

Bill clears his throat. "Your mother and grandfather are an integral part of what happens next." Bill crinkles what sounds like paper from his end. "I don't think it'll foul up Bruno's plans if I tell you that the dead girl in the cellar is Benita Alvarez's sister."

I gasp.

"Was she at Josh's office to kill Benita?" Alec straightens his spine. "For Stella or another reason?"

"Until the hair and print evidence are confirmed, we don't know if Sorellina was at the office. I should've heard from the ME by now. He might have forgotten to call." Bill pauses. "Here's the plan I suggest you follow. When Bruno calls, he'll ask you to come down to the station; he won't miss a chance to talk in person when you're in his city. Don't go to the station. Give him an excuse, like security or Annalisse isn't feeling well so you can't leave. After King's homicide, he should believe you. If Giuseppe Bruno wants to talk, he has to come to you, but set the meeting where you can talk privately. We have no idea who's in Bari and how many thugs or observers there are. You shouldn't take a pistol anywhere, and neither can Brad, so keep firearms hidden from Bruno. If you have knives, hide them as well."

Brad and Alec exchange glances.

"Please don't go to the cellar again or tell the carabinieri what happened to Annalisse—unless there's no way out of that conversation. If you have to explain Annalisse's abduction, take an officer to the *first* door you visited. Not the actual cellar door. That way, you aren't lying. Avoid lies at all costs. If you go down that path—well, just don't. If it's impossible to be honest, change the subject or stop talking at once. He'll pick up on the tactic of avoidance, so be careful. These guys are trained, and Bruno will know if you're holding back."

"Got it," Alec says.

"Call me after you talk with him. Feel better, Annalisse, and keep your heads up and eyes open. Bye."

Bill ends the call, and we're left to our thoughts.

"Just to be clear." Alec looks at his screen. "We *are* lying by omission."

"I don't see that as a choice," Brad says honestly.

"When Bruno calls, which excuse will you use?" I ask.

"He'll believe we're afraid to leave the bed-and-breakfast at night after what happened on the beach." He worries his hands. "Man, I wish Bill had talked to me before calling the police. We don't know what he told the officer. I hate speaking to authorities as blind as a mole." Alec shakes his head. "Bill's never kept things from me before."

"It involves your mother, so it's a big deal. He tried to phone you beforehand." Even though I'm supporting Bill's choices, I agree with Alec. It feels like backstabbing. We're in trouble, and our detective friend is safe in the States. On every call with Bill, I'm usually listening in. Bill doesn't want me to hear; that's why he wouldn't give Alec details.

Stop it.

I remember the rosary in my tote that I promised a place in the suitcase. "This gem finds a new home effective immediately." With crucifix and beads in my hand, I place the pouch in a ziplock bag and bury it between folded jeans. "I'm carrying enough bulk with my Nikon."

Alec pinches his brows and paces in front of the bureau in stockinged feet. "When is Bruno supposed to call?" He wrings his hands again. "The aircraft is on the tarmac ready for us."

"Speak to the police, then decide. We'll endorse it." Brad gives him a fatherly pat on the back. A gesture that's new to me. What advice would Pearce have given his son? The entire Zavos dynasty rests on his shoulders—still. Nothing is ever simple for this man to move on to a different future.

The screen on Alec's phone lights up, and it rings. He nods to me, motions me to come listen, and draws a long breath.

"Zavos."

"Mr. Alec Zavos?" booms out of the speaker.

"Yes."

"This is Giuseppe Bruno of the Bari police. I'm sorry to disturb your vacation, but it is vital that I speak to you. Are you available to come down to the police station now?"

"Officer Bruno, in light of the beach murder, I don't travel alone without my armed guard. I'm happy to speak to you privately at il Gatto Bella. Do you know where that is?

"*Si.*"

"I can meet you in their small lounge at the entrance. Is that all right?" Alec is in charge of the conversation by not giving the man a chance to rebut. "What time?"

"On my way now. *Grazie.*"

Alec places the phone carefully on the bureau, but I notice a slight case of jitters.

"Very smooth, *signor* Zavos."

"That was the easy part." Alec slides by Brad to visualize my sutures. "The rest is anyone's guess."

TWENTY

Sitting in a stiff leather armchair, staring at a doorknob, Alec awaits the Grim Reaper. An interrogation by the police that holds their future and security. He hated leaving Anna and Brad upstairs in the room. Her intense green eyes that he loves so much, fused with so many emotions: anger, uncertainty, and frustration at staying in Italy when they all want to go home. He came close to bringing her to the lobby with him, but Bill was right; her injury would draw too many questions they couldn't explain away without mentioning the cellar and the woman left there.

His relationship with Anna keeps him centered and aware of their joined fates—her bad decisions and good intentions aside. They're what make her unique and one of the reasons he was drawn to her from the beginning. She reacts as a sleek thoroughbred would, ready to bolt at the starting gate, unsure when to run and how far the finish line is. Jumping into high gear is what Anna does, and there's no stopping her once she's in motion. He's gone back and forth in his mind...

Why didn't he stop Anna from running outside the pub? She has more mothering instincts than she realizes. He's witnessed her maternal ways with friends, the horses, and her sheep. She'll make the best mom, and they belong together always, even though she hasn't admitted it herself. Yet.

Anna's turned him down twice, and he keeps putting her in danger.

He's ignoring the other subject that has him deeply concerned. Why hasn't his mother told him about the family secrets?

"May I bring you a magazine or newspaper, sir?" The plain yet attractive girl has impeccable English and no Italian accent. She lifts the vase with a half dozen pink roses and dusts beneath it nervously, sending her rag over the entire coffee table twice.

"Thank you. I'm good. I won't be waiting long."

She folds the cloth in her hand and hangs around as if she'd like to talk. "If you change your mind… I should know you but can't place how." She taps her bottom lip.

Alec decides to let her wonder and smiles instead of giving himself away. He's taken from watching the door temporarily and welcomes the diversion.

"Your first time in Bari?" She tries another maneuver and sits at the far end of the sofa, crossing her legs.

"I have roots here."

A uniformed officer steps inside, removing his cap. He has to be Giuseppe Bruno, a large guy with a strong presence and a lot of wavy gray hair.

The receptionist wipes her hands on her shirt and straightens her name tag. "Uh, sir, may we help you?"

"Mr. Zavos?" he booms out, fully aware of Alec, having done his share of investigation on the family by now. "I'm Giuseppe Bruno."

"If you need anything, let me know." The receptionist hurries into the dining area.

"Please. Let's talk." Alec motions to the matching armchair across from his. "How can I help you, Officer Bruno?"

He studies the surrounding foyer. "I received a call from Bill Drake." Bruno's stroking Alec for some kind of a reaction, but his dark eyes are easily readable. A plus.

"We went to school together. He's a friend."

"I see." Bruno's fidgety and awkward, but his English is strong. Another positive. He's not trying to intimidate Alec with an authoritative presence and has a pleasant manner, which helps relieve some tension.

"We have a touchy situation. In the making for many years." He glances around the room again. "I know of no other way to say this, so… your friend Drake told me you fired an officer from your business… located in Palermo. Signorile, is that right?"

"Yes. You're referring to Josh Jennings. He was Signorile's CFO."

"He's wanted for murder; is that true?" Bruno's niceties end here.

"No, not quite. I believe a body was found in his office, but he's not been charged, to the best of my knowledge."

Bruno notes the comment in a spiral-bound book and lays it across his knee.

"He paid the business bills while he worked for you?" he asks.

"Approved them. Yes. From the first day my father began the corporation."

"Were you aware Mr. Jennings also paid the Cosa Nostra while he was in your employ?"

"I suspected he was siphoning money away from Signorile accounts. I fired him when I found out. We're still investigating how deeply Josh was involved with the missing money." Alec scoots to the edge of his cushion and lowers his voice. "Can you confirm that he was paying the Mafia?"

"Points that way. Protection money, and we may know why."

Sitting back with his arms folded to cover the gooseflesh, Alec asks, "Why?"

"What I'm about to say must remain between you and me. I must have your full cooperation. Lives depend on it."

In case he was being recorded, Alec nods.

Bruno gets up, verifies no eavesdroppers are present, and returns to his chair.

"Are you recording our conversation?" Alec asks.

"Should I?" Bruno's bantering again, looking for cracks in Alec's exterior.

Offering a blank expression, Alec considers his options before saying, "If the Mafia is involved in Signorile business, I would appreciate knowing how that's being done, Officer Bruno. I run a legitimate business."

Bruno has changed his seat to the sofa. "Breaking up the Mafia is an ongoing part of what I do. It's not impossible to turn a member to work with us, but it's very rare. This is difficult, you see, because of the oath each family member takes."

"*Omerta.* I've heard of it."

"Right. The oath of secrecy, silence, and obedience. A person who tells of the clan's business will never get a good night's sleep again. Mob hits are unpleasant to investigate. I won't go into their tactics here. It's very bad." Bruno licks his cracked lips. "On one rare occasion, we got lucky. A member deep into the top level of the Manetti family, a relative of his, came to us. She wanted to protect this member."

A shiver ripples Alec's spine, and he draws a haggard breath. Annalisse's research is about to be revealed as truth or fiction.

Bruno holds Alec in his cool, steady stare. "Something wrong?"

"I think I know where you're going with this, but please continue."

"When your friend Drake phoned me about a number of things, more pieces fell into place. We thought Antonio's daughter had died."

"Antonio who?" Alec decides to force the officer to give details.

"Your grandfather, Antonio Giambruno. He went undercover for Bari police while he was a member of the Mafia."

"Then it's true; my grandfather is that man."

Bruno purses his lips and wipes his temple. "Your mother is Sophia Giambruno, his daughter."

"I grew up thinking Mom's maiden name was DePalma. When she married Dad, she took his Zavos name. Mom goes by Generosa now, not Sophia."

Bruno nods. "*Si*, Drake said this when we talked. Your grandfather feared for your mother's life and changed the family name so she couldn't be... ah, *collocato*. How you say?"

"Located, found."

Bruno smiles. "That's right. She hides."

Alec nods. "We did research of our own and found the connections online. What you're telling me confirms our findings." Alec wasn't sure if he should be relieved or more frightened for his mother. "Tell me about my grandfather. How did he get involved with the Mob? He's not a Sicilian. I thought they were strict about blood relationships."

"We know Antonio had a deep friendship with one of the Manettis. They took him in as part of the family. Your grandfather did good work for the police until one event that involved your mother. It left us no choice but to prosecute and send him to prison as captured Mafia. That allowed us to keep our covert operation in place. When your mama met Pearce, she moved from Italy. *Capisci?*" He holds out his hands.

"I understand, but I wish we weren't involved. My grandfather risks his life and snitches for you, and a prison sentence was the best protection you could offer?"

"It was complicated." Bruno clears his throat. "Your father is Pearce Zavos, who has passed." Bruno lowers his eyes. "*Mi dispiace*. Did you know Pearce also knew of your mother's heritage and paid the Mafia when they threatened to kill her? Monthly payments in US cash. One hundred thousand per month."

"We found no paper trail but sensed the irregularities."

"Jennings knew the arrangement because Pearce directed him to pay the Mafia outside of the corporation. Under the table, as you would say. As long as Manettis got the money, they let Sophia Giambruno live. When you fired your CFO, we believe this opened your family to great harm. Pearce never mentioned these payments to you?"

"Why go after Mom? A vendetta for Antonio? He went to prison; isn't that enough?"

"Your grandfather took something from them, then died in prison before he returned it."

"What is it?" Alec asks, recalling what the Sister told them.

Bruno lifts one shoulder. "We hear rumors but don't know for sure. When Antonio passed, and she didn't attend the funeral, we were told Sophia had died. When Drake called, we had hope again."

"Hope?"

"To bring down the Manettis for good."

I'm glad Anna isn't here. Bill was right to have me do this solo.

"Where is your mother now?" Bruno asks.

Alec's gut tells him it's unwise to offer more than necessary. "She's well."

"Has she spoken of your grandfather?"

"Very little. I knew he went to prison but didn't know why." Sinking deeper into the cushion, he addresses Bruno honestly. "This feels like a bad dream."

"Your mother is smart not saying too much."

"I need to verify everything with Mom. May I phone Drake?"

"Not at this time." Bruno sighs. "As you know, we lost a tourist on the beach, and we think the Mob is involved. There has been more activity in Bari since your arrival."

"We've had a feeling of being watched."

Bruno's eyes glisten. "Yes?"

If Alec allows this line of questioning, he's on the road to making mistakes. "Nothing specific. Just a feeling."

Bruno touches his weapon and adjusts the leather holster.

A stupid slipup.

Alec grips his chair. "This thing my grandfather took from the Manettis. Is there anyone we can ask?" He's using Bill's tactic of changing the subject. "If we find this *thing* and hand it over, they may leave us alone, or is that wishful thinking?"

"They will take both. Money and what Giambruno stole, then kill you for knowing their business. The way we end it is by taking key family out for good. I know this is hard to hear, Mr. Zavos. From their side of it, you owe the Manettis a lot of cash. I don't know how much, but the Mafia won't forget your debt to them. It's very dangerous. The Birdman is in poor health and from mixed reports may already have died."

"Who takes over the family if that happens?" Alec asks.

"Leo has two living brothers, Carlo and Mario. It won't be Mario because he's simple-minded and can't communicate. Carlo is the logical choice, but there is an outside chance Leo will appoint his only son, Joseph."

Joey from Staten Island.

Alec looks away from Bruno too late. If he has to, he'll mention that he's heard the name Joey Calico.

"You know him." He folds his hairy knuckles in his lap. "We'll get to that later. Mr. Drake tells me you're finalizing a sale of your business, and the death of Mr. King has complicated matters for you. I read something about this sale."

"Drake has told you plenty, I see."

"The safety of Bari is my job."

"I was supposed to meet Oliver the next day. He sat on the board for the corporation acquiring Signorile. I assume Oliver came to this bed-and-breakfast to discuss the sale, but we never had a meeting." He leaves out the part about his mother sending him here. "Running into him was an unexpected surprise."

"Did your father ever talk about turning over Signorile to the Manettis?"

"The Mafia? No. He would never agree to that. Dad had big plans for Signorile. He didn't want to off-load it. Global Star tried several times to buy it, but he refused."

"The Mafia might have known about your sale plans with Global Star even before it came out in the news. Killing Mr. King bought them time if this is true. I bring this up because Mr. King's unfortunate death may open an opportunity for us." Bruno leans his pointed chin closer, and his leather belt squeals in protest. "The large sum you owe may be a way to take them down."

Alec transfers to the chair across from where Bruno sat earlier. The heat radiating from the cop's body doesn't help Alec stay sharp.

"Is everything fine?" Bruno raises hairy brows quizzically.

"It's warm in here."

He folds his hands over one knee. "I'd like you to offer Signorile to the Manetti family."

"Are you insane?"

Bruno falls against the sofa cushion. "Mr. Zavos, I—"

"I mean no disrespect to you or your ideas, but what you're asking me to do... is impossible. Give them my father's patents—his work—to a crime family?"

Bruno nods. "It must sound like that. We have a small chance in the next days. If the Birdman has died or is close to death, his funeral will bring the clans together in Sicily."

"That sounds like an old ploy they'll be ready for. I've heard of ambushes like this in America with gangsters. Look, I have no intention of going to Sicily on this trip, especially with Anna along, and in light of what we've uncovered—you've uncovered."

"What have you *uncovered?*"

"Sicily is out of your jurisdiction, isn't it?" Alec asks with respiration climbing. This conversation is on a bullet train, and he's outside the caboose, hanging on to the railing by his fingernails.

"It is out of my provinces. I want the Manettis here, in Bari, not Palermo. They'll come if they stand a massive gain and if you insist."

There's more to it beyond police business, I'd wager. "They won't leave their turf if the boss is dying or dead. Sicilians are a tight clan. The Palermo police can haul them out at the funeral down there. Why get me involved?"

"You *are* involved. I want to drive out the Manetti *ratto* from every crack in Bari. I want the *capo mandamento* in prison. Moles inside are paying officers and breaking up the police unit. The carabinieri are dealing with the *traditore*. Mafia movement in Bari is heavier than we've seen in decades because of *you*, Alec. Are you willing to risk Sophia, your mama?"

"Nothing is certain, and I'm being blamed without proof, Mr. Bruno. *Circostanziale.* It's circumstantial theory. Because the Mafia activity has grown, you believe it's my fault."

He utters a resigned sigh. "This is a lot to think about. How do you know this feeling of people watching you?"

Bruno should be told about the cop on the motorcycle who abducted Annalisse. He knows he has bad cops inside his station. Bill has already brought him in on the Alvarez murder and who knows what else? Tell the truth; but how much is enough? If he doesn't say anything, Bruno will suspect he's hiding facts he wants. Alec's goal is to conceal what happened in the cellar at all costs. Don't lay a course for lies.

"We had an incident a few hours ago that makes me wonder if we're being followed." He steadies his nerves and continues. "While having a drink in a bar not far from the square, a young girl was crying, and an adult was abusing her in public. When the girl was struck, my girlfriend ran outside to help her. There, she was forced onto the back of a motorcycle by police."

"Forced how?"

Alec explains how Anna was pushed and what they went through to find the little girl.

Bruno scribbles more notes in his book. "One man or more? Do you have descriptions or license number?"

"Two men, I think. It happened so fast. The cycle was light blue, leather bags on either side. Driver had buzzed, dark hair. No helmet." He shrugs. "I was running while watching Anna and didn't notice the other guy leave; couldn't read the license. He drove off fast."

"I'll check the duty log." Bruno makes a check mark in the book. "Continue. You searched for your girlfriend by yourself?"

"I was with an associate who travels with me. A guard."

"In your opinion, the crying girl aided the kidnapper?" He stops writing and squints at him with renewed interest.

"At first we didn't think of it that way. The child ran off soon after the cycle arrived. Once Anna was driven away and we lost sight of them, we started looking for the girl. When we found her, she ran from us, so yes, I'm certain the child was working with the abductor."

"Little girls run." Bruno shakes his head, dismissing Alec's suggestion summarily. "You found your girlfriend, yes?"

He nods.

"Why didn't you report the incident since it involves police?" Suspicion clouds Bruno's eyes.

"I was out of my mind with worry. We couldn't waste time making a report. If we hadn't found her, I would've gone to the police." *This next part is tricky.*

"I will need to speak to the young girl," Bruno says.

"I don't know where she is. She ran away after showing us the street."

He swishes at the air with an open hand. "What street? Explain."

"The place where Anna was taken. Luckily, my girlfriend escaped. Anna fell off the bike when he slowed and took a turn. He just drove off and left her."

His brows shoot together. "He took your lady friend and let her go? For what purpose?"

"I don't know, but I'm glad he did. Maybe he changed his mind, or something spooked him. I wasn't there." This sounds far-fetched, so Alec adds more color. "We found Anna sitting on the steps with a scraped jaw and a bad headache. She gets terrible migraines and has to sleep them off."

"Is that where she is now, sleeping?"

"Yes. I left my guard with her. That's why I asked to meet here so that I can stay close to her."

Bruno looks through the window, deep in thought, and then studies his watch.

"I'm sorry, Mr. Zavos, but I have to see this street... tonight. It won't take long."

What if he's one of those compromised cops playing a role to get information for the Manettis? "We won't be able to see anything in the dark. I don't know if I re-member where we were anyway. We looked down so many alleys in that area, I probably won't be any help." The forehead rub is added for effect.

Bruno pulls out a flashlight. "I have this." He grins, and Alec's chest tightens.

"Do I have time to go upstairs?"

In a stomach-turning moment, Alec's aware he can't avoid leading him close to where the body is.

"No time." Bruno sounds firm and won't be swayed.

"Is it safe for me to leave this building? They've already tried to take Anna."

"Who? Do you know?" Bruno asks, digging. "You're with me. We are safe in the police car."

Alec visualizes every movie where an unsuspecting driver gets behind the wheel, starts his car, and turns into a fireball after a blast. He imagines the acrid smell of burnt leather floating from the chair.

"Let's go, Officer. I can't be gone long."

They find the pub from earlier, and Alec points out where the girl stood while having her meltdown. Driving down residential areas he and Brad visited hours ago, in the dark, everything looks different. Many times, he considers purposely giving Bruno the wrong street and guiding him to another door, but in each instance, Bill's warning keeps Alec from doing it.

Stick to the bare truth.

Officer Bruno stops the car beneath a streetlight and turns to Alec with a shining yellow glare on his face and a shadow beneath his brim. "Mr. Zavos, what's making you so nervous?"

"Other than riding around with police?" He fidgets with his seat belt to cover his angst. "When you told me about men being paid off in your unit, how can I trust you?"

"I see. I have forty-two years in, and I plan to collect my old-age pension, not spend it in prison. *Capisci?*"

Sounds like something an honest cop would say.

Alec adds more cover to explain his nervousness.

"What if Anna hadn't fled the motorcycle? I was way too slow to react at the pub. Tracing our steps tonight, I didn't realize how freaked out I'd be reliving Anna's abduction. When I lost Dad on our yacht last year and almost lost Mom, if something had happened to Anna today, I'd—"

"Concentrate on where you found your *la fidanzata*. Your woman." He pulled out onto the empty cobblestones, and they were on their way to the street where the girl took Brad.

"Turn here." Alec directs Bruno toward the dark, narrow roadway. "I think this is right. It's dimmer now—hard to be certain."

Bruno slows and parks close to the building where the sidewalk begins.

"When we get out, stay beside me. Is that place where Anna was sitting?" Bruno motions through the windshield to the first stoop.

"That's it, yeah."

"Follow me."

They walk quietly while Bruno clicks the wand and flashes his light ahead. "She was here?"

"Yes." He glances at the door many yards away, not at the actual cellar door Anna was behind. "I think we're in the right place." Alec's index finger shows the way to safety, door number one.

Bruno shines his beam on the arching wood Alec approached first when the girl sent them there. An undeniable odor swirls the atmosphere the closer they get to the building. No mistaking decomposing flesh nearby. Bruno lifts his head and sniffs.

He smells it too.

A claw hammer hooks at his ribs between heartbeats. Safety is running back to the patrol car and planting his butt in the passenger seat. He nearly went there but kept his wits about him instead. Did he show him the right door? This was such an idiotic idea.

Play stupid and don't bring up the odor.

Bruno tries the door, it's unlocked and opens, and Alec breathes some relief. They didn't come through this one, he's sure of it.

"Step inside and pull it to you. Stay here. I'll take a look."

"What are you looking for? Anna didn't go inside," he lies.

"One minute." Bruno walks through; in lieu of waiting, Alec follows.

Trying to breathe normally, Alec feels the darkness weigh him down. He's expelling air at a faster rate than normal. Alec stops for a long while. "Officer Bruno?"

The officer finally appears from below, bathed in a light beam.

"Nothing here but a dusty basement. Let's go."

They enter the outside air, and free of that place, Alec reflexively groans.

"Claustrophobic?" Bruno asks.

"I like to see where I'm going. It's an old habit." His uneasy laughter echoes off the stone and brick.

Bruno inhales through his nose. "Smell that?"

"Yeah, smells like moldy bread," Alec lies again. *If he goes to the next door, he'll find Sorellina.* "It's getting late, Officer Bruno. I should check on Anna."

Bruno ignores Alec's objection and waves him toward the cellar. Decay grows stronger with each step, and dread creeps a sticky path across his skin. He's shivering as if someone threw a soft drink on him and then turned on a fan.

"Come inside and follow me. This door isn't shut. See there, it's ajar." He shines the light on the gap.

They locked it.

He visualizes the mechanism—lifted and not locked. Brad latched the door; he confirmed it. Someone came to this place after they left.

"Isn't this breaking and entering? We don't have a warrant." And this isn't the United States. Laws are different here.

"Mr. Zavos, please be quiet and watch yourself." Bruno's flashlight brightens the staircase, and they descend the same brick steps Anna walked, one at a time. The decomposition is sweeter, like a homemade jerky, in this part of the stairwell. His tongue sours. *That's sickening.*

Alec closes his eyes for a brief moment and tightens his abs, expecting the optics of a bloated corpse at the bottom. There's no preparing for Officer Bruno's reaction when he finds her.

"Are you coming?" Bruno directs the beam in Alec's face, and he stares straight into it, temporarily sending white dots dancing around where his sight used to be.

When his focus returns, the floor appears past the brick. Bare floor. A damp cellar with barrels lining one wall. Where'd she go?

"It stinks down here. What are they making in those casks?" The comments are convincing enough while covering his relief. Dead people don't get up and walk out on their own. Was she alive after all?

Officer Bruno continues his investigation around each of the oak barrels and hauls up a huge dead rodent by the tail.

"This must be what we're smelling. Coypu." He sniffs the biggest nutria Alec's ever seen, pulls away, and drops it on the floor. "To the car."

Springing up the steps, Alec shoots out the door before Bruno hits the first rung. Whoever claimed the woman's body might have left the rodent to cover the stench. The criminal discovery he'd feared didn't happen, and it won't without remains. Anna's off the hook for any suspicion of murder for now.

Their situation has changed again because someone knows Sorellina's dead.

He has an unimaginable decision to make.

Bruno won't be happy when he's told that Signorile isn't Alec's to sell.

CHAPTER

TWENTY-ONE

There's a light knock at the door that I recognize as Alec's.

"Anna, it's Alec. I have Officer Bruno with me. Are you sleeping?"

"I'm up. What's taken so long? I was about to send Brad to look for you."

Brad gets the door for me since my jaw is throbbing something awful, and I'd rather not move my head from its comfortable lounging position. Why did Alec bring this monstrous cop in full gear to our room after Bill said not to?

The officer's meaty arm leans against the threshold as Alec politely kisses my cheek.

"How's the headache?" Alec adds in a whisper, "You fell off the motorcycle. Migraine."

Tugging on his earlobe, I bat my lashes to let him know he's understood. "It's a dull roar, but I'll survive. How are you, Officer?"

He slowly closes the door. "I hear you took a fall today. Can you tell me anything about the man who kidnapped you? Identifying marks? Did he talk to you?"

Alec told him about the cyclist after all.

"The wind made it hard to hear, and I was too shocked and angry to notice much. He mostly ignored me."

"Anna, what did he look like? If you can recall the basics. I know it's not easy to think with a migraine." Alec narrows his eyes as if he's trying to tell me to be careful, as Brad skulks into a corner.

"No helmet, short, dark hair. Italian accent, of course." I splay my hands. "Sorry, that describes most men in Italy." I smile demurely, and Bruno returns it. He's not taking notes, so I've told him nothing more than he already knows.

"You have an injury. Did you get it looked at?" Bruno's hanging jowls and darting eyes give him a bulldog look, like he'd rather be sniffing out the creeps in town. His pointed chin doesn't fit though.

"The bandage makes it look worse than it is. I'm fine, thanks."

Alec turns to the officer. "There's nothing more we can tell you."

"Would you mind grabbing my purse on the dresser, Alec?" I may as well do a little playacting to move the conversation to a close. "I'd like my headache and queasy stomach to be over soon. The pills are in there."

Alec picks up the bag and drops it in my lap. "It's lighter. What did you take out, the Nikon?"

"Yeah, I had second thoughts about the camera in my tote and the rosary in my suitcase, so I switched 'em. The purse weighs less, but I wish the crucifix wasn't so huge. It doesn't fit anywhere. I'll remember to thank your mother when we get home." My laughter brings a glassy-eyed glare from Officer Bruno. "Did I say something weird?"

Everyone is gawking at the officer.

"Why thank Alec's mother? Did she give it to you?" Bruno takes out a notebook and scribbles a few lines. "May I see this item?"

I'm aware of being put under a magnifying glass. "The old rosary beads are pretty common. Not much to see."

Officer Bruno moves next to my chair, watching my actions closely, driving Alec to step protectively between us.

Unzipping the pocket, the beads slowly unravel from the immense cross. "It's a handful but not heavy. The best I've been able to determine, the beads are olive pits or bone."

Officer Bruno allows the strand to stretch to the floor and pores over each one, flipping the Madonna medal as I have.

"MC. I can't read the rest. May I take this with me?" Bruno's almost drooling over the rare article.

"Absolutely not. The rosary was a gift to me. Why do you want it?" Jumping up, I grasp the cross, dragging the bead string over the tile and stuffing it back into the pocket of my tote. *Mine.*

"Be careful with those." His dark brows arch high and bounce.

Alec encircles me with his arm and asks Bruno, "For what reason? We know they're old. Please explain."

Bruno's attention shifts to me. "I had an earlier conversation with Mr. Zavos about an item taken from a crime family."

He tells us about a dead Sicilian Mafia member. Bruno's account is familiar, but I try not to show it.

"Until now, I wasn't sure this rumor could be true. We assume the article taken was not money, but no one knows for certain." Bruno looks at Alec. "I've heard about a religious relic that belonged to an astronomer, but we dismissed it as gossip."

"Anna's crazy about historical pieces because she's an antiquities appraiser. My mother passed it on to her a day before our trip and told Anna a sister gave it to her in Bari. How's it tied to the Mafia?"

Bruno wrinkles his forehead and slides one hand into his pocket. "That doesn't match what we've heard."

"Of course it doesn't." Alec leaves me to sit on the bed. "It has nothing to do with the people you think it does."

"Mr. Zavos, may I interject here?" Brad waits for the go-ahead, then adds, "On the off chance you have *the* stolen item, do you want to be caught with something the Mafia wants? My strongest advice is to leave Italy at once."

"May we leave?" Alec asks Bruno.

He checks his watch. "Not tonight. We still have the Oliver King investigation, and you haven't been released by the officers on that case. I'll give you an authorization, but the *notaio* is closed until morning. Without it, you may be stopped at the airport. You arrived here private, not commercial, correct?"

"Yes. We have the corporate jet."

"I'll pen your request this evening." Bruno starts for the door. "Don't be foolish. Stay in your room tonight. We'll arrange your flight tomorrow."

"Wait. There's one more thing you should know." Alec scuffs his toe along the floor. "I haven't told this to anyone. I no longer own Signorile. That's why it's impossible to use it as a bargaining tool with the Mafia."

"Seriously? When did that happen?" I don't care if disappointment seeps into my tone. "I've been worried sick for you, Alec. With all we've been through, you couldn't trust me or Brad to keep your secret. That hurts."

The short meeting at the estate before we left for Italy. That's what they were doing in Alec's study with the attorneys and a notary. Preparing and signing documents.

"I didn't tell you because the deal made with Global Star Class hasn't been confirmed until I talk to Mom. You see, *she* owns Signorile. I'm superstitious about jinxing the sale if it hasn't finalized yet. Oliver King would know, but we didn't get a chance to talk. Keeping the details to myself seemed the right thing to do, but I see now it was a bad call. I'm sorry, Anna."

In a room full of stunned looks, the information hits Officer Bruno the hardest. I felt something in the works when we boarded the jet to meet Josh. Once Giuseppe Bruno leaves, Alec will be ready to spill what he's been keeping to himself since our arrival.

"Who's running Signorile now?" Bruno does an about-face as he reaches the door.

"Consider it on autopilot. My suggestion is to go with your original ambush idea in Palermo. It's the most straightforward plan, but we won't be a part of it. We'll be packed and at the airport by sunrise tomorrow. We leave with or without your authorization. Good night, Officer Bruno." Alec opens the door for a stupefied policeman at a loss for words and closes it behind him.

"Wow." Sitting in the chair feels good to my thighs. "I think he dropped his silver fillings at the door. We'd better check."

Alec spent the next hour going over the arrangement between himself and Gen. Although some intricacies of his corporate world flew over my head, the transfer made perfect sense. Gen already has a working relationship with Serge LeBlanc through the gallery, so any difficulties with the acquisition of Signorile by Global Star Class were made simpler by her involvement. Gen's late husband's business dealings were easily explained away, once Josh admitted to Bill, more or less, that he took the team's money. We can only surmise that Alec's dad thought Josh came by the loan money legally. The tabloid photos and story were sensational journalism, nothing more, thanks to Alec's ex, like the last story in *Reveal Reality*. Josh's facts may be squishy, but if anyone could convince LeBlanc of Pearce's innocence, it would be Gen.

"Oliver King might have come here to confirm the sale or celebrate with you." I'm saddened by that thought. "Such a shame. He seemed nice."

"His death was tragic." Alec reads from a small menu on the nightstand. He nods with a sinful gleam in his eyes as he rattles off a few sandwiches in Italian from the trifold card. "I have some other news." He's sitting on the bed cross-legged. "Sorellina's body was removed from the cellar, or she walked out on her own."

Brad's eyes flare. "Not possible. She had no heartbeat."

"How could you take Bruno there?" I ask Alec in horror.

"I let it slip that we felt as if we were being followed and had to explain why. That led Bruno to tell me about bad cops being paid off. He doesn't trust his own men."

"Do you trust Bruno?" Brad said what I was thinking.

"Could he be a Mafia informant? Please tell me that's not possible." I'm sick to my stomach at the thought and get up to pace the floor. "That's why he wanted the rosary. To use it to snare the Mafia."

"It's worse than that, and no, I don't think Giuseppe Bruno is a snitch for the Mob. He believes my grandfather stole a piece of history important to the Manettis, and they're searching for it to this day. The nun said as much."

Alec goes on to affirm the search for a missing Giambruno daughter from Bari, related to a man who died in prison.

"It fits, Alec."

"That's the conclusion I came to as well."

"What do you think happened to the woman in the cellar?" Brad is heavily invested in this conversation and takes over my empty chair. "Do you mind, Ms. Drury?"

"I mind being called Ms. Drury. Annalisse, please? You performed surgery on me, for Pete's sake. We should be on a first-name basis."

Alec laughs, and Brad manages a weak smile when he rarely lifts a brow my way.

"Someone tried to cover the decomp odor with a dead nutria. They look like giant rats. We found one in the cellar."

"It wasn't there earlier. We would've seen it." Italy is overrun with water rats.

Alec's phone rings, and he grabs it off the night-stand, glancing at the ID. He taps Speakerphone. "Hi, Bill. Sorry I forgot to call, we—"

"How fast can you pack and get to the airport?" Bill's tone raises my hackles.

"What's wrong?" I ask, glancing at Alec, who's also grown tense.

"I called Bruno to give him an update...and I have some, uh, startling news. They didn't want to tell me—Bruno is dead."

"No, that can't be." I'm the only one able to speak. "He left here a while ago."

"Slumped over his steering wheel about a block from the station. He was shot in the head. They wouldn't give me any details other than the window was down and he was seat belted inside. Pack up and check out *tonight*. Don't wait until tomorrow. It's doubtful anyone will expect you to leave in the dark unless the bed-and-breakfast is being surveilled. Can you do that?" Bill asks.

I run for the dresser drawers and remove garments, making a clothing pile on the floor near the suitcase.

"Bruno said we needed notarized paperwork, but we aren't going to get anything more from him, so we're outta here. Anna's already working on the suitcases."

"Call me from the tarmac. Good luck."

Alec ends the call and springs off the mattress.

"I'll stay here until you're ready. It won't take me two minutes in my room; I travel light. If that's fine with you." Brad slowly dons his jacket and stands at a parade rest, expressionless.

"I'll call the pilots and have them meet us at the plane," Alec adds, punching the first number to the screen.

"What about Stella? She's a couple of hours away. We won't have time to drag her out of the vet hospital this late. Alec?" Tears blur the objects in the room. I already know the answer.

"We'll make arrangements to have her shipped over, honey. We won't leave her here. Because Stella's developed an infection, she needs a doctor's care. They'd rather not release her this soon."

"An infection? When did you check on her?" I could've but didn't call the vet hospital myself. Stupid me. We've been caught up in ourselves and forgot about Stella. All except Alec; he remembered. My heart knows he didn't want to worry me about her infection, but I'm still disappointed at being taken out of the loop. Again.

I turn away, and my lungs are heaving with regret. I accidentally graze my hand against the bandage, then bite my tongue, sending pain ricocheting to and from the facial nerves I didn't know I had.

"Ow. Dang it." Zinging a pair of shorts across the room like a slingshot, the tears I've held back stream down my cheeks.

Alec lifts me from my buckled knees. "Anna, I've got this. Slow down. We have to focus on getting to the plane, but stay calm. Can you do that for me?" I'm in his arms in seconds.

We jog past the white posts lining the charter side of Bari's airport, toting luggage and ourselves onto a newly surfaced section in private aircraft parking. This is a small airport designed more for tourist traffic than its three hundred thousand locals. I'm grateful for fewer flights and little humanity during a weekday evening. Tourist season is winding down as ocean temperatures change and the days get shorter. There's a catch in my throat, and my spirits lift as I see Alec's Challenger parked where we left it a few days ago, straight across from the control tower. Runway lights dot the landscape, and blue taxiway globes seem to suspend in midair like during the Jewish holiday of Hannukah. No one is strolling the tarmac in the darkness from flight arrivals, which is fine by me. I won't breathe naturally again until we've taken off or, better yet, when we touch down in New York.

When we make it to charter parking, there's a crazy combo of jet fuel and dirt swirling in my mouth, not unlike the Manhattan taxis and their exhaust fumes. As I stare across the granite-colored tarmac, the interior lights are on in our plane. A thud, and the glistening hull door cracks open. Someone lowers the boarding steps for us, and relief washes over me. I glance behind at the path we took from the gate. No one has stopped us from leaving, and our pilots were allowed to file a flight plan, as usual. There are no official vehicles for carabinieri or Bari police in the lot. Maybe Officer Bruno lied to us so that we wouldn't leave the bed-and-breakfast before he could work on his rosary theories? Officer Bruno, close to retirement and too close to us for his own good. Since Turkey, we have that effect on people.

I have tons of questions only Gen can answer, but that'll have to wait until we get to the estate. Having Alec unable to contact his mother when security took their phones has made him moody and anxious, although he won't admit it. I've been plenty punchy myself.

The unknown and outlandish Sister Mary Natalina is mind-boggling and may require Gen's help to unravel the nun's knowledge of the rosary and why she brought her own family into this. I have to remember to mention that strange blue birthmark on her hand. That may trigger Gen's memory. The sister said she wouldn't mention the rosary to her family, but she might have changed her mind and alerted them.

"Annalisse." Brad takes me from my reverie, tugs at the luggage handle I'm gripping, and rolls the soft side bag up the steps. It's easier to move than planned because we didn't hit any shops.

We moped around and did nothing but eat because that's what *I* wanted. Alec would've taken me anywhere. In hindsight, we should've canceled the whole Bari excursion once we'd talked to Josh in Lecce. No, much earlier than that. After the tabloid printed Pearce's picture, and what's with the strange bird feather and pin? There's something missing from the Alvarez case that's clawing at my sense of logic. Stella belongs to someone, but Sorellina didn't seem that concerned for a pet owner and never cited the cat's injury. She didn't know about the broken leg. Supposedly, Stella belongs to an abusive man because Benita Alvarez told Josh so. Could Stella's abuser be the same person who put Sorellina in the cellar with me?

Whatever the missing link is, Bill will figure it out.

"Ready to go, babe?" Alec wrinkles his nose.

"You bet." I scrunch mine in return.

Alec inches me in front of him, and we climb aboard and buckle into our comfortable recliners.

At the end of the runway, vibrations shake the cabin while we wait through the run-up checklist where both pilots go through a manual to ensure all operations used during flight are in perfect order prior to takeoff. Alec encourages me to go to the cockpit and watch them on every trip, but I always decline. It's too technical and would give me more theories and reasons to believe we will crash. Dreading the fall from the sky keeps my acrophobia amused enough.

The jet brakes shimmy prior to takeoff, then I notice reflections in the window from a slew of vehicles entering the empty lot at the terminal.

Polizia and Carabinieri are inscribed on each car.

"Alec. Look." I direct him to the vehicles as our plane pivots into place on the runway numbers. My stomach sloshes side to side as the brakes release and our tires thump down the asphalt.

Brad's watching the cars too while whistling our founding hymn, *My Country 'Tis of Thee*, but as a Brit, he knows it as *God Save the Queen*.

CHAPTER
TWENTY-TWO

Hours into our flight, after unbuckling myself from the rigid recliner, I swivel toward Alec dozing off in his comfortable section of the couch. After a full-body stretch and a few deep knee bends, my envy gets the best of me while watching the rise and fall of his chest—a man sleeping in total relaxation. Some might call it the sleep of the dead, but it's more like the sleep of the unknown. He hasn't made a twitch or turn in the cushions—just soft, even breathing—since we reached altitude.

We've been here before.

His dark lashes flutter, and he slowly draws up one corner of his mouth. Wrinkled clothing worn since yesterday, along with the sexy, unshaven appearance of the corporate guy who's stuffed too many meetings in one day, make me wonder what he's smiling at in the exhausted state he's in. Alec's ruggedly handsome like his Greek father, more now than before, or his dark stubble is playing tricks on me. When we met last year, I saw his mother's fire and determination and his dad's sense of duty, but most of all, Alec is his own man who respects his friends and places them at the front of the line without being obvious he's taking a back seat. I see that now. He's been in plain sight while I've been searching someplace else, like Kate who took off after that gut-wrenching letter she dropped on me. Who does that?

I did that.

To him.

Alec brought me to Italy not to unload Signorile like he sold the trip to me but to introduce me to places I've heard of only in books. Places he's already traveled to—for me to experience with him. He and his mother had worked out the business aspect long before we left. The thrust behind Alec's drive isn't money and power. His ambitions are more similar to mine than I've understood.

A reminder to myself that a thousand women would uproot themselves from their current lives for a future with Alec Zavos. To have the affection of a life force who has proven many times that he's supportive and loving. Oblivious, I've taken so much love for granted, and I've pushed it aside. For what? Better timing? Accepting his mother's offer as business partner and at the same time declining a marriage with a man whom I deeply love and admire. What message have I sent to Alec?

On bad days when I'm missing my friend, Samantha, my loneliness is so devastating that I sit on the bed and stroke Boris, just to sink my palm into his healing fur. I yearn to possess what I already have… Alec wants me in his life. Me. Sometimes a scatterbrain but *a well-meaning one*, his mom likes to say. Thank God he sees me for who I am.

Samantha was right about me. I lose my best friend, almost my only friend, and simply close the door on others. Except Chase. I'm surprised he hasn't run away as well. All I've done is put Alec off, turn him down, or complain that he works too much. I'm lucky he's still around. Smiling to myself, I recall the abbreviation Samantha used for me. TSTL, too stupid to live. She's gotta be looking in right now, rolling with laughter.

Aw, Sam, I wish we could laugh about it together, and I could tell you how right you were.

It's hard to shut down thoughts and rest because we're flying.

"Can't sleep?" Brad asks. "I don't sleep well on aircraft either." He unbuckles and sits on the sofa across from me. He likes to make direct eye contact when he speaks, I've found. "How's your jaw? If it's bothering you, I can fix that."

"You're a godsend, Brad. The ibuprofen is enough to keep me from thinking about it. Thank you though." My leg's going to sleep, so I shift and cross the other one. "I've wondered what really happened to Sorellina at the bottom of the stairs. Could she have been alive and walked out of there?"

"No. She was removed to cover the mishap."

"Mafia?"

"I don't know her motive for being in the cellar, nor would I speculate on the players. Pardon me for saying this... I'm glad she's gone, and you weren't implicated."

"I wish I could snap my fingers and our jet arrives in New York in the next fifteen minutes. Long flights, any flights, mess with the vibration of my entire body. Being out of contact with Alec's mother for so long is hard. I don't get the reason for keeping Gen quiet. Bill wasn't *that* convincing about taking phones away from Helga and Gen. We don't know if they're okay. What if there's an emergency?" I ask.

"They have added security and that Mr. Mason." Brad's telling me what I want to hear, but he's forming his own ideas behind calculating eyes. "I wouldn't worry."

"Wish we had more information on this." Opening the pocket where the rosary lies, one more time the cross beckons me. There's a great sense of sorrow in these beads. The sister who owned them felt pain and suffering, perhaps from her alcoholic, sickly sibling or from Galileo, her father, whose anguish she experienced while nursing him. His later years were riddled with illness—shunned and imprisoned at home by the church because of his planetary beliefs that didn't match the pope's. The rosary emits a strong history. It's easy to believe this *is* the missing treasure from the Manettis and it did belong to Galileo's daughter. The inscribed initials are enough to convince me.

"May I see that, Annalisse?" Brad calling me by name feels foreign, but I like the way he says it.

"I wish I had the jeweler's loupe from the shop. There may be details we've missed." The rosary tumbles from my hands into his.

Brad observes the cracks and fine details between the beads and spends time on how the crucifix attaches

274

to the five-decade rosary. He's forming his own opinion about its history.

"Very old craftmanship. So fragile; you must be careful with it. Have you ever been to the British Museum? If not, you have to visit sometime; I know you would enjoy it."

"I've heard London museums are fantastic. I could spend days wandering the eons."

"And not see all of it. Millions of articles on display span centuries. Natural history, military history, there's so much to see. I've been through them on many occasions." Brad carefully wraps the beads around the cross and hands them to me. "I'd put that into a safe when we get to the estate."

Alec's smiling in his sleep again, and I'm dying to know what he's dreaming about instead of worrying like I'm in a flimsy paper airplane zooming above the clouds.

"We have so many unanswered questions that are driving me crazy. We're missing something important. What do you think, Brad?"

"I believe if you find the person who committed the crime in Lecce, you will have the answers to the rest."

"Sorellina is Benita Alvarez's sister. Let's begin there." At the bottom of my purse is a small tablet and next to it, the blackbird pin. "This bird business means something too." I toss the pin to Brad. "If we record everything chronologically, something will gel."

"I'll help if I can." Brad sinks into the sofa cushion, gazing at the lapel pin.

"If you recall anything as we talk, please interrupt so I can add it. I value your opinion. Okay, from the top: Alec walks into the gallery with the tabloid. Pearce is accused of embezzlement. Alec worked with Bill Drake years ago on this same possibility. When Alec fears his dad might have taken money, he has Bill stop his investigation."

"I didn't know that," Brad says, leaning his head back.

"Alec feels that Josh Jennings is the one person left with direct knowledge of how Signorile began financially. Josh contacts Alec and we fly to Lecce and find him in the middle of a murder investigation, because Benita was found in Josh's office. Huh." I lift my pen when I recall something. "I'm sent the bird feather and find the bird pin in my purse while on the plane. I didn't notice the bird earrings when the woman dressed in red came into the gallery. Sorellina did have bird earrings in the cellar."

"Keep the birds in the back of your mind. Go ahead, Annalisse."

"What time is it?" Alec asks, groggily.

My lungs deflate. "Oh shoot. I woke you. I'm sorry, hon. Good dreams? I have to ask since you seemed to be enjoying yourself."

He muses for a while. "Who knows? After I close my eyes, I don't remember what goes on." Alec yawns. "How long have I been out?"

"I'm guessing an hour."

His silver eyes brighten. "The nap helped."

"Was there hatred between the two sisters?" Brad asks.

"Sibling rivalry is always a possibility. Benita had Stella Notorious Kitty with her, and Sorellina asked about the cat on two occasions that we know of. Could they have been in love with the same man?" My shrug makes Alec grin. "The deadly triangle. Women go insane when they're fighting over a guy."

"Or she's a ballplayer who knows how to swing a bat."

I'm not laughing, but Brad finds Alec's taunt mildly pleasant.

"Seriously though, the blow to Benita's head is what finally took her out. Drugs in her system made her compliant, a substance like gin in her hair, and wrists clawed up with razor wire is quite an operation for one person, especially when you said Sorellina was a petite girl. Not to mention tying Benita to the chair. If Sorellina planned to kill her sister in Lecce, someone else was also there to help her." Alec's conjecture brings agreement from Brad.

"If Sorellina had an accomplice, that person might show up after Benita's drugs took effect. Benita might not have seen a helper." I'm madly scribbling on the tablet. "Who would work with Sorellina to commit a murder? The boyfriend who chooses Sorellina over Benita? The owner of the missing cat or someone who wanted to make sure Benita was dead, like Josh? Alvarez might have made plenty of enemies. Extorting Josh for money could've been her style."

"Premeditated." Brad shifts his weight on the couch. "The deed was planned."

Alec releases his belt and straightens his spine. "If Sorellina offed her sister, this world is safer without her in it."

That's a strong statement coming from Alec.

I'm taken to the top of the stairs again, fumbling with the tiny key knife hidden in my hand, watching a woman torn by uncertainty. To kill me and run, or stay and face Alec on the other side of the door. She could've grabbed my leg as I kicked, if she were ready for it, and we both would've landed at the bottom of the staircase. A chill shakes me out of the realm that didn't happen.

My fingers tug at a key from the pocket lining—the tiny knife so underestimated and ready to spring. "Sorellina's passion for all things red went to the extreme, like the blood on the floor in Josh's office. I wouldn't put it past her to hang around and watch her sister suffer and take snacks for later." The shudder closes my eyes for a second. "She's my first honest-to-goodness experience with bloodlust. I may never look at blood the same way again. Ick. Sorellina is a common denominator: the attempted robbery at the gallery, her relationship to Benita, her friendship with Joey Calico, and her appearance in Bari."

"We may be making her fit the profile because she had opportunity," Brad says.

"Yeah, she'd have a lot of ground to cover—flights alone are expensive for someone who doesn't appear to hold a real job. We can hope Sorellina's death is the end of our part in this, and that she was the mastermind of the killings." I feel that sentiment is optimistic.

"Other than Oliver King and Giuseppe Bruno. Sorellina was already dead prior to Bruno's shooting in his patrol car. There may be two separate operations. Benita and the cat being the first and Mafia business the second." Alec gets a nod from Brad.

"On the other hand, having the Mafia behind every killing wouldn't be a shock, given what we've heard from Officer Bruno and Bill," I add.

"Anna in her rose-colored glasses." Alec smiles. "We left loose ends in Italy. The endgame hasn't been reached." Alec sighs. "I'll feel a lot better when we see Mom and confront her about the Giambruno legacy."

"Why you, Annalisse?" Brad asks. "Picked up by police and dropped in the cellar with that...girl."

"Anna might have been seen carrying the cat crate from Josh's office or into the vet hospital." Alec pierces me with a sharp glare. "I know those sad green eyes. Have I ever let you down, babe? The hospital will call when Stella is ready to travel."

"Why kill Oliver King? Isn't his death related to the Signorile sale and not the cat?" I ask Alec. "How do the bird feathers, earrings, and pin fit the narrative?"

"That began at the gallery. There may not be a connection," Brad says quietly.

"The girl in red showed up there first. So did the envelope with a single feather. Anna noticed the bird earrings in the cellar." Alec's put it together.

"It was me who had the encounter with Sorellina at the shop. *I* was given the rosary beads. *I* insisted we take Stella. *I* was on the beach and saw the jogger when Oliver was knifed, then taken to the cellar, and found vague rosary ties to Sister Mary Natalina. I'm in all places where meaningful events took place."

"The motivation is money. It's always money and sometimes revenge thrown in." Brad speaks in low tones. "It's possible that forces have collided, and there may be many motives joined together for one goal."

"The Mafia protection payments haven't been paid, and Bruno wants Signorile sold to them to dispel the debt. Where would a shady idea like that come from, unless Bruno had ties to the Mob?" Alec looks up at the headliner. "Dad, if you're listening, the Cosa Nostra will *never* get Signorile from me."

My breath catches at the sweeping misery fused into Alec's words. Losing parents to criminals is a wound that rarely heals completely. The pain comes back with each little reminder of those whom we've lost. Alec's jaw clenches, and tears are working on me too. Clearer thinking and wiser decisions.

His.

Mine.

Ours.

The circumstances shrouding us involve a complicated riddle of multiple deaths and few clues, connected to—whom? Gen, Alec, Josh, or is it me driving a killer? It can't be me. I've never met Benita Alvarez.

In a sheepish grin, I pat Alec's thigh. "Incoming."

The space between him and the armrest barely contains my hips, but on an angle, I manage to snake myself around him to unleash a smoldering kiss. We've had so few intimate moments together on this trip, I couldn't help myself. Alec tastes of sweet caramel and the coffee candy he ate before he fell asleep, and it's heavenly.

When we eventually come up for air, he's rosy red, the shade of intense joy.

He observes me quizzically. "I don't know what I did to deserve that."

My hand laces with his, giving me time to whisper in his ear, "Thank you for being my umbrella in the rain—my storm shelter against the elements. Faults and all, I'm yours—I love you, Alec."

I dip my lips to his, ignoring Brad's eyes on us, then stop before making contact. *Bill, we forgot.*

When I jump into a recliner, I feel Alec's wanton stare on my back.

"Anna, wait. Don't go."

"Did you happen to text Bill when we boarded? Our call from the tarmac?" I know Alec forgot once we saw the police lining up at the terminal building. We were too happy congratulating ourselves on our stealthy getaway to think about Bill.

Alec gapes as he looks for his phone.

"Let him know we made it out of Bari. By now he probably figures we ran into officials."

"We did, sort of." Alec turns on his phone and grimaces. "He's going to think I neglect him on purpose." He scrolls. "He left a message. I'll drop a note to meet us at the plane when we touch down. If he can." Alec looks at his watch. "Eleven hours to New York, give or take. Minus two."

While Alec messages, I ask Brad, "How can I thank you for what you did in Bari? Name it." I gesture to my bandage. "If anyone had found the woman's body…" I stretch over and ask softly, "I'm gonna have nightmares about Sorellina's knife. What did you *really* find at the bottom of the stairs?"

Brad shrinks and turns away.

We aren't friends, and I'm a fool to think so.

"Bill's taken care of." Alec glances at Brad, then me. "What happened?"

Brad quietly returns to his original seat near a window, putting space between us.

"What's that doing out?" Alec's looking at the prayer beads strewn outside my tote bag. "Still trying to uncover its secrets?"

"Riddles, you mean? Why was Giuseppe Bruno taken out, unless he knew too much? Gen didn't lie about how she ended up with the rosary. She looked me in the eyes, Alec. Your grandfather might have landed into Mafia territory and been in prison because of it, but your mother not telling you is hard to wrap my head around. I trust my own historical research and won't get pulled into another officer's little notebook— about us and some Mob family. Some theories are just too weird to believe."

Alec's staring off toward one of the circular windows.

"Alec?"

"Suppose the rosary did belong to Galileo's daughter, and the Manettis had it because of its historical value. What if Granddad gifted it to the novice, Sister Mary Margaret, to bury it forever? The sister might have felt it belonged to Mom, so she gave it to her, having no knowledge of its origin. That would take my granddad out of the picture. Bruno said the Mafia wouldn't stop looking until they found this missing *thing* stolen from them, and they would kill anyone for knowing their business. He predicted his own ending. What I don't understand is how Granddad figured out the rosary was our heritage. How did he know to steal the beads out of a safe? Are the beads the missing item, or is it something more valuable like gold?"

"What if the Manettis are also related to the Galileo family? The sister said something about that." I feel like we've landed on an iceberg in the North Atlantic. *Shake it off, Annalisse.* "No one knows we have the rosary."

"Unless…when Bruno was found in his car, didn't he have his notebook? He had it on him when he left our room." Alec's point strikes a nerve.

Brad nods. "I see. The officer's killer might have searched him and found his book."

"With our names in it, including his notes on the rosary beads and crucifix." I groan. "Just because we're almost home, doesn't mean that we're almost safe."

Alec takes a long breath. "Bill doesn't know to ask about the notebook. If it was recovered on Bruno, the Bari police have it. If not… we may not be done with the Italian authorities yet, babe. The little gathering at the airport may be a prelude for the main event."

CHAPTER
TWENTY - THREE

Sitting underneath crooked limbs in the shade of orange groves with crates of oranges at his feet, Joey Manetti forgot how awesome blood oranges are. He picked fruit as a kid like many of his friends and didn't notice the oranges much because it was dirty work, and the branches scratched and tore at his arms. Sticky juice runs through his fingers from the bumpy peel he's holding. There's nothing like the candy of home, melting on the tongue to bring you back. Blood oranges always taste sweeter in Sicily. How does a citrus massage feel? He'll have to request that from his gorgeous masseuse when he gets back to Staten Island. Someone has this fruity oil. If not, he'll make some up and bottle it under the Manetti label. Citrus is the family's lifeblood—the Manetti trees that his papa planted with his own hands. He and his mama raised the lemon and orange groves from tiny sticks and seeds given to them by neighbors. It's taken fifty years to build heavy lemons and giant Taroccos on this farm. Manetti Sicilian citrus is superior to the rest—and it finally belongs to him.

A scooter turns down the row at the far end of the grove—the pain in his butt that won't go away since he got here. So much for a little R and R before the task at hand—the gathering for his papa's rosary.

Uncle Carlo's Vespa whips between the tree trunks, and he stops near the one next to his, leaning the bike against the bark. He's sweaty and hasn't put a razor on his face for three days and is still in the same lounge pants and robe. Doesn't anybody bother to shower and get dressed during mourning? Carlo shames the family.

"Uncle Carlo, where are your shoes? You have slippers on."

"I heard something. We'd better talk."

"How long before the... you know, the thing?" Joey drops the last orange segment in his mouth and wipes the red juice on his jeans. "Shouldn't you be getting ready?"

"Joey, get off your butt when I talk to you." His uncle lectures as if he were a child.

Joey fondles the horn on his necklace and jumps to his feet, literally inches away from stepping on Carlo's toes. At that angle, on higher ground, he's looking down at Uncle Carlo's eyebrows, smiling at his unease at having a towering presence so close—Joey smells the extra garlic his uncle added to his *trapanese* pasta for lunch.

"If we're going to view Pops before my sisters arrive, we should be there by three. I don't want to be late. Is the limo ready?" Joey asks.

"That's a concern. I don't think using the limo is a good idea. The heat—"

"I know, the heat is on, so what's new? The heat's always on." His foot grazes the dirt and leaves a cloud behind. "We should go in the limo and be comfortable. Pops would approve it."

"We'll stick out at the funeral home with nobody else there. I don't advise it, especially with blood on our hands and a dead cop." Carlo makes a sound like a toilet flushing.

"Who bit the big one?"

"In Bari. The scum was going to rat us out. One of our men inside took care of it. See, Joey, it pays to have people hooked up in the police. Our insider warned us about this cop. We got his notebook, and guess what it said? Giuseppe Bruno, the cop, was onto what Giambruno stole. It's the closest we've been to getting it back for the family. Too bad they got sloppy and killed him. He would've been more useful alive. Too much killing in Puglia lately."

"I'm already working on the prayer beads with our cousin. We don't need law enforcement help. It's too dangerous around police." Joey props his foot against the tree trunk and pushes. "So, what's in the cop's book?"

"Dates, times, and locations. Bruno made sure he didn't name names."

"What good are locations... for what, his favorite cannoli stop? Sounds like a bunch of nothing to me. I'd like to see this book. *You* take care of it after the funeral. I've got more pressing things in New York to iron out." Body odor from Carlo's robe hits him full-on.

"Get a shower; you'll feel better. I want to leave in thirty minutes."

"Hey, I'm still your elder. It's only me, Mario, and you—let's take the Maserati. It's more incognito." Carlo's lips tighten as he folds his arms across his chest. "We should do this."

"BS. I'm not sitting on my uncle's lap in a two-seater sports car. No way. What about the war with the Fricanos? They know our Maserati. The seating is too tight for the three of us, unless you want me to stay behind, which is fine by me." Joey's silently hoping he'll agree, but his uncle doesn't crack a smile. "Okay, so me staying behind is a bad idea. Where are the family cars anyway? They aren't in the garage."

"That's because your uncle can't be trusted to practice too close to the house. Not since the explosion when Mario messed up the wiring. Leo didn't have time to show Mario how to inspect and correct the bomb setup. That's up to me now." Carlo points to the end of the groves. "The cars are covered in the old goat barn. We haven't driven the Maserati coupe in a while, and it'll be good to take it for a spin." Uncle Carlo cinches his robe with the belt.

"We go in the limo. Forget about it, and tell Mario to spray it for bugs. No telling what's crawling around in that scuzzy old place." Joey picks at the scaly bark, leaning into the tree. "The Bari murder is a long way from here. The police are looking for the cop killer four hundred miles away."

"Joey, there's paper on all of us, you included. We have to be careful; these cops talk to each other. One stupid move, and we go down, bullets flying."

Joey taps his watch. "Twenty minutes, Uncle Carlo. I'm leaving with or without you. Have Uncle Mario get the limo out and clean it up."

"*Stupido.*" Carlo pulls an orange off the tree and throws it three rows over, when Joey knows he'd rather do that with his head. "*Pazzo.* You never listen." Carlo raises his hands, then maneuvers his slippers through the weeds to the Vespa. "I'll be ready. So will the limo. Are you goin' with stained pants?"

"I brought slacks."

The only noise Carlo makes is a grunt, and he speeds off down the aisle, spitting dust from the tires.

Scrolling his contacts, Rave's number springs up for the call. The Raven's late for check-in, and Joey wants to know why.

Finally a connection, then a sigh. "*Come va?* What's the word? Tell me something good." Joey waits for his answer through dead air. "Rave?"

"Can I call you back, Joey? I'm in the middle of something." He's huffing and puffing like he's running a marathon.

"*Bocca al lupo.* A full report when you call." The joker's been out a few weeks, and already he's handing out headaches.

"*Crepi il lupo.* Back in thirty minutes," Rave says. The call ends.

I wished him luck for what? Pete, what are you doing?

Sprawled out against the soft leather with straight bourbon in his glass, Joey feels his uncles' vacant stares at his drink, counting how many he's had. Their glares are working out if he's sober, like it's a problem when he's not driving. They've been following his moves since he walked in the door from the airport, and he's sick of it.

"What's up?" Joey holds his drink so that he can hear the ice tinkle against the crystal. "It's after lunch. Is there a law against having a bourbon in the afternoon?" The gulp burns the back of his throat, but it's a good singe.

"*Ubriaco.* You drink too much. By dinner you can't walk straight." Carlo sneers in his pious way.

He should talk, pouring whiskey into his morning coffee and sucking it down all day as if nobody notices his breath. Jealousy ain't pretty on an old man, but Joey enjoys the irony. Carlo expected to own the Manetti spread and become head of the family, waiting on the Birdman hand and foot as a manservant from the old South would. Instead, the plan blew up, and Uncle Carlo can't stand it.

"Surprised you didn't bring your k-kitty along." Uncle Mario wrinkles his nose. "Your cat stinks like the p-potty box."

Joey gets it. He doesn't like cats. His loss.

The limo driver knocks on the glass divider, and they're off to the funeral home to make a showing for Pops. Joey doesn't look forward to seeing him all made up like a fake doll in the casket. A shiver runs down his back when he thinks that one day it'll be his turn to entertain the gawkers.

Joey's phone rings, and it's the Raven calling back. "What's so important you rushed me off last time?"

"I had an appointment with a cat."

"Hey, good deal. You found her." He takes another sip and smiles. "What's—"

A rumble, static, then the line cuts out. *Where'd he go?* Peter Gregory, aka the Raven, holds his phone out, stares at it, and places it against his ear again. Did the phone die? Can't be. The line at the top says it's at eighty percent. What happened to Joey Calico?

Peter tries Joey again.

It doesn't ring.

Another time, and the same dead air. Nothing.

"Maybe his battery died, or it's a bad connection. The satellite dropped, or the tower went out. Whatever. I couldn't care less how cell phones work, and I don't have time for an internet lesson on how sound moves over the ocean." Peter turns off his phone so that he won't forget to later and then shoves it into the waterproof sleeve. "Something sure as hell happened. He'll leave me a message when he can."

The nineteenth-century pocket watch his brother-in-law Harry Carradine gave him is working great when he remembers to wind it. It's the last personal item he had restored before they hauled him away in cuffs and closed the shop. At least Joey stuck some of the art in his vault for safekeeping before Westinn shut its doors. Not enough to open a new gallery in Manhattan, but there may be enough pieces to start a small shop in Jersey, if he can get his hands on the cache.

"Shift change in ten minutes." The watch case snaps shut. "Time to wrap this up. Better get down there and disable the alarm system for the homecoming. There's plenty to do."

Gwen couldn't finish it, but he will. *Sorry, sweet thing. I wish you were with me for the finale.* He thought the job was done in Bari. This whole thing is so scrumptious, he can't stop thinking about it. Christmas comes early for ol' Pete. It's gonna feel so good to see them squirm, with Pete at the helm again.

"I never expected a twofer when Gwen asked me for help with Benita the catnapper. Ben, you weren't getting away with Stella that easily."

Joey has spies everywhere.

You stole my cat, you witch.

Everybody pays for taking property that don't belong to them.

Peter had eight long months to plan how he'd take smug looks from the snooty gallery people who prospered while he sat in prison.

"Won't you be surprised to see me after all this time, Ann, with your hoity-toity Greek millionaire who's using you for his pleasure. Let's see how much *you* like being on the receiving side of the pepper spray."

CHAPTER
TWENTY - FOUR

Upstate New York

The Mulsanne's seat adapts to my body like a comfy, broken-in driving glove, and my eyelids are heavy from daylight streaming through the windows, warming the leather. If it weren't for the pebble swimming in my eye, I'd be taking a nap. What I wouldn't give for one restful night's sleep at Alec's estate. We're all so drained from our "vacation," there's no need for a repeat trip in our future. As nice as the bed-and-breakfast was, we didn't have time to enjoy the grounds or the authentic architecture both inside and outside our room. How could we? Oliver's murder on the beach and Sorellina's knife to my throat ended every last hope of one romantic, stress-free day in Bari.

I glance at the back of Brad's head in the front seat and smile, feeling safe with Alec belted beside me and his bodyguard at the Bentley's wheel. We may never know what Brad actually discovered in the cellar when I ran out of there. That evil person groaning on the floor after her fall might have been Sorellina in the death throes. There was always that risk of a falling injury, but the knife in her chest after being kicked hadn't made my wildest dreams. A living being with blood in its veins, about to take its last breath, is a hard thing to watch. Glad I missed Sorellina's end.

She's not worth thinking about.

She's gone, and it's over.

"You haven't said four words since we left the airport. What's on your mind, Alec?" My eye is driving me nuts as I rub it again, which only worsens the burn. "Where did I put the darn mirror?" Looking in the bottom of my purse, it dawns on me. "I stuck it in the drawer with the pistol when I added all my makeup." A lot of good it did. I barely used lipstick. "Would you look for a bug or a grain of sand in my eye?" I draw down my lower lid and turn so Alec can check my tearing left eye.

"It's red, but I can't see anything obvious. Close your eyes. Rubbing isn't helping." He kisses my brow. "We'll wash it out with some saline when we get home."

Through blurry vision, I study Alec's profile as he looks beyond the window. He's been zoning out since he mentioned Officer Bruno's little notebook. We don't know what's in it, and if it lands in the wrong hands…

His phone sounds like an angel's harp, the new tone he set for text messages. *We can all use a little divine intervention*, he'd said.

When he doesn't look up, I ask, "Who's that?"

He scans the screen some more and rests his head against the seat back, staring at the roof in silence.

That's not good.

Alec passes his phone to me so that I can read the breaking news headline about a car bombing in Palermo.

I don't want to see boring news because my teeth ache from the constant pain in my jaw. "Do you know the victims?"

"Drake sent it. No identifications yet. Man." He swipes through his hair. "I can't rest until I know who was in that car. To hell with it." Alec's phoning someone. "Bill, it's me. Are you at Brookehaven yet?" Alec listens and nods. "Okay. We've got plenty to talk to you about too. Have they given out the victims' names?" A pause. "When you hear anything, let me know." He checks his Rolex. "We should be rolling in about forty minutes. See ya then." Alec ends the call and purses his lips. "No identifications made to the media yet. They'll keep it quiet until they can identify the remains, and the next of kin is notified."

"Bill's already at Brookehaven?" I ask.

"No, but he'll beat us there. I'm calling Vincenzo at the plant. I have to know if any of my guys could've been in that blast." He finds his manager's number and calls with a smile as wide as I've seen all week. "Vincenzo, *buon pomeriggio*, it's Alec. Is everyone all right at Signorile?"

The conversation lasts about three minutes, and Alec tucks his phone away in the door pocket.

"They heard the blast, but Vincenzo says everybody's okay from assembly." Alec exhales loudly. "We got out of there just in time."

"Sicily is hundreds of miles from where we were."

Alec gives me the look.

"When this is over—I mean really over—and it's confirmed you and Gen are out of Signorile entirely, take me to New Zealand where no one knows you or your family." I give him my look. "As long as there are no Zavos ties, we may need the diversion before you start your vet practice at Brookehaven."

"You're on." His rumbling laughter is comforting, and his palm cradling my knee feels even better. "No mix with business, only pleasure. We go for the breathtaking snowscapes and giant flocks of sheep. Fair enough?" He unbuckles his seat belt and slides next to me. "There's important, unfinished business between us." Alec pinches me, playfully.

"Ah, no business, remember. There you go, breaking your own rules."

I must have dozed the last half hour of the ride with my head on Alec's shoulder, but the thing in my eye still plagues me. Out of habit, I rub my lid, and it waters from the corner.

"Almost there, babe. Feel better?" Alec moves hair out of my good eye. "You're squinting. Your jaw's sore, isn't it? One of the first stops after we dump off the luggage is to get it looked at by a professional. Stitching you up in a hotel room in clean conditions is one thing, but the chance for infection from Italian cooties isn't worth the risk. Let's set up an online doctor visit and see what they say."

"They'll want to look at Brad's handiwork in person."

He grins. "I'm counting on it. They can also prescribe the right meds for you."

"Can't you dig in your vet meds and find something similar? I don't have it in me to wait in emergency or sit in a doctor's office. I've heard of some vets using their supplies for themselves." I gently tug on his shirt button.

"And get my license pulled? Not me." Alec shakes his head. "My vet stash is for the animals. Forget about skipping the doctor visit. Infections are bad news, and you don't want one near your jaw." He's scrutinizing the bandage, twisting his mouth the entire time. "Gauze looks clean, but I don't like the redness on your throat. If we can get in to see someone today, you'll feel better, and so will I."

"'Kay, Doc Zavos. Whatever you think, but I hope they don't want to redo any stitches. Once is enough. Is that Bill's blackout SUV by the brood mare barn?"

My gesture points to the new digs for the Walker Farm sheep. Alec graciously loaned me his stables while the new barn's being built. Jeremy Walker, Kate's son, couldn't wait for us to take the sheep and horses from the place. He'd asked Alec to purchase the farm, but I couldn't allow Jeremy to rip off a buyer just because I wanted the property, and Alec has the money. Alec planned to purchase Walker Farm for me, but I declined it at three times the value.

"Looks like Bill's car. Why is he parked way out there?" Alec's surveying both sides of the estate. "It has to be his rig. I don't see the other security. Mason might have taken off when Bill arrived. Brad, drop us at the stables, please."

"Alec, I have to get inside and find a mirror. My eye is watering so badly I can't see anything out of it. I'll check on Gen and Helga, then I'll meet you at the stables. Okay?"

It takes Alec a few seconds to ponder, but he eventually agrees to drop me off at the house.

"Don't be long. I'll check in with Bill, and we'll wait for you there." Alec launches a lightning-quick kiss that makes it to my ear, and I'm out of the Bentley with nothing more than my leather bag.

I can't wait to get this demon out of my eye. Jogging up the walkway, a sixth sense slows my pace.

One of the estate doors to Brookehaven is open a crack. Why isn't the alarm blaring?

Helga knows to set it and lock the doors at all times, especially with Gen there and Boris inside.

"Helga?" I call out in a normal voice, creeping up to the landing. In a crouch below the kitchen window, my phone's on long enough to text Alec. If Helga accidentally didn't close the door hard enough, I don't want to get her in trouble with the boss man. Alec's door lectures aren't fun. That doesn't explain the security though. Maybe it's a silent alarm. What if things aren't okay inside the house? I erase the earlier message and tell him to grab Bill and come to the house as soon as he reads this. Did Alec take his phone out of the car door pocket?

My Smith and Wesson is in the home secretary drawer along with my compact. I need to get there first.

The only noises around me are birds chirping and falling leaves hitting the walkway, helped along by a slight breeze. Neither Helga nor Gen are talking indoors, which is unlike the two of them together. Naptime? It's possible in the middle of the afternoon, although Gen's hardly fond of sleeping during the day. If Helga is in the kitchen, she'll see me.

With one good eye, I scan the driveways from the estate to the stables for unusual vehicles, but there aren't any cars other than Bill's SUV. No one is walking around either. The guys could be anywhere.

Slowly lifting myself but staying low, I creep to the door and push it open just enough to snake my way inside, checking for human beings in the dark entry and kitchen with the light off.

That kitchen light stays on until Helga turns it off at night before bed. This is unusual.

The hair stands straight on my arms as I look around a vacated house. No sounds of Helga's humming or footsteps on the upper floor.

I stop short of clicking the main door closed behind me and shut one eye to get an unobstructed view.

"Helga?" I whisper, standing tall. "Gen?"

Setting my tote on the floor, I carefully pull out the drawer on the secretary and feel around the side compartment.

My gun's missing.

The mirror is still here. What did I do with it? I'm sure I placed it in the drawer. Someone moved it. Helga might've if she saw it out of place, but why would she bother with it while we were gone?

Something yellow flaps near the refrigerator, and I hold my breath.

"Helga?" I whisper.

The familiar full cheeks appear near the stainless door, and she signals me closer, but Helga's watching the ceiling near the hallway. There's something terribly wrong going on in this house, and it appears Helga is hiding from someone, watching high above my head.

I snag the mirror and quietly scamper into the kitchen next to Helga.

Her grayish brows shoot up when she sees my bandage.

"Don't worry." I place one finger over her mouth to silence any comment and give her a hug. Her round belly is quaking in terror. Water pours down my cheek from my bad eye, making it difficult to think of anything else. Speaking softly, I ask Helga to look into it and clear it for me, if she can.

In a few seconds, she finds an eyelash and shows it to me.

Yes. Instant relief. My brief respite from the irritant frees me to think clearer.

Helga tilts her head toward the wall phone, walks to that counter, and draws out Alec's junk drawer about ten inches. My shiny .38 is neatly tucked next to the flashlights.

Quickly I snatch it and close the drawer.

We run back to the original spot near the refrigerator. It's the only corner hidden by the entry and sitting room. Helga knows that too.

"He's watching but not all the time. Up there." Helga looks to the spot she indicated earlier.

No movement was detected on the upstairs landing when I entered.

"Where's Gen?"

Helga lays an index finger over her mouth like I did moments earlier and pushes me hard against the granite.

Someone's nearby.

Footsteps are closing in from the hall, and the memory of the wolf man in the mask is as fresh as the day we encountered him months ago. He'd watched us inside the estate when we were searching for Kate. Who is here now? *Please come back to the house, Alec.*

The treads are made with leather or rubber soles, perhaps sneakers, but not boots. Treads of a lightweight person or someone walking on the balls of their feet. It's not Gen's walk.

Helga's shakes are overwhelming her, and she's gripping my arm in her puffy hand as a vise would.

We hold hands, and I offer a little smile for confidence even though our situation is serious. "Do whatever they say. I won't leave you like last time. Promise." She nods with a deadpan, zombie-like look.

The intruder's shoes halt at the tile entry, and whoever it is shuts the door and fools with the entrance lock.

If the door was left ajar on purpose, they have sealed us inside.

"May as well come out." A soft-spoken male then giggles like a young girl. "Party time."

That sounds like—no, can't be.

Shoving Helga behind me, my heart thuds wildly like a cottontail racing through a meadow with a fox in pursuit. "Lowlife!" I yell at the top of my lungs, causing Helga to jump.

There's a swishing along the tile that stops at the counter where all that's visible are the toes of his loafers with copper pennies in the slots.

Loafers?

Ralph Lauren's Polo cologne hits my nose.

Dear God, what's he doing here?

TWENTY - FIVE

A .45 revolver with a wooden grip pokes around the refrigerator door, and the man himself steps out into view. He's lost every bit of thirty pounds since Westinn Gallery, and the added bags under the sneer haven't lessened his wicked appearance. The stringy comb-over has disappeared, and in its place is a completely bald cranium, with tufts jutting out from his ears. An aging Hollywood star he isn't. He has two starburst scars on him that I don't recall from before. One on his forehead, the other pocks one cheek. Neither of them he received from me and the pepper spray I gleefully used to bring him down on the Westinn office floor. Prison has provided a pitiable edge to Peter's persona, not unlike a vagrant who scrounges the seedier neighborhoods of New York, looking for a meal in a dumpster dive. This Peter has morphed into a character to stand clear of in a dark alley.

"Who let you out?" I ask, recalling the jail releases throughout New York due to overcrowding and illness. I slip the .38 in my front waistband and ruffle the flowing cotton tunic over it, double-checking that it's hidden.

"No kiss for Uncle Pete?" He forms his lips as if he's a kissing gourami aquarium fish.

Helga gasps and comes out from behind. "What have you done to Gen?"

"Oh, be quiet, biddy. I knew you'd be trouble. We'll fix that. I'll follow you two to the cat room. Get going."

"Where's Boris?" I'm seething over this jailbird taking charge in Alec's house, thinking about the term Gen used at the shop when talking about the feather in the envelope. My sense is Peter and that feather have something in common.

Peter motions with his .45 and steps aside as we pass, inhaling through his nostrils so loudly that I swear he's conjuring up old memories. "Still wearing the same body cream. Glad to see some things never change."

Gross. Same hound, different year.

He reeks of male odors. That hasn't changed either.

When he managed Harry's gallery, and while I worked at Westinn, we'd cringe every time a client walked in and asked to speak to Harry about his brother-in-law. In most cases, Peter had made an error in his valuation or had offended the customer in some other way, such as his arrogant rudeness. Sometimes they came into the shop to complain about other things like his odor. Peter used cologne to cover his wretched smell, but the coverup was worse than the BO. It didn't matter how many candles and air fresheners we bought; it was not enough scent to take the rancid fried burritos and last week's garlic chicken out of the air. Harry spoke to Peter about it repeatedly, to no avail. Suggestions were met by Peter's cavalier message to get lost, or he'd tell us about the shower he'd taken. We all longed for the days when his awesome mother was alive and living with him—a nursemaid to her son because he'd refused to become an adult on his own.

Evil men with body odor seem to follow us to this house.

Where is security and the Mason guy that Bill was so hot about?

Sour bile inches up my throat while I hook my arm through Helga's for support. More for me than her. I didn't expect to be in the same space with Peter again, and I'd forgotten how dirty his loathsome form makes me feel.

Helga opens the door to Boris's Shangri-la while he's at Brookehaven. The room's been closed for a while because the urine odor from his cat box is overpowering. I want to run inside and embrace my kitty, who is hiding under the bed, but I can't take the chance of my .38 getting exposed. Peter is too close. I have to pick my moment so that no one gets shot. He doesn't know I carry, so there's my advantage.

Where are Alec and Bill?

"Get inside, lardo, and shut the door." Peter kicks Helga's ample backside, and she falls headfirst onto the bed. Then he slams the door, pointing his pistol at me. "Lock it, Ann. No games."

"I'm sorry, Helga," I say through the door.

I do as he asks and consider my options. We're surrounded by little tchotchkes, too valuable and lightweight to disable the jerk long enough to take his weapon without getting a bullet myself. In my sleep-deprived state, I wouldn't want to chance a mistake and Peter doing something foolish like shooting at Helga through the closed door.

Gen has a medical condition he doesn't know about.

"How long has Generosa been... detained? I want to see her right now." With folded arms, I sell my obstinate-child routine.

"Still got some fire in ya, huh, Ann? Save it for later. Where's Richie Rich Zavos?" He turns slightly and glances through the bay window. "With the horses, is he?" He falters on the last syllable.

His shaky voice gives him away.

"Gen. Where is she?" I plan to be the dominant player.

"Snooty as ever."

He has something long and cylindrical in his back pocket. I need to get it in case it's another weapon. I carefully slip a hand into my own jeans nonchalantly and find the key knife, folded. It's been there since the cellar. I slowly draw it out and swipe my forehead to palm the key. Two potential instruments to inflict harm as backup for each other.

"It's hot in here. Why don't you tell me what you want, Peter?"

He gets into my face and grazes my bandage with the pistol barrel.

I flinch and hold my breath, watching the gleaming steel follow the line of adhesive tape.

Peter laughs. "She got ya, didn't she? Ha. At least Gwen took a piece of ya before she... bit it. Yo, the Raven is happy."

"You sound like a gang member. I don't know any Gwen, crazy jerk." He's tied to her. *Stay calm.*

"You know her, Ann. I came for my cat."

He owns Stella, not Joey Manetti. Broke that poor animal's leg and would like to break my neck.

"I don't have your stupid cat." I flip my wrist at him.

His snarl turns uglier. "Down the hall. You and me have a rendezvous with fate."

"Quit with the melodrama."

The pistol barrel gouges the base of my spine and I'm thrown forward.

"I'll show you a melodrama, smart girl."

In your dreams. I hope Brad's stitches don't pop from my teeth clenching.

He's marching me down the cool, dark hall to the solarium, and I hear crying.

"Gen?" I ask at the doorway.

"*Bambolina,* you're home. Thank God. Be careful of the raving lunatic. He put me in here."

Peter pushes harder with his pistol, and I stumble through the solarium entrance into Alec's beautiful space of light, with hanging plants and watercolor pillows. The exact opposite of who is taunting us.

"Gen, are you hurt?" I run to the massive sofa where she's shackled to the leg. The heavy chain is about a yard long, and the room smells of uric acid. Gen's hair hasn't been combed in a while, and she's sweating profusely. Mascara rings form ovals beneath her eyes. "Do you need your meds?" I whisper, realizing the odor is drifting from the cushion beneath her. "Where's your purse?"

"Get away from the stinky broad." Peter jerks me to the floor, and I land on my shoulder, jolting my sore jaw. "Ugh." I sputter out a gasp and cough.

"Don't hurt her, you... you..." Gen's so mad but won't cuss, when I know she wants to.

There's a rustling noise somewhere, but I can't tell if it's in the hall or outdoors, then I think back on something he'd said. He mentioned a raven.

Peter glances over his shoulder in the general vicinity of the sound, and I see that his gun doesn't have shells in the cylinder, but I can't be sure there isn't one in the chamber. He might have no access to ammo because he's a felon. My gun is fully loaded, or at least it was before we left for Italy. A pistol has a certain weight when all the shells are in place.

I bounce next to Gen, and she asks about me. "You're hurt. Honey, what happened to you?" Her eyes well with big tears and so much emotion; she clutches me and sobs.

I have to find her Gaucher's prescription before I lose it too and we're both useless to save ourselves.

"Quit blubbering and stay here, and keep away from the windows. I mean it." Peter exits through the only way out and locks us inside the solarium.

"Where are your meds?" I ask Gen.

"In Alec's master bathroom. I'm all right now that you're here. Where's Alec?"

"He's coming." *I hope soon.* "The bandage is nothing. Should've seen the other person." I smile a crooked grin, and she cackles.

"Oh, you."

I lift my blouse, exposing the .38's grip. "Peter isn't aware. When I raise the couch by the arm, can you unhook the chain from the sofa leg to get yourself free? I'll hold the weight while you pull the links."

Gen looks at me, curious.

"We don't have much time."

Gen hesitates, then stands and studies the stain where she'd had an accident on the cushion. "I ruined Alec's—"

"No matter. C'mon, hon. Please hurry." Poor thing. Peter hasn't allowed her a bathroom break. I run to the arm and lift the beautiful peach sofa that weighs a ton, waiting for her to kneel. "That's it. Slide the links out. You've got it." I let the couch settle on its leg once again. "I'll do the rest. Sit where you were. I know it's wet, but we have to look the same as when he left us."

She descends into the mushy cushion and crinkles her nose. This has to be one of the top three most embarrassing moments for Gen since I've known her. The other two were when we escaped Bodrum Castle.

"I'll fix it to look like it did." On my hands and knees, I scramble to the sofa leg and rearrange the chain as if it's still attached to the wood.

"When Peter shows up, I have no idea what he has in store for me, but I also have... remember this?" I hold up the key knife extended, then close it, handing it to her. "Keep it in case I need help."

"Oh yes. You used it to cut our duct tape at the towers. How clever of you to keep it all this time."

"I didn't see any bullets in his pistol."

Gen claps softly. "That's good, isn't it?"

"There's still a chance he has one that I can't see. I have to treat his gun as a loaded weapon with one shot in it. If Alec and Bill don't find him first, I'm going to maneuver him as close to you as possible."

Gen flattens a hand on her chest.

"Don't worry. He'll have his back to you. Peter has something in his back pocket. Do you know what that is?"

"He keeps talking about spray. He's mad about the spray."

"That time he attacked me, I covered him with pepper spray, and he suffered. He may want to do the same to me. Peter's vindictive enough to use it to take his revenge. Let's assume he has a can of pepper spray or Mace. Can you get it from him if he's close enough?"

Gen nods. "I will so you can use it on him again. What am I going to do with the little knife?"

"Jab him in the seat of his pants as you slip the can straight up and out of his pocket. I'll go to work from there." I have no idea how long it's been since Gen has taken her pills, but they aren't far away. Hopefully, this ordeal will be over and—

Peter barges into the room, securing the lock. "There's little time."

"Time for what? I'm not leaving Gen, so whatever you want, you're gonna have to come here to get it."

"Fine." Peter sniffs and he approaches Gen, sticking the pistol barrel against her temple, creaking the hammer back.

"If you hurt her, I won't cooperate." I'm as forceful as I can be with a tremble in my voice.

Gen covers her face. "No, please. Don't hurt us. I'll pay you whatever you want. We won't tell."

No. I hadn't thought about Gen using her wealth as a ploy. Peter doesn't turn down free cash.

I step in front of him so that he shifts the pistol from Gen and defensively points it at me.

"Back off," Peter says, stepping away from the couch.

My leg is touching the sofa cushion, and I'm contemplating whether Gen is working our plan or too frazzled to remember Peter's back pocket. If he uses the spray, he could disable both of us. Shifting my eyes until she meets mine, I finally have her attention.

"Peter, Gen's connections in the art world can get you reestablished in the community. Another town. A new gallery, new clients, and an awesome place to live." My half-step slide toward him receives the desired effect.

He's listening.

I steel myself to an attack instead of concentrating on the potential for one bullet two feet from my face. The hidden pistol he doesn't know about is giving me super courage.

He treads backward while he considers the offer.

Instead of retreating, which most smart people would do in this situation, my steps bring me closer to his weapon because he's not in the right position for Gen to act. He moves every time I do, so I alter my direction some, correcting Peter's stance to within Gen's reach.

"Now. We need to go now, Gen," I say quietly.

When the words register with Peter, Gen holds an aerosol can and jabs him in the rump with the key knife, hitting her mark.

Peter bounces and yelps in unison, long enough for me to take out my revolver.

"What did you stick me with?" Peter trains his shaky pistol hand on me while rubbing his butt and putting distance between himself and Gen.

We've caught him off guard.

My .38 is pointed at him in the mirror image. "Time to drop your weapon. You've lost, Peter. But you always lose."

"Where'd that gun come from?" he asks me, wide-eyed in disbelief. At this range, he can see that the pistol I'm holding is loaded.

As he's staring down my handgun, Gen springs and thrusts the puny blade into him, ripping a jagged cut down his forearm.

"Auff." In horror and pain, he clutches the wound. "Damn you!"

With the help of my shin bone and low kick, his gun is skittering across the floor near a potted plant. Pain cascades through my ankle, but the self-defense move is effective.

His gun doesn't fire—lucky us, or it could've been empty all along.

While I am mentally praising myself and trying to ignore my aching foot, Peter lunges at me, screaming, and we collapse, the pile of ugly pressing on my chest.

"Can't breathe," I manage to get out as he's squeezing the air from my throat with both hands.

Kicking and bucking to remove the leech strangling me, I swing my gun arm around and clap his ear with the metal barrel, hard enough to roll him to one side and get my feet beneath me in a crouch.

"Stop." This time it's me who clicks the gun hammer back with my thumb where he can hear the sound. Through laboring breaths, my thoughts fuse. "Don't make a move... Rave. That's what they... call you, isn't it?" I remembered Bill said one of the Manetti guys referred to it. Peter called himself the Raven earlier.

"How do you know that?" he squeals, rubbing his ear. "Where's my damn cat? Are you just going to stand there and let me bleed all over?"

I'm reminded of Sorellina's bloodthirst and would love nothing more than to bring her up and shove it all back at him, but she's dead, and I won't go there.

Standing over him with the pistol, I give Peter the smile of a victor. "Don't get up. Unlike your weapon, mine's loaded. Make a move and I'll add a bullet to the arm that's bleeding. Good job, Gen." I watch her for signs of fainting. "You okay?" I ask her.

She holds up a black can with big white letters. Pepper gel.

"Works for me. It's your turn." I snag a pillow from the sofa and toss it at Peter. "I'd cover that wound if I were you. This might sting."

"Now?" Gen asks me.

"Please don't," Peter begs with his hands clasped. "I can't go through that again. I won't give you ladies any more trouble."

"Now we're ladies? Bah. Dirty pigs who chain up women don't get a second chance." Gen drags the chain at her ankle across the floor reminiscent of Marley's ghost, Scrooge's business partner. She flicks open the container.

Peter is lying on his back, howling with his eyes closed, expecting the worst.

Gen points and sprays his face and torso gingerly for a few seconds.

"That's enough, Gen. The smell will get unbearable soon." I step back and take her with me.

"Did you really think you could take your revenge on us?" I ask Peter and wonder what's taking Alec so long. Peter may not be alone.

Snot pours from Peter's nose like it did the last time, and he slings the bloody pillow to his face. "I'll laugh," he blubbers behind his pillow, "when the Manettis put a hit out on you…"

"Anna!" The hardwood is pounding with an army of feet, and Alec's calling me from the sitting room. He bursts inside, with Bill racing on his heels.

When my gaze settles on Brad outside the solarium windows with his pistol raised, I lower my gun.

"Babe, Mom— Did he hurt you?" Alec's scrutinizing the blood pool on the floor and my clothing. Peter's blood is all over me. "Where are you cut?" He checks my face and the rest of me, groaning.

"Not my blood. I'm fine, but your mom—"

"Nonsense. I've caught my second wind." The faint smile from Gen is naughty.

"Let's get out of here. My eyes are burning." He looks at the chain on his mother's leg and his shoulders drop. "He did that to you?"

I calmly take the pepper spray from Gen and hand it to Bill, who has drawn his weapon on Peter as he writhes like a rattlesnake run over by a car.

"We'll leave this with you to keep handy for *Mr. Gregory's* interrogation. I don't care if it's not admissible evidence, he doesn't go with the cops until we hear the entire story. Stella belongs to Peter."

"Seriously?" Alec and Bill ask in stereo.

"Matt's knife and pepper spray saved us twice. I wonder what the good captain in the carabinieri would say about that?" I ask Alec.

Gen lifts her brow at me. "I don't get that one."

"Your pistol helped a little. Mom, we'll explain later," Alec says, tightening his lips to secure inappropriate laughter.

"Someone should tend to Peter. He's figured out that his pillow is covered in capsaicin. Burns like fire. Too bad Gwen isn't here to help clean up the bloody leftovers." I promised not to mention her, but it slips out to Gen's horror. "We'll explain that too."

"I'll look at his arms and apply pressure," Bill says.

"I'm not stitching him. Neither is Brad," Alec says smugly. "Paramedics can do that when they arrive."

"What kept you guys? I texted you before I walked in the house," I ask Alec.

"Never got the message. I left my phone in the Bentley. When we found Mason, we ran over here. Totally my fault."

"Where is Mason?" I ask.

CHAPTER
TWENTY - SIX

From Helga's account of what happened, Peter entered the house through the solarium hours before we arrived and threatened to hurt Alec's mom if Helga made any attempt to leave or tell a soul he was inside. Behind his back, she thought she could overcome her fear of firearms long enough to confront Peter but lost her nerve after moving my Lady Smith to the kitchen drawer.

Peter's the color of rooibos tea, red from swelling, and the whites of his eyes look like giant strawberries. After we allowed him to wash, the pepper seems little more than an annoyance. He's been zip-tied at his extremities and bound in a corner bedroom. Sullivan County deputies and an ambulance were called to investigate more than one crime scene on Alec's estate.

Unanimously, we choose Bill to handle the opening questions since he has the details on the Alvarez murder. Bill's wearing the hidden, clip-on recorder that worked so well when he and Alec found Kate at the spa weeks ago. Peter has no idea he's on the record— our best shot at any confession, if he talks to us at all.

Nothing we do here will be admissible, but I wanted to know Peter's role, for myself.

"We found the charred remains," Bill announces to Peter.

Peter cocks his head slowly like an aging toucan on a branch, putting his beak in the air.

"The SUV at the mare's barn belongs to Derrick Mason. It's registered to him." Alec faces me since this is new information. "I found blood on the seat and located Bill wandering the pasture, and we walked the drag marks to a smoking corpse in a shallow grave, too hot to get near."

I cover my mouth. "Mason's charred body?"

"You can't pin that on me," Peter utters, defiantly.

"Mr. Gregory, everything said to us is off the record and can't be used against you. The authorities will read you your rights and take your official statement." Bill's hair is in a strange shag cut, and he's dyed it a chestnut brown since we were in Italy. Is this his new undercover look? If so, it's a bad one. It's as if he's taken the shears to it himself, whacking chunks and leaving ladders and hunks behind. Bill sits on the mattress near the bedpost, while Alec and I stand beside him. "Mr. Gregory, did you know Benita Alvarez?"

"I don't."

"How about Josh Jennings?" Bill goes down another road. "Gwen Alvarez?"

"Ha. A lot you know. Gwen's name *isn't* Alvarez. I don't owe you any explanations and take the fifth."

Peter's bulging eyes are glued to me. Creepy, calculating, faithless eyes that I've never trusted because they're constantly shifting. Through gritted teeth, I consider a ploy to dig at the heart of his ego that I know so well.

"Bill, he's a waste of time. Cowards always are. Harry and I found it hilarious that Pitiful Pete, we called him, still lived with his mother because no one else would have him." I turn to Alec and add laughter for ambiance. "We nicknamed Pete *PP*, the laughing-stock of Westinn. You never knew that, did you?"

My remarks flare Peter's nostrils. It's working.

"Harry looked forward to afternoons when you left for the bank so that we could air out the gallery from your drunken stench, or was it bad aftershave?"

"I wear cologne, not aftershave, and you know it, Ann." Peter spits on the floor and struggles against his bindings.

"He doesn't have the brains to plan a killing, Alec. Sorellina used him to get to Benita, and he ate the bait. Stella's ours now because Peter's going to prison for being an incessant screw-up. A fitting conclusion for a loser." I exchange glances with Alec and Bill and wait for Peter to blow.

"I got Harry, didn't I?" Peter blurts. "It wasn't the Ruski brothers who poisoned him like everybody thinks. I put the stuff in his beer every day at closing time. Simple. Harry croaks, and the gallery is mine."

He couldn't stand not being important to the discussion. His story confirms one of the scenarios we'd considered for Harry Carradine's poisoning. The Russian Mafia supplies the polonium to Peter, and he administers the miniscule doses to his brother-in-law in liquor. A year later, we have the confession for Harry's murder. I hope Peter is charged in the homicide case Mooney left open. You're welcome, Colum.

"You'll say anything to get off the subject, Gregory." Alec breaks my thoughts.

"Gwen *Hanson* hated her half sister. When Benita stole my cat and fled to Italy, we joined forces and took her out. Joey gave us his blessing since he was done with that ditzy broad. Never understood that attraction."

"Joey would be Joseph Manetti of Staten Island?" Bill asks.

"None other."

"How did Gwen know Benita's whereabouts? Josh said Benita was in a hurry and didn't tell anyone she'd left the States." Bill twists his mouth quizzically.

"Easy. GPS and a tracking bug on her phone, since he gave it to her."

"So, Gwen drugs her, ties her up, and wraps the concertina wire by herself?" Bill presses further. "I don't buy it."

He's making him confess.

"The wire was extra. My calling card from time served at Rikers. It was hard to find, but we managed. The deep cuts helped the process along after I disengaged the security cameras. What is it with companies going cheap on security? Crummy equipment is easy to override thanks to pointers I got in jail." He beams with satisfaction. Peter is actually proud of his part in a killing. "How d'you like my little calling card? Figure it out, Ann?"

"What card?" I'd like to punch the smugness from his lips.

"C'mon now, the raven feather. I left you a note. Don't you bother to read?"

That's who sent the feather. Who got a note? Not me.

"The bird pin is yours also?" Bill asks.

Peter lifts one shoulder and sneers. "I don't know about any pin."

"Who used the bat on Benita Alvarez?" Alec takes my hand, and we put more space between us and Peter.

"Benita took Stella away." Peter shrugs. "I didn't find my cat, and crushing her skull was the least I could do. Left my signature on her wrists too. I'm surprised you didn't hear about the Raven. I was all the talk on my cell block." Peter drifts off for several seconds, blinks his eyes and rubs his lids with his secured wrists. "I have a rep on Block 8 for scratching an inmate with my homemade claw." Peter grins at me and licks his chops as if he's about to tear into a meal. "You're as good as dead, Ann. Joey has allies in New York. He may be in Italy, but he's a far-reaching dude. If I'd been in that cellar, *you'd* have the knife in your chest instead of her." He swallows an emotional gulp, and his eyelids fill. "The Manettis won't rest until—"

"Past tense," Bill huffs. "They're resting quite comfortably, what's left of them."

Peter opens his mouth when Bill strikes a nerve.

"Joey and his two uncles have been... fired... terminated. The next of kin riding in a second car confirmed the bombing victims in the limousine. Immediate family were about to pay respects to a dead Mob boss, Birdman Manetti." Bill's stark smile brings a grimace from Peter.

"Horse teeth," Peter mutters. "Nothing happened to Joey. You're trying to trick me."

Bill taps his phone and reads aloud the headline from the latest article put out by the AP on the bombing.

There's acceptance and sadness in Peter's gaze. He starts to say something, then changes his mind, meshing his fingers instead.

"They want the heirloom back. The sister said you have it." Peter's subtle smile is irritating.

Sister Mary Natalina told the Manettis after all.

As I view it, it's not the Manettis' heirloom. We've seen no proof that Alec's grandfather took the rosary beads from anyone, only rumors and conjecture. There's more research to do.

"Shouldn't the deputies be here by now?" Alec asks Bill.

"Bill, what happened to Alec's other estate security? Where are the usual cars—dismissed by Mason? That's a strange way to surveil the estate."

"Where are the men from security, Gregory?" Bill's pinpoint stare shoots toward Peter, who's giving us his Cheshire cat impersonation. Bill turns to Alec. "We'd better explain our security protocol to the officers. There may be more homicides we don't know about."

"Security, ha. Your system sucks too. Anyone can break into this place. All the money in the world, and you pick the cheesiest alarm on the planet." Peter hasn't lost his touch making people feel small.

A wave of nausea gushes over me. What if something had happened to Gen or Helga? After the wolfman incident, Alec and Chase discussed many alarm systems. It used to be a comfort having people watching from the road, but there's too many areas to hide with easy access to the house. Video surveillance and men in vehicles have been a dangerous choice for Alec, but how high tech can he get? Derrick Mason should've stayed inside with Gen and Helga. There's a possibility he tried, and they shooed him outdoors.

"Don't sweat it, Richie Rich. The guys should be up from their naps by now," Peter offers to Alec. "They're a bunch of lightweights. I hope you don't pay 'em much."

"I'd worry more about the friends waiting for you in Italy. We have a bilateral extradition treaty between our countries. Too bad for you," Bill says.

I avoid looking at Peter but can feel his stare.

A knock on the bedroom door.

"May I bother you?" Helga asks.

Alec runs to let her in. "Is Mom all right?"

"She is wonderfully well. I came to bring you this." She's holding something in one of her cross-stitched dishtowels. "I found this in the solarium on the floor. I didn't touch it. Utterly horrible." When Helga's upset, her German accent is more pronounced.

Alec cradles the object and recoils. "Bill? Your thoughts."

We join Alec at the door. Helga is right. She's holding a primitive weapon made from junkyard scraps. Bird talons attached to sticks, woven together by twine and scrap wire, on a wooden handle.

"What does that look like to you?" Alec asks Bill.

"It's mine. I want it back." Peter hops in his seat, scuffing the chair legs along the hardwood.

Bill raises his hand over his weapon. "Calm down before I accidentally shoot you in the nuts."

"Oh, please do it, Bill. Save the taxpayer any chance of him reproducing." I'm snickering at Peter's knees drawn slightly to cover his groin area. "What a sick weapon. This is what you used in prison? On Benita?"

He'd planned to use this on us.

"I hear sirens." Helga's clunky shoes clack out of the room. "I'll make some coffee."

"Anna, I need some fresh air. Let's talk to our good friends at the sheriff's department." Alec reaches for me.

"Good friends?" Peter cocks his head. "A suck-up. I remember that about you."

I stray toward the broken-down man in the corner, who's wearing a snarl and blood-soaked bandages. "Harry gave you a livelihood you didn't deserve, and you blew it. Pathetic." I follow Alec into the hallway and close the door, leaving the stain on humanity behind. I smooth back my hair and hold my head high, relieved to be wearing a clean blouse and a new bandage on my throat. Peter's film coats my teeth and skin; the shower is going to feel good.

As Alec passes Helga at the coffee maker, he rubs her shoulder. "They aren't making a social call. Please don't go to any trouble. Rest."

"It's here if they'd like some. I know your mother could use a strong cup after her bath. Making her favorite blend. I'll get to work on Annalisse's Manhattan and a strong martini for you. You've both earned it. Bill may need something lighter. He has a bad stomach."

Alec gives her a kiss on the cheek, and she blushes.

I know the feeling. He's such a handsome guy.

In moments like this, I see him for who he truly is. That's thanks mostly to Gen and his father, Pearce. They've become more like family than… I can't relate to any of my own blood relatives. Relative. Kate's it, and she left me to sort my mixed-up past, alone. My fantasy dreamscape is here with Alec and the wonderful people who've welcomed me into their hearts.

"Earth to Anna; are you ready to do this?" Alec carefully touches my jaw and assesses his patient as an MD would. "Your neck is red where he squeezed your throat. May have some bruising by tomorrow. I want to be sure that Brad's stitches are holding and that you're put on meds."

His soothing voice makes me want to snuggle up next to him and spend the day in bed together. I'm definitely crashing from my adrenaline high.

The ambulance stops in the drive and quiets the siren, followed immediately by two black-and-white sheriff's cruisers.

"Okay, Doc. I'll get checked out, but don't forget to mention our missing security crew to the badge and gun boys." I turn and wave at the closed door to the room where Peter and Bill are. "Good riddance, nutcase. Harry's celebrating tonight."

"As will we. Wait until you see the new stables. Hank's been busy this week. They're almost finished." Alec opens the door to a flurry of uniforms and flat-brimmed campaign hats.

CHAPTER
TWENTY - SEVEN

What a gorgeous sweater day to christen the new sheep barn and celebrate my thirtieth birthday. Alec, Helga, Gen, and my close friend and business partner, Chase Miller, have overwhelmed me by throwing an authentic Italian dinner party, including piles of mussels and greens in the orecchiette pasta we brought home from Italy. More mouthwatering and sinful than the restaurant meals we hastily left behind in Bari. Less stressful too. The inside of a barn that smacks of seafood aromas instead of stalls with manure piles, I'll take any day. Alec still feels bad about our disastrous seaside adventure two months ago, but there is nothing to forgive and no one to blame for an attempt to mix business with pleasure. We'll stick with a straight vacation next time. I'm flanked by new friends, Bill Drake the investigator and a very formal, and sometimes stuffy, Mr. Edwards, driver slash bodyguard. I consider Bradley my friend even if he's *a bloody hard nut to crack,* to use a phrase he fancies.

Peter Gregory was extradited to Italy the moment Bill forwarded his recording to the carabinieri head of security in charge of criminal investigations for the Puglia region. Peter, having been recently released from Riker's Island, made it easy for US authorities to ship him overseas for his crimes there. One less criminal discharge the City has to deal with. In the meantime, the New York murder investigations involving Harry Carradine's and Derrick Mason's deaths are pending in the courts while police gather more hard evidence and strengthen their cases against Peter. His relationship with Gwen Hanson, also known as Sorellina, is sketchy. Bill thinks Peter set out to impress Gwen during her sisterly feud with Benita, or he and Gwen were pushed together by accident because of Stella. The actual truth rests with the deceased Manetti family lost to the bombing. Peter refuses to speak about his affiliation to the Mob for fear of being their next victim. Italian authorities will have to sort out the group of homicides at the hands of Gwen, Peter, and possibly the Cosa Nostra, including Gwen's own death, but circumstantially, we believe they are connected to the cat and the sale of Signorile for the unpaid protection money.

Josh Jennings was relieved of his ankle bracelet but not until he made financial restitution to Lecce police for the manpower spent during the Alvarez case. Even though Josh was cleared of Benita's murder, he was the last person to see her alive and had left a nonemployee alone in the building after hours. Lanny Quicken Racing has dropped the suit against Alec and is pursuing Josh for the funds he stole from them as their CFO.

Bill disclosed Josh had an affair with Alec's ex-wife that had ended badly for her. Ex-wife Tina retaliated when Josh's wife found out about them and forced an end to their affair. Josh had admitted to Tina he'd embezzled the racing team funds, so, hurt by the end of their fling, Tina offered *Reveal Reality* the photo and article, assuming it would bite Josh and implicate him, which it did. Tina's vindictiveness at dragging Pearce's name through the rumor mill bruised Alec's feelings, as it had mine, the last time she played in the tabloids with old photos taken during their marriage.

Alec is so furious at Tina, he hasn't been able to talk about it. We can expect Tina to use other pictures to attack Alec and his family in the months to come. Alec is preparing since it's a means of income for her, having been attacked by two stories so far. It's mind-blowing that Alec once found love with a hateful woman like Tina.

The Maria Celeste Gamba-Galilei rosary is safely locked in Alec's den. We plan to confront Gen about my Galileo findings, but I'm waiting on Alec for the right time. Since our return, Gen's hinted at something she wants off her chest. We're hoping she's ready to tell Alec what really happened with her father.

Stella was flown to New York a few days after we left Bari and is recuperating well due to her young age. Alec removed her cast, and she walks beautifully without a limp. She and Boris are inseparable buddies, even though he hoards the cat treats and takes the best morsels for himself from Helga's canned food portions. Roly-Poly Man can't help himself because I've spoiled him. Stella stays with Helga until other arrangements can be made, but I anticipate Stella becoming the Brookehaven house cat from now on. Helga lights up when Stella curls in her lap, expressing the love only a purr pile can show.

Beside my plate is Alec's birthday present: an itinerary to Christchurch, New Zealand's South Island, during their autumn season. Fewer crowds and comfortable temperatures. I'm finally going to see this magnificent country for its mountain ranges and wild rural regions, and I'm so relieved to have the added months to work out how I'll withstand an eighteen-hour flight. I get goose pimples thinking about it. We haven't figured that part out yet, but Alec promises it won't be an issue. He has more faith in me than I do.

It was Alec's idea to boot the animals to the pasture and have a picnic celebration inside their building in case the pre-Christmas storm arrives earlier than forecast. The chocolate sheet cake Helga baked for my birthday is half gone. What's left looks similar to a porcupine, stuck with the remaining fifteen rainbow birthday candles. I know I ate two pieces but barely recall downing the first, thanks to her scratch cakes that are light-as-air heavenly. Helga is a masterful baker. Her flaky German pastries are to die for.

The tiny white scar where Brad did surgery on me in our room at the bed-and-breakfast is barely noticeable—my reminder of that insane day in the cellar. I know the scar is there and so does Alec because he kisses that spot each night we're together. Since the car bombing, we've shut off Gen's international news apps to keep as many facts about the Mafia from her as possible. She feels responsible for the murder of her friend

Oliver King. It turns out he had come to Bari at Gen's request after all. The Bari police have one of the biggest Mob families taken down, thanks to rival Cosa Nostra or Manetti's own goons fighting for control. There's been no word on Officer Bruno's notebook, but he got his wish to take out the Mob, giving every ounce of himself for it.

Gen successfully delivered the Zavos corporation to Serge at Global Star Class the day we returned home. Her initial agreement went through without Oliver King's blessing, which is sad for Oliver. The police report says that his senseless knifing is officially unresolved—a random malicious act. We know that isn't so. I'm here for Gen and Alec should either of them want to revisit that terrible night on the beach and compare theories.

"Hey, birthday girl. I see the gears grinding in your mind. Care to walk off dessert?" Alec asks from across the table.

I look at the long table of grazed leftovers, where we hardly made a dent in the salad side dishes. I'm so full but wish I had room for more. Hm. Something Samantha would say. She must be watching over the festivities.

"I miss you too. Thanks, Sam," I whisper. "Alec, Helga needs help carting this food back to the house." I stretch and pat my belly. "I feel like an old toad on a lily pad. Why didn't you stop me from having that second piece of cake?" I see that he's drifting off.

"Who do you miss?" He's unaware I was having a private talk with my departed friend.

"Don't you think about clearing the table, dear." Gen overhears and never misses anything. "We're just getting started." She passes a quick glance to Alec sitting next to her.

The person on my right, quietly indulging in his second round of lobster, belches under his breath. Poor Bill. Dueling seafood dishes are sparring with each other.

"Did you bring any antacids with you?" I ask in a low tone, stretching toward Alec with my hand out.

He rolls a pack across the blue tablecloth toward my hand, and I slide them in front of Bill.

He nods his thanks and shakes his head. "Sorry to be so wimpy. I don't eat rich foods very often."

"We know," Alec says with a grin.

Gen takes a page in a clear sleeve from her purse and gives it to me. "I kept this in safekeeping. I would leave it in its protective sleeve. What am I saying? Of course you know that."

The wrinkled and stained parchment is faded and delicate. A nun stands beside a chair, carrying the strand of beads we've all come to know since showing it around on the plane and elsewhere. I scrutinize the paper, holding it closer so that the shiny glare on the crucifix clears away. The onyx piece is unmistakable. The etching's title describes the nun.

"Gen, it's the provenance we lacked. This is wonderful." My heart skips a few beats. "This close-up confirms they belonged to Sister Maria Celeste. Your beads—in her hands." I'm so awestruck, words stick in my throat.

"Your beads," Alec corrects me.

"I'm proud of you, dear." Gen's glowing in her knowing smile. "I almost told you in my office. Forgive my fibbing about not knowing their origin." She takes a long breath. "Where the senses fail us, reason must step in. If I'd told you who they belonged to, Alec would've lost you forever in Italy."

She's repeated that saying.

"Pardon me." I grab my phone and do a quick check to verify. "One of your clues. Galileo said those words."

"I can't fool you. Did you also figure out the black-bird pin? I dropped it in your purse."

Alec and I trade glances.

"It was you?" I ask.

"Remember that bird feather in the envelope? What I didn't show you was the note that came with it. It was so disturbing that I destroyed it. Burned it in the wastebasket," Gen says matter-of-factly.

The charred odor in Gen's office I thought imagined was real.

"Well, what did it say?" Alec is as curious as I am.

"Since he's in custody... It was all over the news that inmates were being released throughout New York. I couldn't find the articles in a hurry, so the bird pin was the only thing I found to go along with the bird feather. I know Annalisse can't help herself when it comes to a good mystery, and since she hates to fly, this would occupy her time. I wasn't worried about Peter's threats with Alec, Bradley, and Bill along." Gen lays a fork in her plate.

I'm sensing she's second-guessing her methods.

"You knew Peter had threatened Anna and didn't think it was important to tell her? Mom, that's not like you. He attempted an assault on her last year." Alec's raising his voice, and people are noticing us.

"It's fine, Alec. We didn't know Sorellina was Peter's accomplice until we got to the estate. Oliver, Josh, the police, not a single thing would've changed had we known about Peter's threatening note."

"Alec, I didn't want to scare Annalisse. The trip was supposed to be fun; looking over your shoulders at every turn would've been a heartless thing to do. Ruined your trip before it began." Gen is pleading because Alec isn't convinced.

"When Anna saw the door ajar at the estate, and if she'd known about Peter's threats, she would not have gone inside. Instead, Bill and I would've entered the house."

"Then what? A gunfight with Peter? Risking someone getting shot or him getting his hands on a loaded weapon? You know if that scenario had happened, you would have insisted that I wait outside. Peter could've seen me and made his assault there while you were doing a walk-through. Gen's nondisclosure turned out for the best. Her heart is always in the right place. Thanks, Gen."

"The note, Mom. What did Peter say?" Alec asks.

"Ann, my claw is going to rip your guts out. Get ready. XX OO the Raven." Gen closes her eyes. "I read it once so quickly, the words may not be exactly right, but you get the gist."

"How'd you recognize Peter in all that?" I ask her.

"A strong sense it was him. He is the only person who has ever called you Ann. Put that with the prisoner release and his handwriting. He makes strange letter *R*s. Recognize them anywhere from the days when he wrote notes to me from Westinn Gallery. Peter is a filthy man." Gen swabs her forehead with a napkin.

"You recall Gwen, the thief in red from the shop? She was the woman in the cellar and also wore blackbird earrings." Time to change this sore subject. "What can you tell me about this parchment?" The rendering of Sister Maria Celeste crackles in its plastic sleeve.

"My father gave me that before he left us for good, with my help." Gen gets misty-eyed as she gazes off like she does occasionally in her office. "I hope he's forgiven me for what I've done."

Forgiven her for what?

Alec stands over my shoulder to view the parchment for himself, ignoring his mother's comment completely.

"Have you asked Gen about Sophia?" I whisper.

"Mom, can you clarify Sophia for us?"

Gen stares at her son as if she doesn't recognize him. "I see you've been busy. Given events, it's time you and Annalisse knew." She pulls out the chair on the left side of me.

"Are you absolutely certain Sister Mary Margaret gave you the rosary and not someone else?" Alec asks in a lower tone.

"Like who?" Her retort is too sharp. Gen doesn't appreciate being questioned, and we're pushing her actions today.

"We met a Sister in Bari and later went to the church you asked us to visit. This Sister calls herself Sister Mary Natalina. Have you heard of her?" Alec asks.

"She has a blue birthmark near her thumb in the shape of a heart," I add.

"What did she look like?" Gen puffs and passes a palm through the air. "She was dressed like a nun in a habit. Silly me. That has to be Sister Mary Margaret. She has a birthmark like that."

This Sister has changed her identity too. For strangers like us. If her family is tied to the Mafia, this may be the way she hides her kinship to the infamous Manettis.

"Sophia Giambruno," Alec says without warning.

Gen's mouth forms an *O*. Her entire body is shaking, and she's rolling a cigar out of her napkin.

"Mom, it's all right." Alec reaches for Gen's hand, and she turns away. "Is my grandfather Antonio Giambruno?"

Quietly Bill and Brad pick up their plates and leave their seats. Out of respect, the rest of the guests notice Gen's demeanor and follow the guys to mill around the entrance of the barn.

Gen drops her head into her hands. "What I did had to be done." She sniffles. "We tried to keep this from you, Alec, and hoped you'd never find out. Going to Italy is always risky; that's why I couldn't go."

"Granddad was part of the Mafia, wasn't he?" Alec asks. "We ran into an officer who told us Giambruno became a mole for the police, and they ended up putting him behind bars so that the operation wouldn't come to light."

Gen raises her head and swipes her eyes. "When I learned Papa joined the Mafia, I was scared. He was all that I had. I felt so betrayed. I tried and tried to get Papa to leave that organization, but once you're inside, you can never leave. His life was no longer his own, so I went to the police and cut a deal with them. If he turned informant for the Bari police, they would look the other way. I thought the police could protect him. Papa never knew it was me who went to the police about him, and he ended up in prison anyway. It hurts my soul to this day." She takes Alec's hand.

"Mom, you did what was necessary."

"I may not always make the right decisions. Your grandfather protected me with a new identity, new passport. He told me never to return to Bari, and I haven't. Pearce and I were married, and I turned my back on Papa because it had to be this way." Gen leans back in the seat and sighs as big tears cascade down her cheeks. "I haven't thought about this in a long time. It's a weight lifted now that you know, son. Your grandfather was a decent man, but he was weak and penniless. Please don't let his foolish decision blemish your memories of him."

"Gen, did your father take the Galileo artifacts from the Manettis?" I ask.

"Sister Mary Margaret told me the Manettis found out Papa foiled many of their plans by going to the police, and the rosary beads and rendering were items from Carlo Manetti's safe. Papa took them and gave them to the sister to give to me because the Mafia hoards priceless, historical relics. Papa knew they belonged to the Giambruno family. We are one of many relations whose heritage goes back to the Galileo line. The Mafia takes for value or money but mostly for power. I sleep better knowing that Leo, his brothers, and his only son are no longer among the living. We are all safer now."

"Should we keep these bits of history?" I set the page on the table, not feeling good about this. Holding the Mushasha jewels is too fresh in my memory.

"They are yours to do with as you wish. My gifts come without strings. Think about it. If you're uncomfortable keeping the beads, I would imagine the Smithsonian or the Met will take them off your hands." Gen reaches into her sweater and draws out a gift wrapped in turquoise paper. "Annalisse, this is for you. Happy Birthday, my dearest gem. I hope you like it."

We make her cry and question her actions, but she doesn't miss a beat.

It's a rectangular velvet box we use in the gallery for custom jewelry. Inside is the prettiest heart-shaped sapphire-and-diamond necklace I've ever seen. The blue is how I remember the color of the Aegean. Crystal and iridescent.

"Oh, Gen, it's breathtaking. My gosh. Thank you." I give her an awkward sitting-down hug and kiss her cheek, managing to stir a smile from her sad, tearstained face.

"Turn around. Let me put it on you." She snaps the clasp at my neck. "There. Lovely with your dark hair. It looks beautiful on your white sweater, doesn't it,

Alec? Come and see, everyone." Gen waves toward the crowd of people, who are whispering.

A round of applause spatters through the rafters as guests file by for a closer view of the glittering gem surrounded by a row of diamonds.

Chase strays in from behind, startling me.

"I helped pick it out. It isn't your birthstone, but that blue is so *you*." Chase looks past me to Alec.

"You've been making yourself scarce. Did you take some cake? Chocolate, your favorite." Chase has playful eyes and a pink nose from the chilly air. "What are you up to, old friend?"

"Don't you have some unfinished business?" Chase peeks beyond me to Alec again.

"Hey." I swipe Alec in the arm. "Does everyone need to know our secrets?"

Alec raises his hands and steps aside. "Don't blame me."

Chase tosses something dark to Alec.

I hold my breath and fondle the sapphire pendant I'm wearing.

It's the blue velvet bag.

The crowd is watching in curiosity since no one but me has ever seen the pouch before. Several times, in fact—the drawing room, the stable office, and lastly, in the solarium. Alec's beautiful room soiled by Peter's break-in. The space will need new furniture and a complete makeover before I'll enter that part of the house again.

Alec slowly pulls apart the drawstring at the top and takes out a black ring box to a room of sighs and aahs. He studies me as if seeking my approval to proceed and drops to one knee, opening the box.

This chance isn't slipping away again. Not after Italy.

Footsteps scuff the concrete, and body heat closes in on us.

I don't see anyone but Alec holding a teardrop sapphire-and-diamond ring, glistening in the overhead lighting. The perfect pairing with Gen's necklace.

My hands are clammy and trembling. It's hard to see through tears ruining my eyeliner. A thought strikes me and I swallow hard. It could be a dinner ring and not an engagement ring.

Dummy.

He's *on his knee.*

"From that first moment you appeared, I had to find you. Back then, the mysterious woman with green eyes in my dreams had only a face and no name. Annalisse, you're my next breath, my next day, my forever. I love you. I'd be honored if you—"

"Excuse me!" a high-pitched voice yells, and a woman waves from the barn entrance.

Alec springs to his feet, clutching the box, and the rest of us crane our necks toward the person speaking. We don't usually get people visiting this far from the house. The new barn is almost a mile away.

"Are you lost?" Helga asks her because she's closest to the stranger.

"I was told we could find Alec here. A nice man in that big barn down the road said you were here. You're having a party, sorry. I didn't mean to interrupt."

Alec closes the ring box and grabs my hand. "Let's go."

Guests surround a woman about my age, standing with a little boy of maybe eight or nine. As we approach, I see that she's rail thin, bleached platinum, and has a center part with dark roots. Her brows are penciled too harshly for light hair. The boy's a natural towhead with curious blue eyes and adorable dimples that dent both cheeks when he smiles. He's gripping her leg as a lifeline, so he must belong to her.

Alec abruptly halts us and stares as if he's seen a ghost.

"Virena. What brings you out here. I haven't seen you since—"

"Columbia. I should've called, with your party and everything." Her eyes dart from Alec's face to the ring box in his hand.

This person doesn't seem sorry to burst in on us at all. She's blushing all over herself, a few panting breaths away from having an accident on the barn floor. Then she notices me and goes board rigid, dropping her overdone smile.

The boy tugs on the Virena woman's jeans. "Is he my new daddy?"

I'm squeezing the blood out of Alec's hand. What is that kid talking about?

"Shh." The woman looks down at the boy. "Be quiet."

Alec releases me, and we walk toward the woman, side by side.

A freezing gust lifts the tablecloth and distributes paper plates and napkins to the concrete.

"Alec, this is Noah. Your son."

My jaw drops, and I run. Past my ride in the pea gravel, past the parked cars, and away from Alec calling my name.

THE END

Ewephoric Publishing

Dear Reader,

   If you enjoyed *Scattered Legacy,* please consider leaving a review on Amazon, Goodreads, Book Bub, or your favorite book site. Thank you!

Be sure to sign up for free books, giveaways, and news on future releases in the Annalisse Series as well as children's books by Marlene M. Bell.

Visit Marlene's website at:
https://www.marlenembell.com

Twitter:
https://www.twitter/ewephoric

Facebook:
https://www.facebook.com/marlenembell

ACKNOWLEDGMENTS

A thousand thanks to my readers for your helpful reviews during the Annalisse series writing journey. What began as a one-novel standalone took a turn and has blossomed into a multi-book saga. Your encouragement motivates me to provide tempting venues and more peril for Annalisse in future installments. Delicious Trouble (with a capital T) seems to follow her…

Elizabeth Kracht of Kimberley Cameron and Associates is the first editor to read each book in the series. Liz kept me from making a few mistakes in *Scattered Legacy*, suggesting point-of-view changes, major pacing revisions, and a different opening. Oh, those hard-to-get-right openings! Perhaps Annalisse will visit the Cayman Islands in another book. I'm grateful to you, Liz, for keeping Annalisse out front and on point in each book.

Annie Sarac of The Editing Pen waved her magic wand on *Scattered Legacy* after making the *Spent Identity* project shine. Thank you for allowing me to say the words in my own voice — and your humorous comments in the margins are a delightful stress reliever.

Who doesn't love an editor who's saddened when villainous characters meet their demise? The mobsters in *Scattered Legacy* are a charming bunch!

Kristine Hall of Lone Star Literary Life has saved my backside more than once with her top-notch editing and proofreading team. Kristine promotes Texas authors exclusively during book blog tours and newsletters, and I highly recommend Lone Star Literary to garner honest reviews from some of the best, most honest bloggers in the industry. https://www.lonestarliterary.com/lone-star-book-blog-tours

In the late 1980s, I left a lucrative, full-time job in the San Francisco Bay Area. Today, I'm able to create at home—write, take pictures, sell merchandise through a catalog, and spend time with the sheep. My husband's support and love have made this possible. I am so blessed to enjoy this life with you, Gregg! Never a dull moment.

Thanks also to my Advance Reader Street Team for your input and assistance prior to each book release. Followers on social media and my websites: I sincerely appreciate each and every one of your personal messages, feedback, and recommendations!

Any and all mistakes are my own.

TO MY BRAINSTORMERS

This book was written with the advice from family, friends, and readers who are absorbed in Annalisse's journey as she travels between continents. In *Scattered Legacy,* there are walk-on characters without speaking parts, unless you count purring. I'm referring to three cats, Stella, Valentino, and Savina, all with different owners.

For fresh ideas, I went to friends on social media and asked them to toss out names for cats that belonged to Italian households. I wish to thank my cousin, *Karla St. Louis* for the name contribution for main kitty, lovingly known as: Stella Notorious Kitty. The cat has a strong lead throughout this story and required a memorable name. As soon as I read Karla's suggestion, I knew Stella was it. Thanks Karla!

The second cat, Valentino, makes an appearance near the mid-point in this book. Valentino belongs to a woman from the town square church in Bari, Italy. He has a great little mustache that turns up on the ends in Rudolph Valentino style, so Valentino had his identity! Thank you, *Reni Melvin,* for your suggestion.

For the third cat, a dear friend from our days as 4H community leaders offered the name, Savina. It was so different, yet appropriate for the story; I couldn't pass it up. *Natalina Davis* knows a beautiful name because she has a unique first name that stands from the rest. Thank you twice for fictional inspiration, Natalina.

BOOKS BY
MARLENE M. BELL

**Stolen Obsession ~ Annalisse
Series Book One
Spent Identity ~ Annalisse Series
Book Two
Scattered Legacy ~ Annalisse
Series Book Three**

**Trading Paint ~ a short story,
Volume 5 Texas Authors**

**Mia and Nattie: One Great Team!
A Children's Picture Book**

ABOUT THE AUTHOR

Marlene M. Bell writes twisty mysteries and sheepish children's books with a caring message featuring Nattie, their bottle lamb. Marlene's an acclaimed artist as well as a photographer, using her talents to pay homage to the livestock they raise. Her sheep landscapes grace the covers of *The Shepherd, Ranch & Rural Living,* and *Sheep Industry News,* to name a few.

The catalog venture, Ewephoric, began in 1985 out of her desire to create personalized sheep stationery. She set out to design them herself and eventually added gifts from other artisans. Order Marlene's Ewephoric gifts and books online or request a catalog at TexasSheep.com.

Marlene and her husband, Gregg, reside in beautiful East Texas on wooded acreage with their Dorset sheep, a large Maremma guard dog named Tia, along with Hollywood, Leo, and Squeaks, the cats that believe they rule the household—and do.

Made in the USA
Monee, IL
19 July 2022